League of Incredible Vegetables

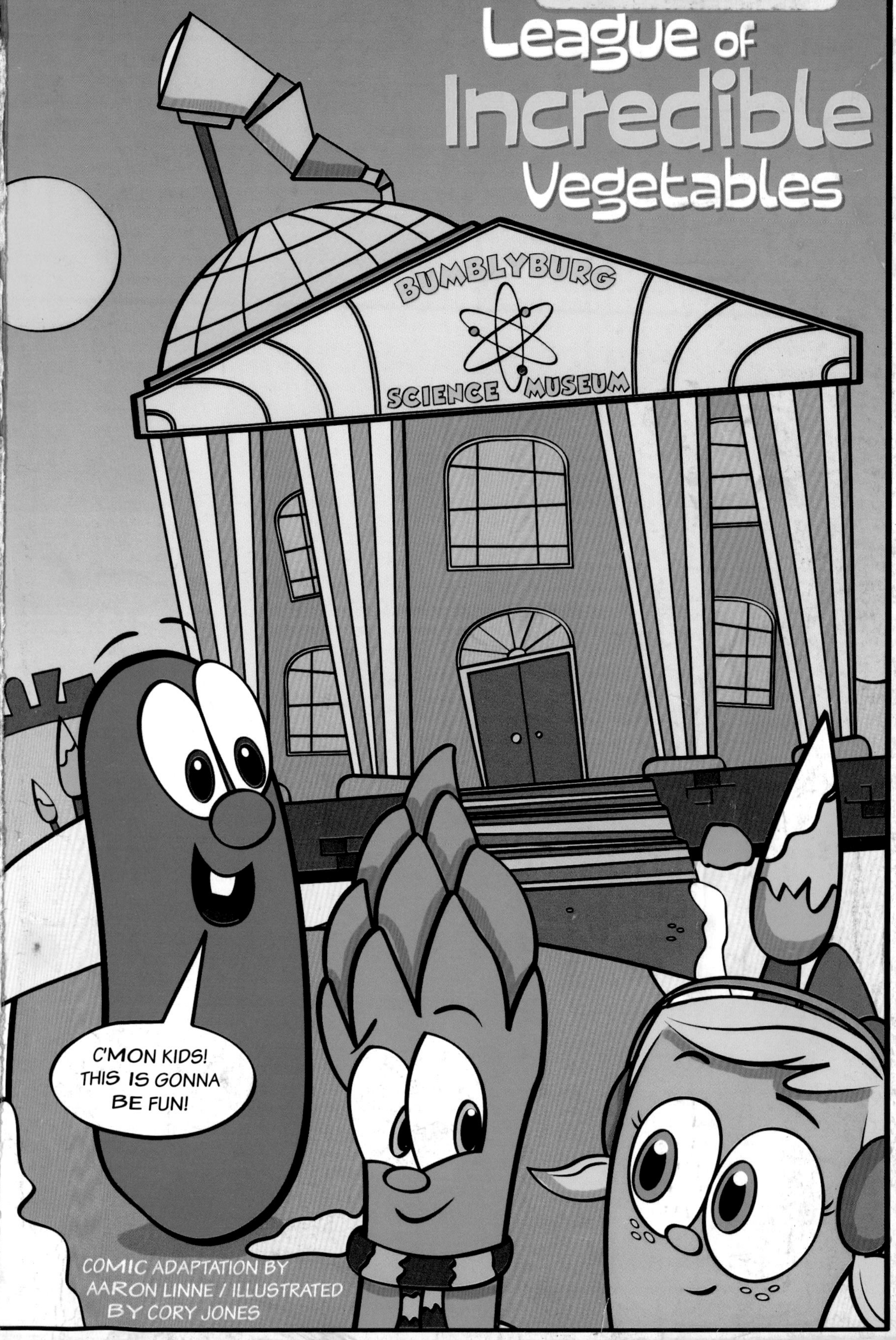
BUMBLYBURG SCIENCE MUSEUM
C'MON KIDS! THIS IS GONNA BE FUN!

COMIC ADAPTATION BY AARON LINNE / ILLUSTRATED BY CORY JONES

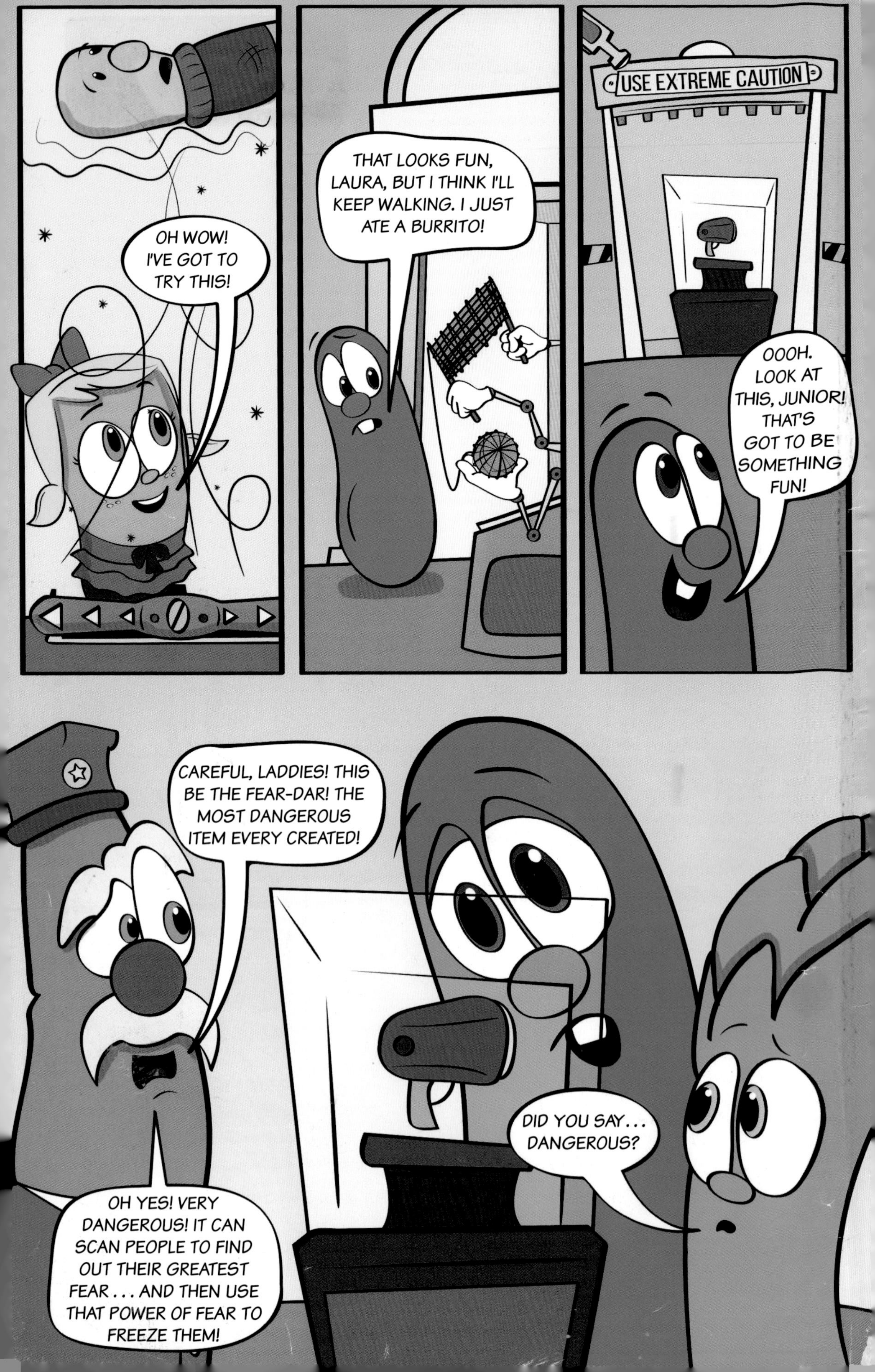

OH WOW! I'VE GOT TO TRY THIS!
THAT LOOKS FUN, LAURA, BUT I THINK I'LL KEEP WALKING. I JUST ATE A BURRITO!
USE EXTREME CAUTION
OOOH. LOOK AT THIS, JUNIOR! THAT'S GOT TO BE SOMETHING FUN!
CAREFUL, LADDIES! THIS BE THE FEAR-DAR! THE MOST DANGEROUS ITEM EVERY CREATED!
DID YOU SAY . . . DANGEROUS?
OH YES! VERY DANGEROUS! IT CAN SCAN PEOPLE TO FIND OUT THEIR GREATEST FEAR . . . AND THEN USE THAT POWER OF FEAR TO FREEZE THEM!

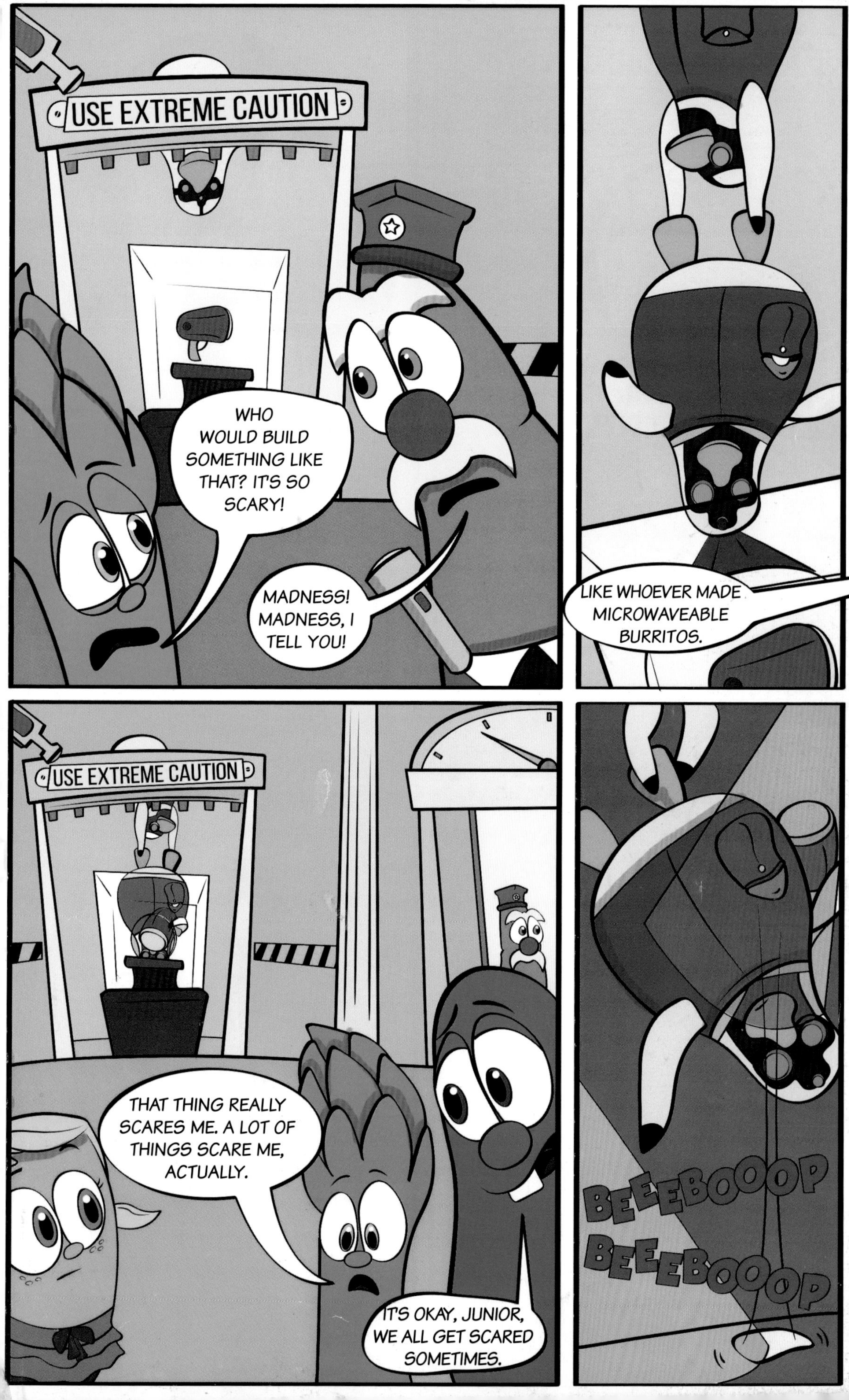
USE EXTREME CAUTION
WHO WOULD BUILD SOMETHING LIKE THAT? IT'S SO SCARY!
MADNESS! MADNESS, I TELL YOU!
LIKE WHOEVER MADE MICROWAVEABLE BURRITOS.
USE EXTREME CAUTION
THAT THING REALLY SCARES ME. A LOT OF THINGS SCARE ME, ACTUALLY.
IT'S OKAY, JUNIOR, WE ALL GET SCARED SOMETIMES.
BEEEBOOOP
BEEEBOOOP

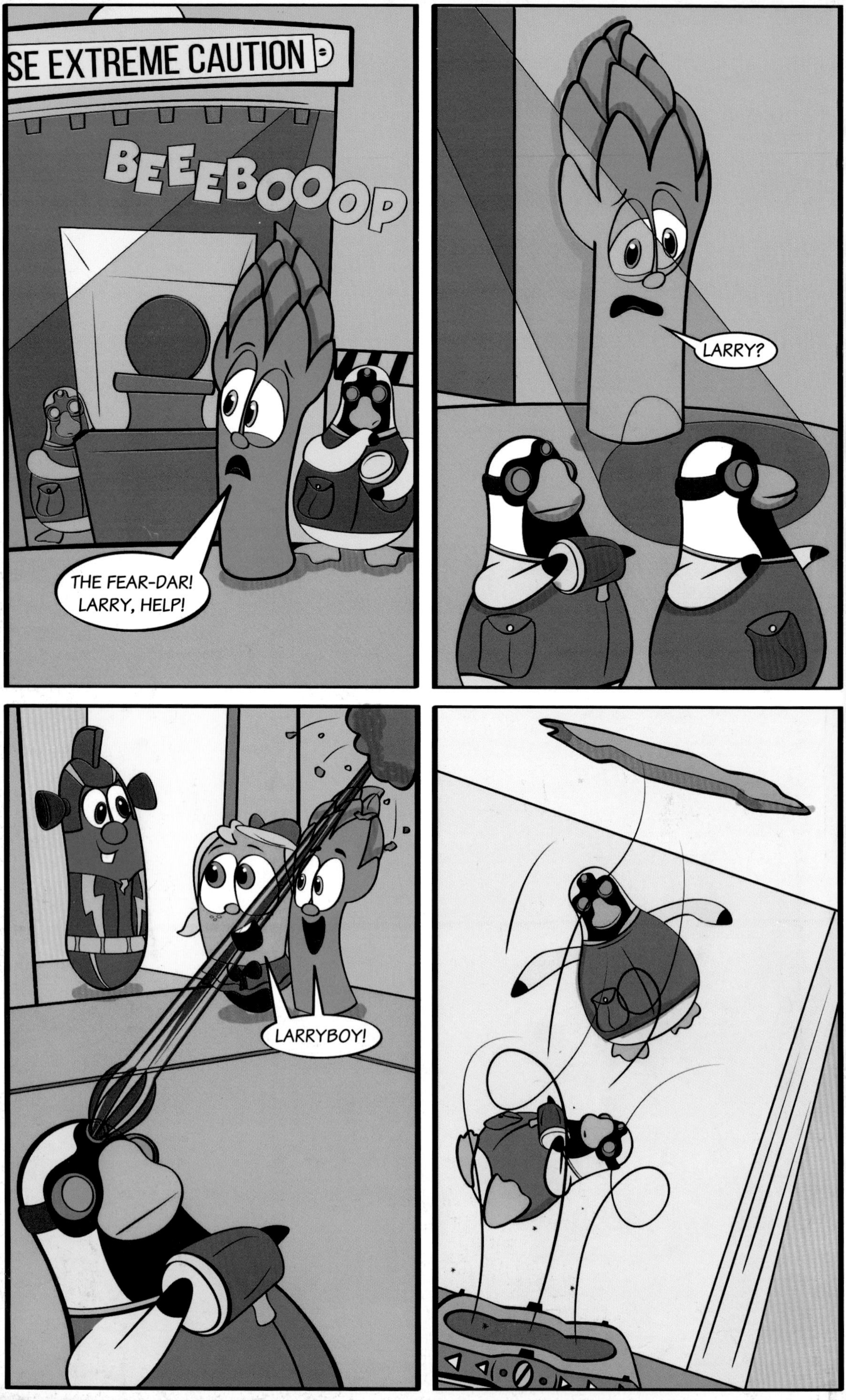
SE EXTREME CAUTION
BEEEBOOOP
THE FEAR-DAR! LARRY, HELP!
LARRY?
LARRYBOY!

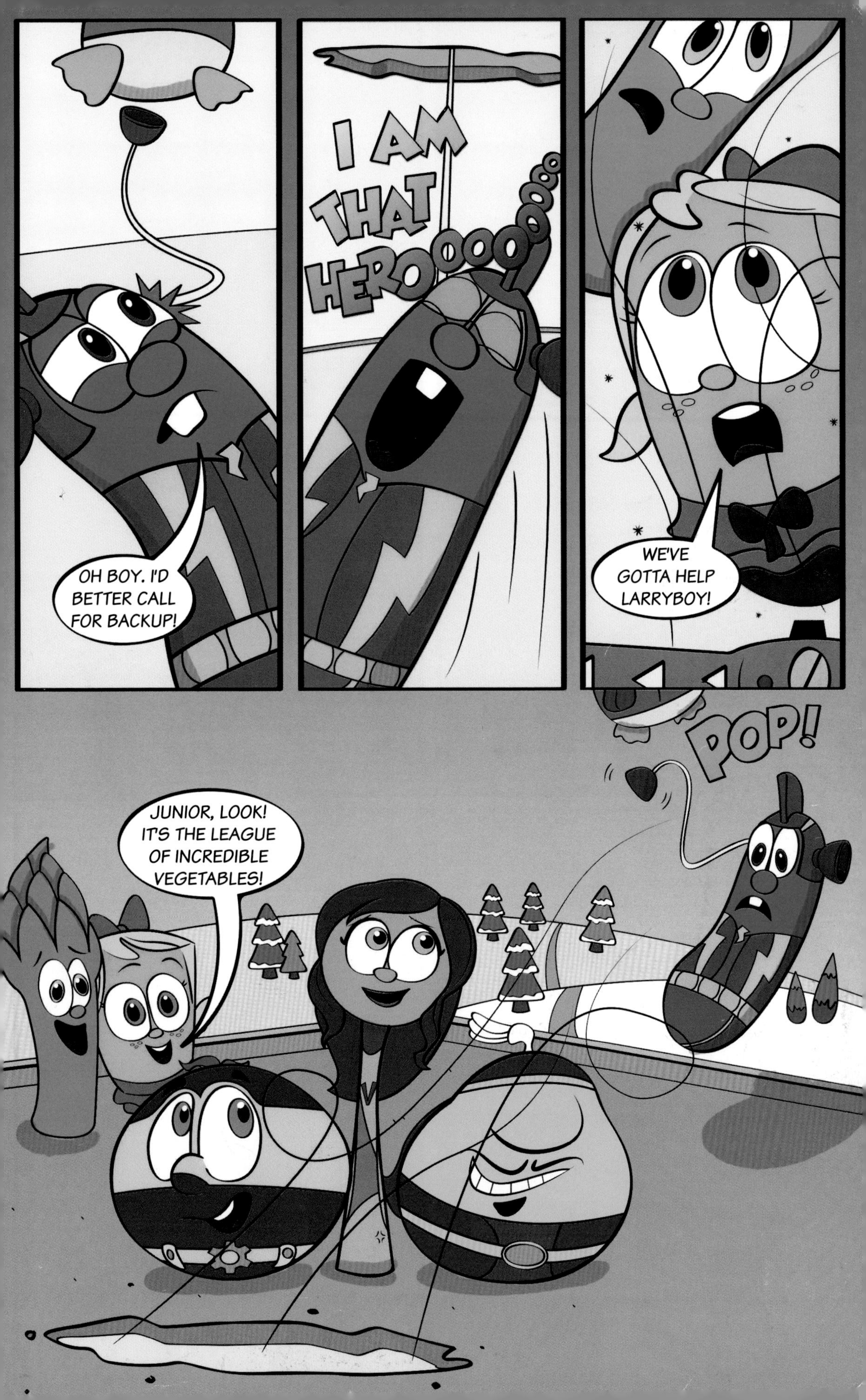
OH BOY. I'D BETTER CALL FOR BACKUP!
I AM THAT HEROOOOOOOOO
WE'VE GOTTA HELP LARRYBOY!
POP!
JUNIOR, LOOK! IT'S THE LEAGUE OF INCREDIBLE VEGETABLES!

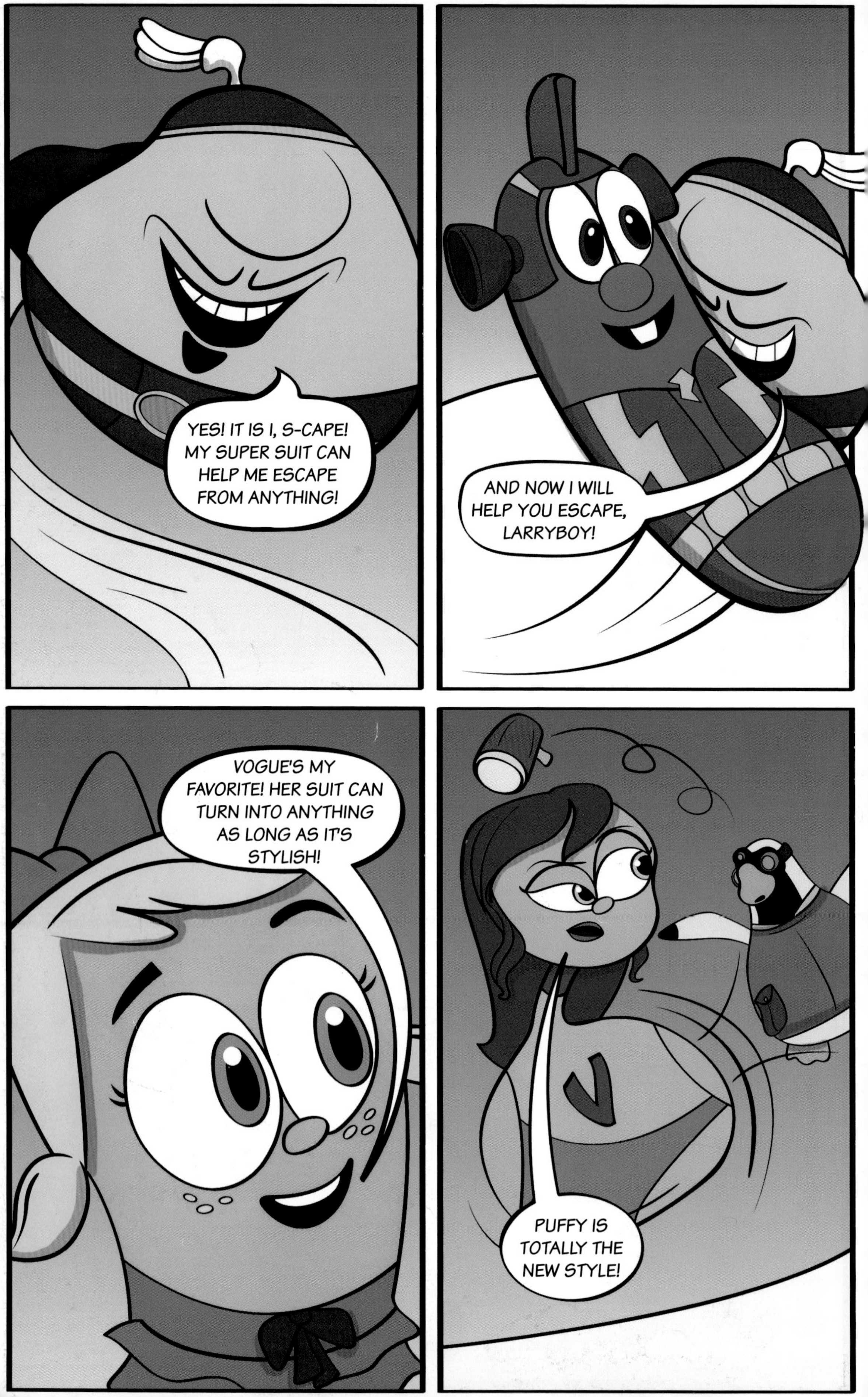
YES! IT IS I, S-CAPE! MY SUPER SUIT CAN HELP ME ESCAPE FROM ANYTHING!
AND NOW I WILL HELP YOU ESCAPE, LARRYBOY!
VOGUE'S MY FAVORITE! HER SUIT CAN TURN INTO ANYTHING AS LONG AS IT'S STYLISH!
PUFFY IS TOTALLY THE NEW STYLE!

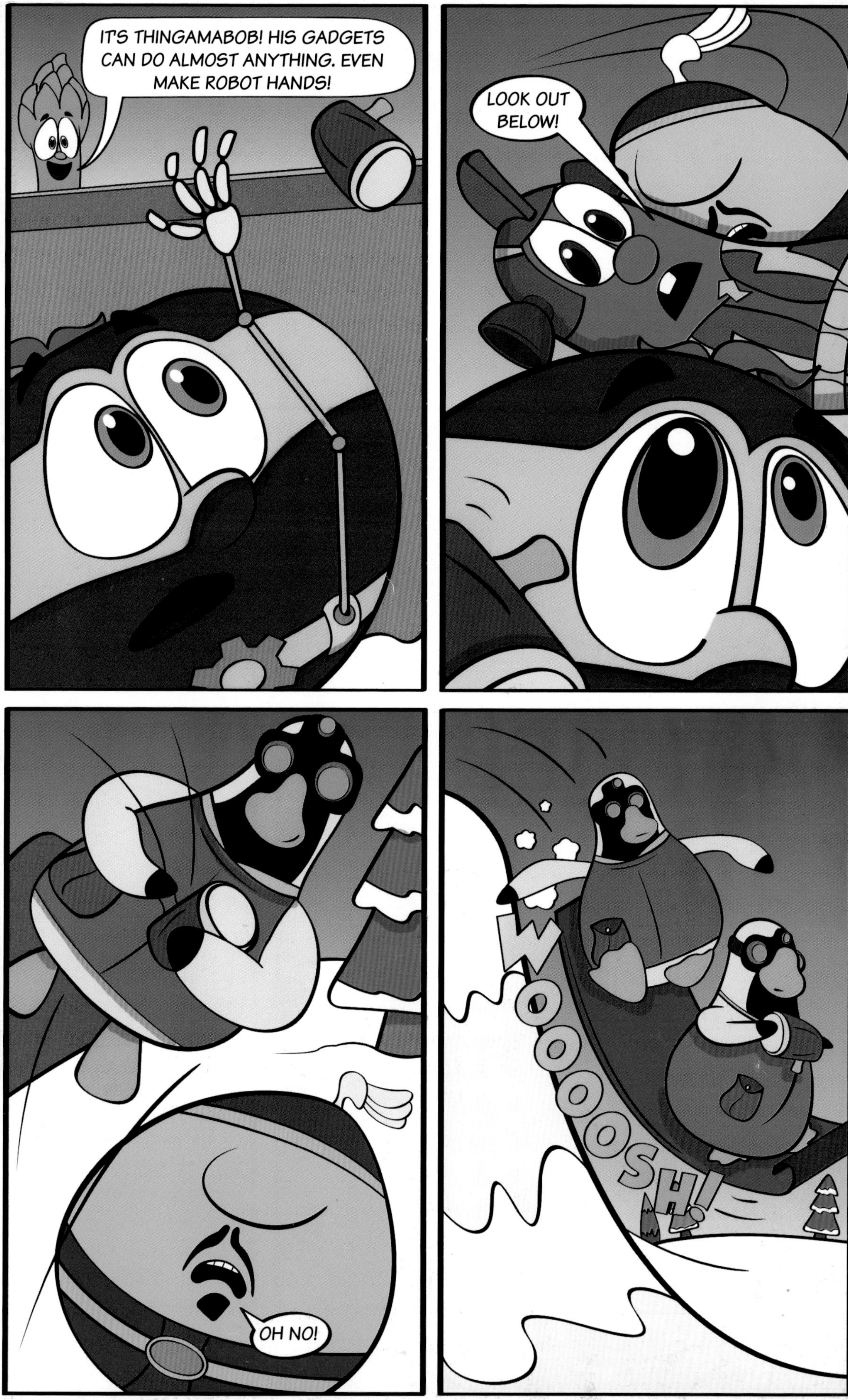
IT'S THINGAMABOB! HIS GADGETS CAN DO ALMOST ANYTHING. EVEN MAKE ROBOT HANDS!
LOOK OUT BELOW!
OH NO!
WOOOOOOSH!

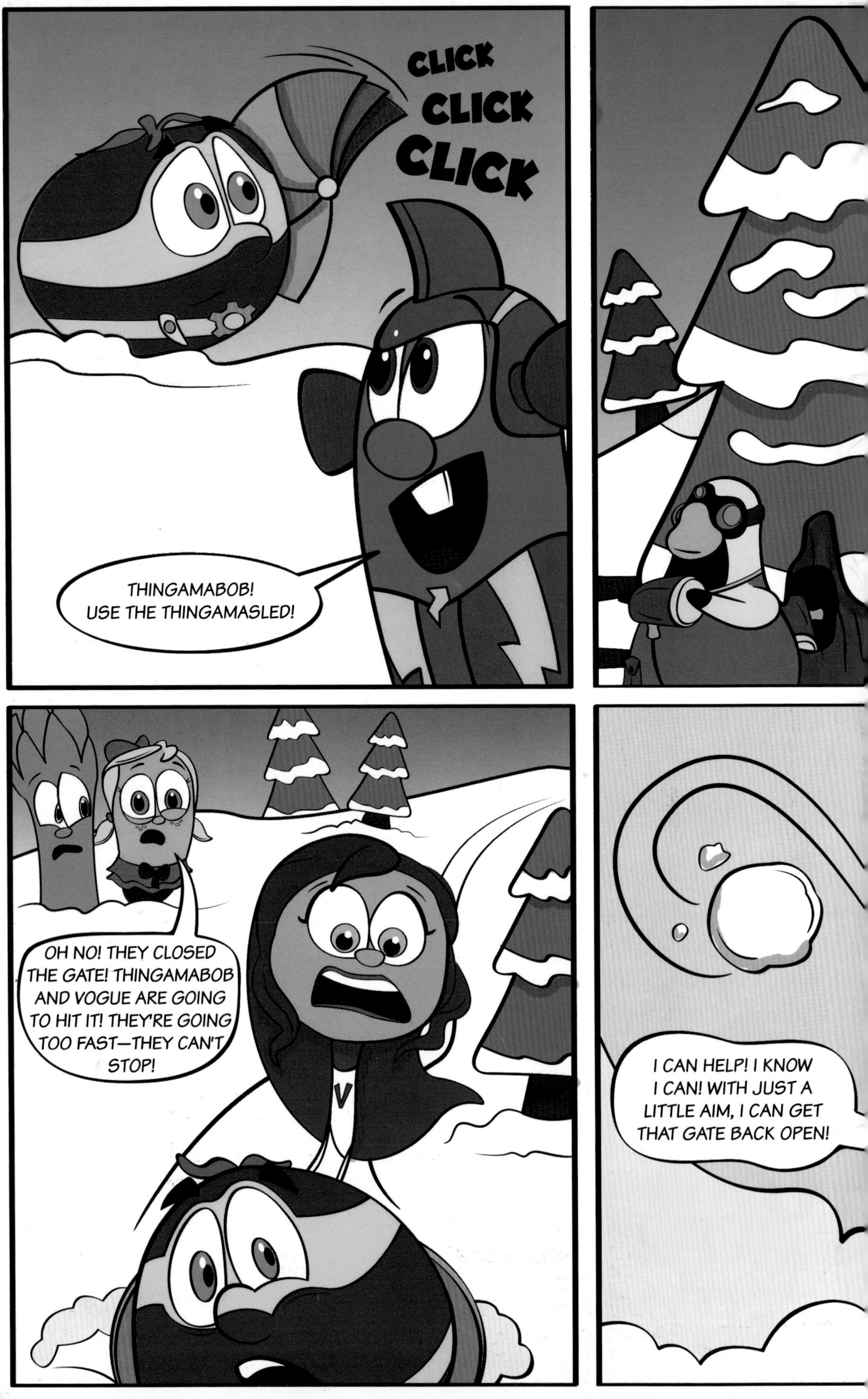
CLICK
CLICK
CLICK
THINGAMABOB! USE THE THINGAMASLED!
OH NO! THEY CLOSED THE GATE! THINGAMABOB AND VOGUE ARE GOING TO HIT IT! THEY'RE GOING TOO FAST—THEY CAN'T STOP!
I CAN HELP! I KNOW I CAN! WITH JUST A LITTLE AIM, I CAN GET THAT GATE BACK OPEN!

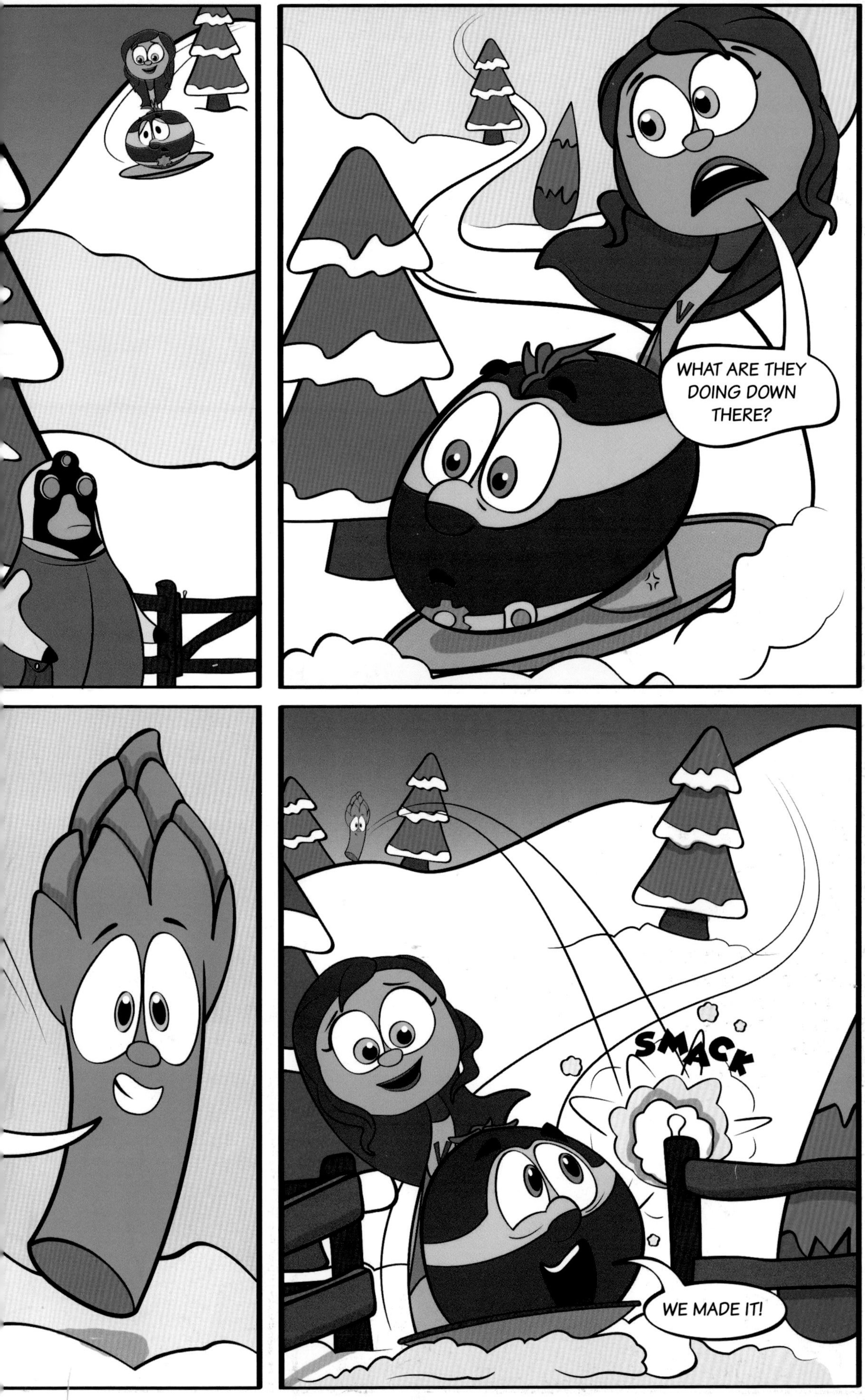
WHAT ARE THEY DOING DOWN THERE?
SMACK
WE MADE IT!

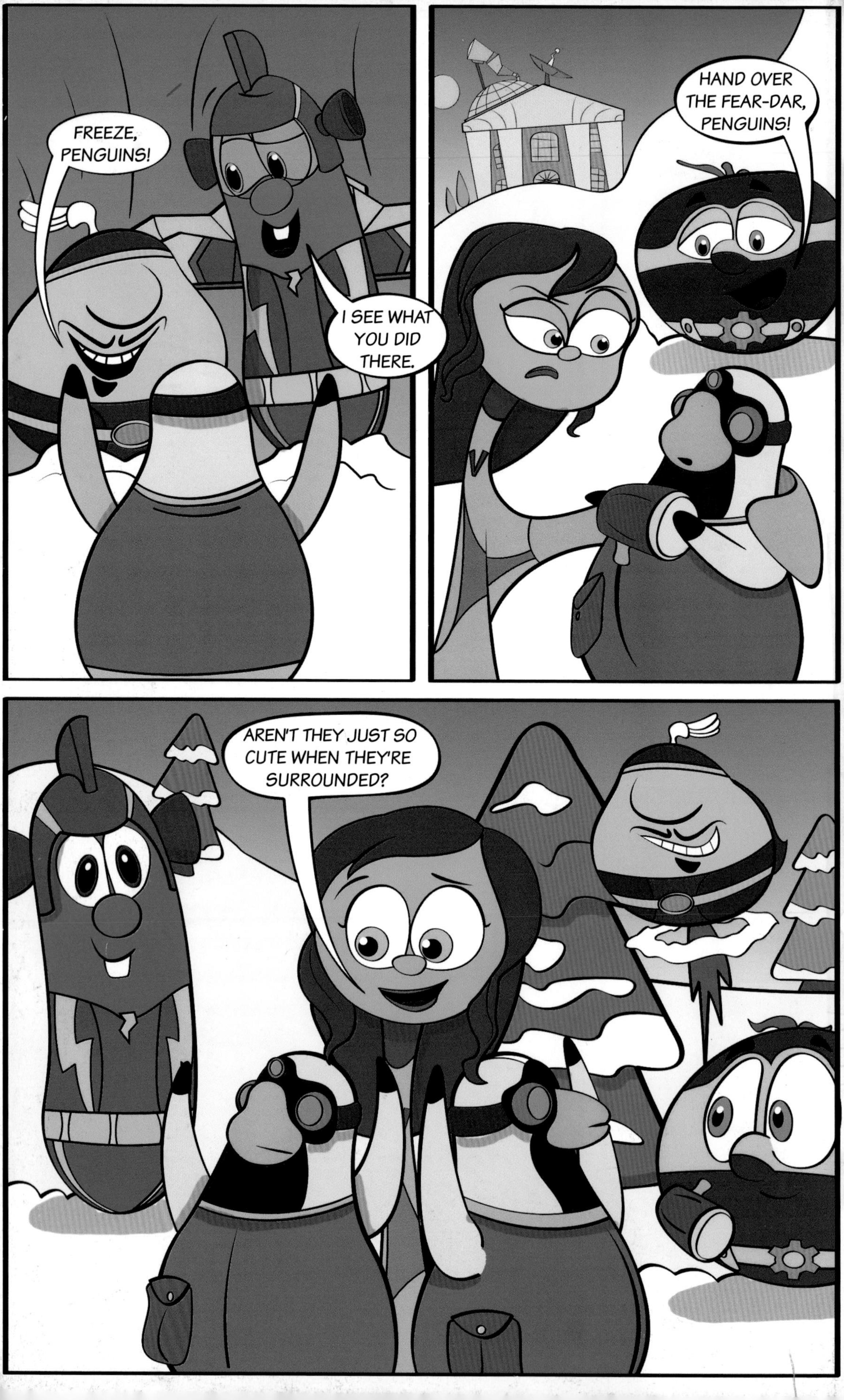
FREEZE, PENGUINS!
I SEE WHAT YOU DID THERE.
HAND OVER THE FEAR-DAR, PENGUINS!
AREN'T THEY JUST SO CUTE WHEN THEY'RE SURROUNDED?

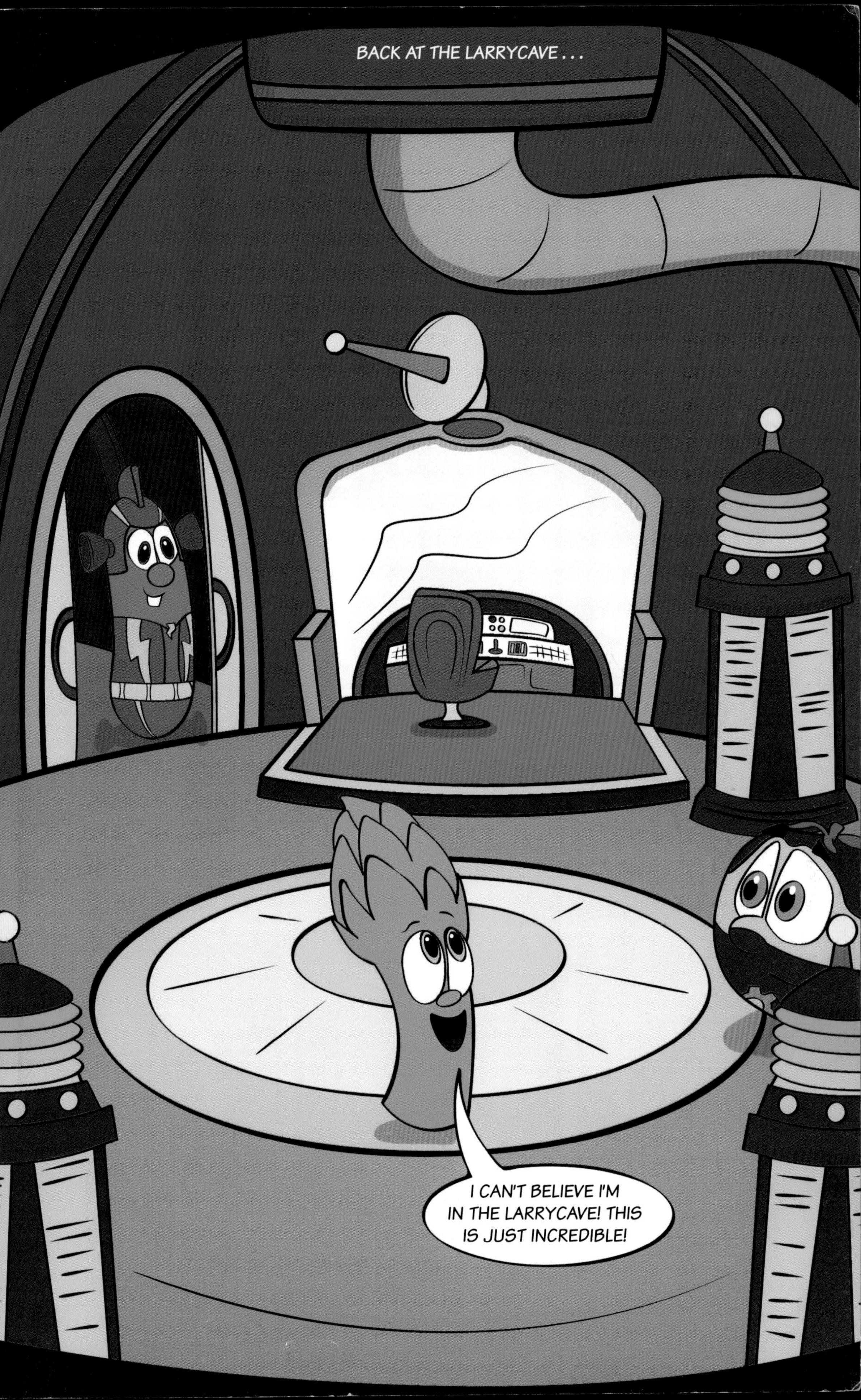
BACK AT THE LARRYCAVE . . .
I CAN'T BELIEVE I'M IN THE LARRYCAVE! THIS IS JUST INCREDIBLE!

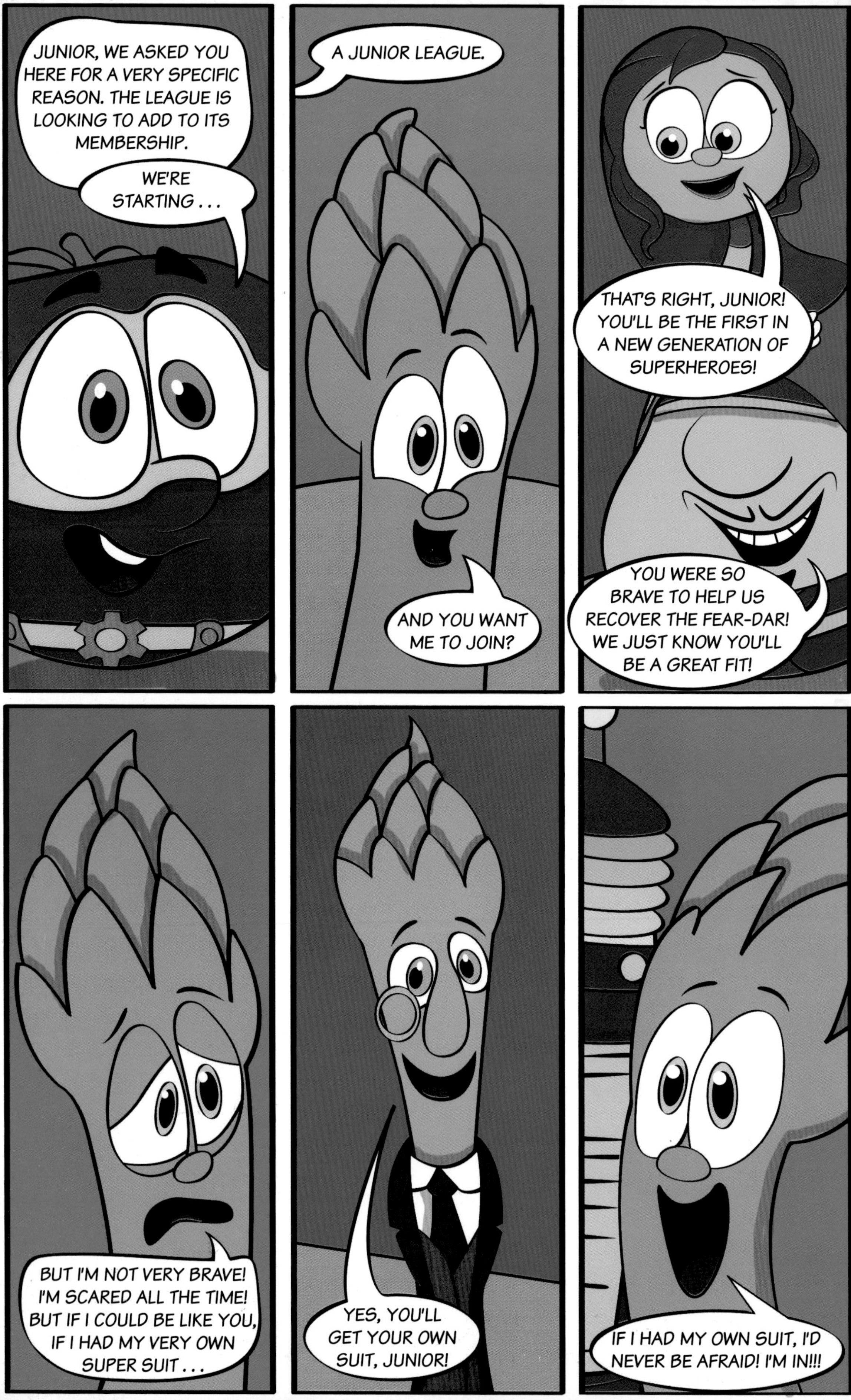
JUNIOR, WE ASKED YOU HERE FOR A VERY SPECIFIC REASON. THE LEAGUE IS LOOKING TO ADD TO ITS MEMBERSHIP.
WE'RE STARTING . . .
A JUNIOR LEAGUE.
AND YOU WANT ME TO JOIN?
THAT'S RIGHT, JUNIOR! YOU'LL BE THE FIRST IN A NEW GENERATION OF SUPERHEROES!
YOU WERE SO BRAVE TO HELP US RECOVER THE FEAR-DAR! WE JUST KNOW YOU'LL BE A GREAT FIT!
BUT I'M NOT VERY BRAVE! I'M SCARED ALL THE TIME! BUT IF I COULD BE LIKE YOU, IF I HAD MY VERY OWN SUPER SUIT . . .
YES, YOU'LL GET YOUR OWN SUIT, JUNIOR!
IF I HAD MY OWN SUIT, I'D NEVER BE AFRAID! I'M IN!!!

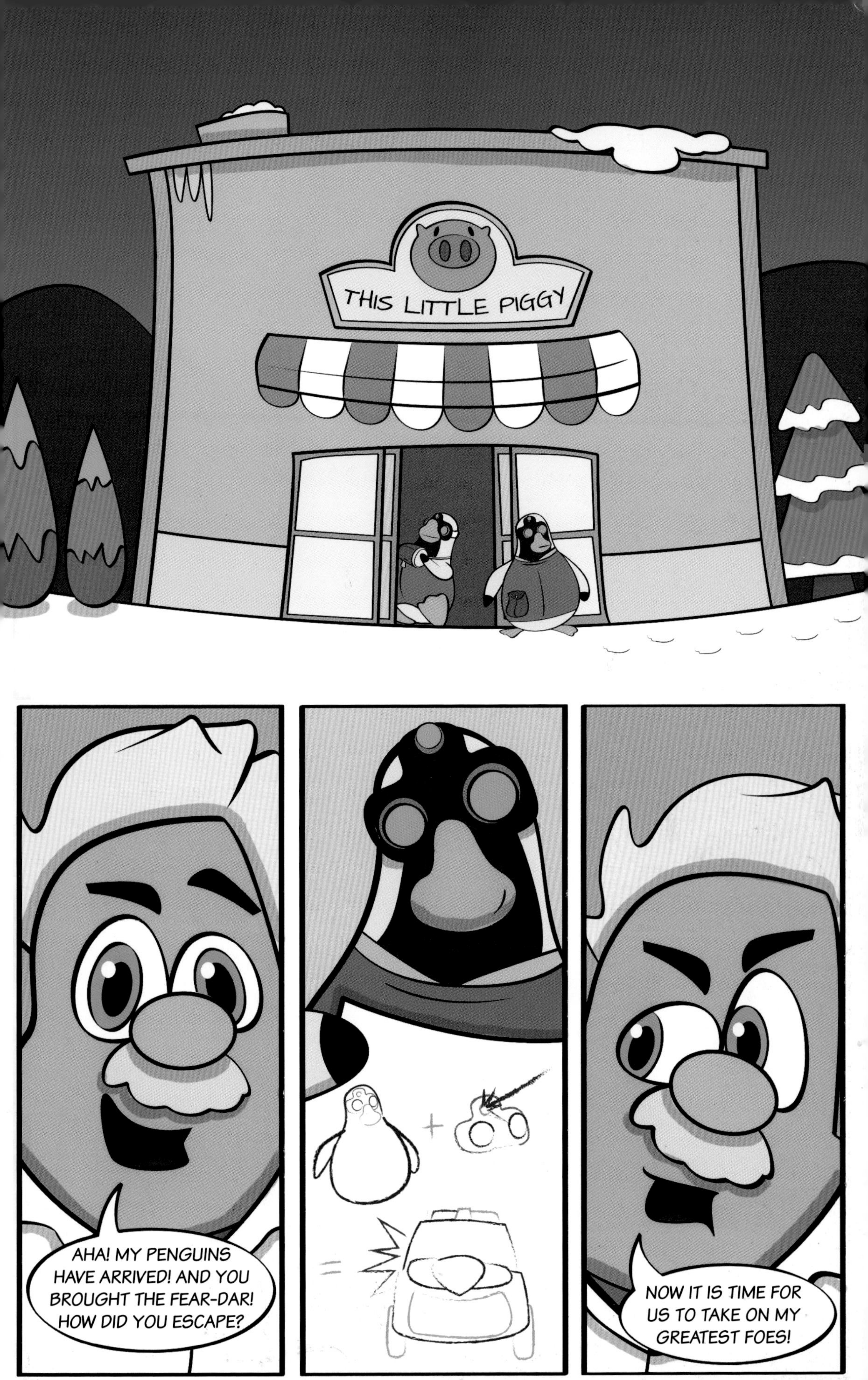
THIS LITTLE PIGGY
AHA! MY PENGUINS HAVE ARRIVED! AND YOU BROUGHT THE FEAR-DAR! HOW DID YOU ESCAPE?
NOW IT IS TIME FOR US TO TAKE ON MY GREATEST FOES!

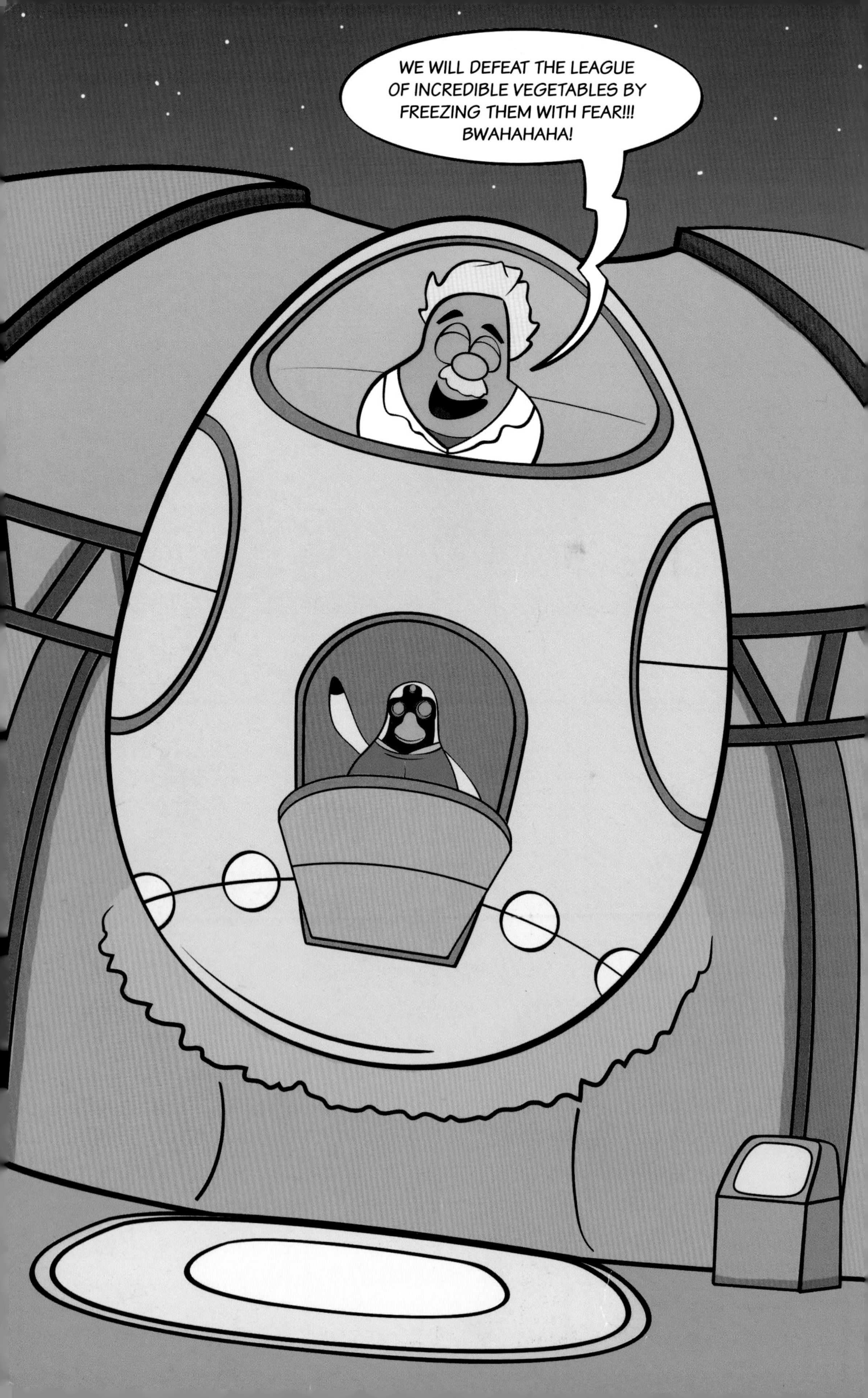
WE WILL DEFEAT THE LEAGUE OF INCREDIBLE VEGETABLES BY FREEZING THEM WITH FEAR!!! BWAHAHAHA!

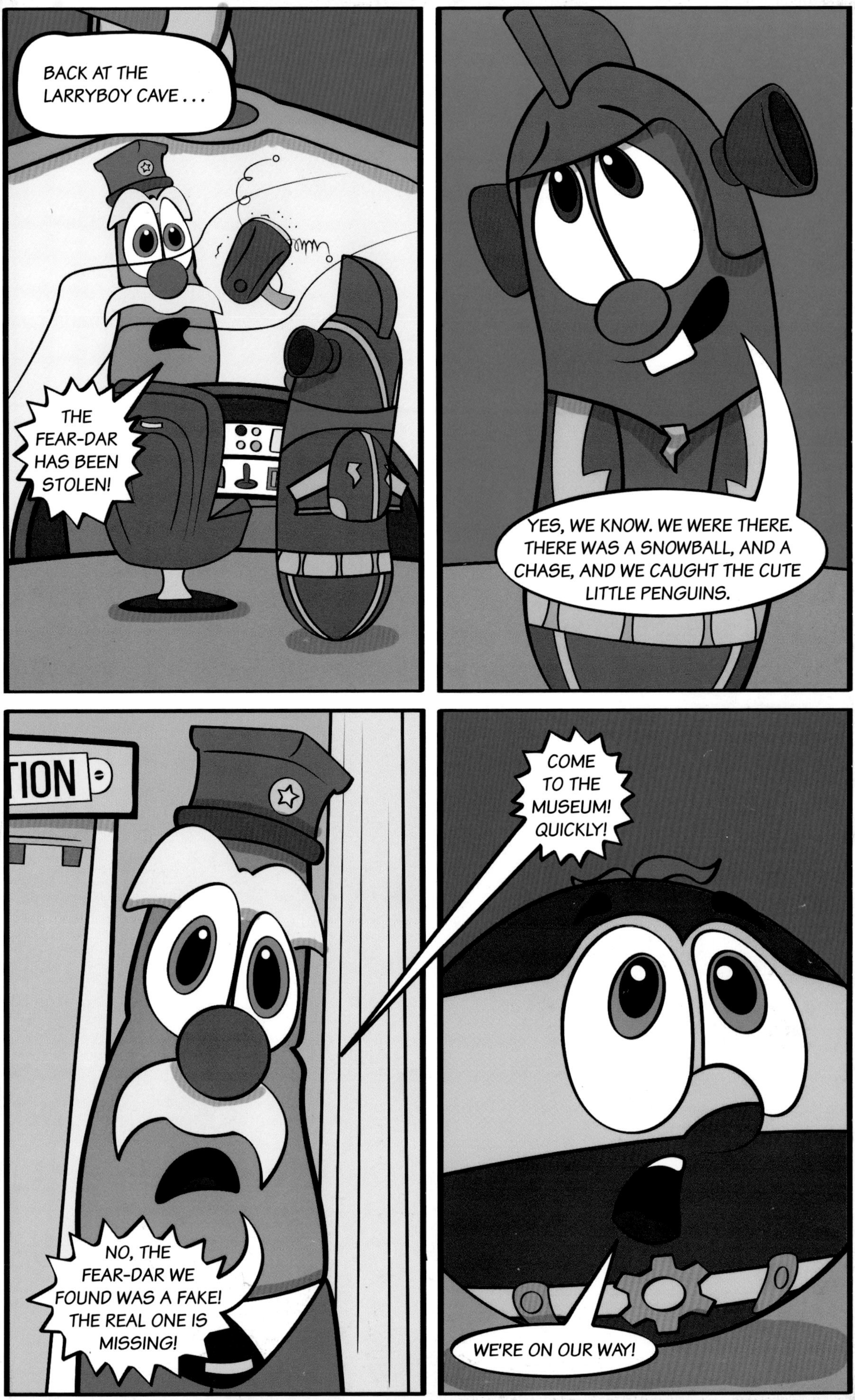
BACK AT THE LARRYBOY CAVE . . .
THE FEAR-DAR HAS BEEN STOLEN!
YES, WE KNOW. WE WERE THERE. THERE WAS A SNOWBALL, AND A CHASE, AND WE CAUGHT THE CUTE LITTLE PENGUINS.
TION
NO, THE FEAR-DAR WE FOUND WAS A FAKE! THE REAL ONE IS MISSING!
COME TO THE MUSEUM! QUICKLY!
WE'RE ON OUR WAY!

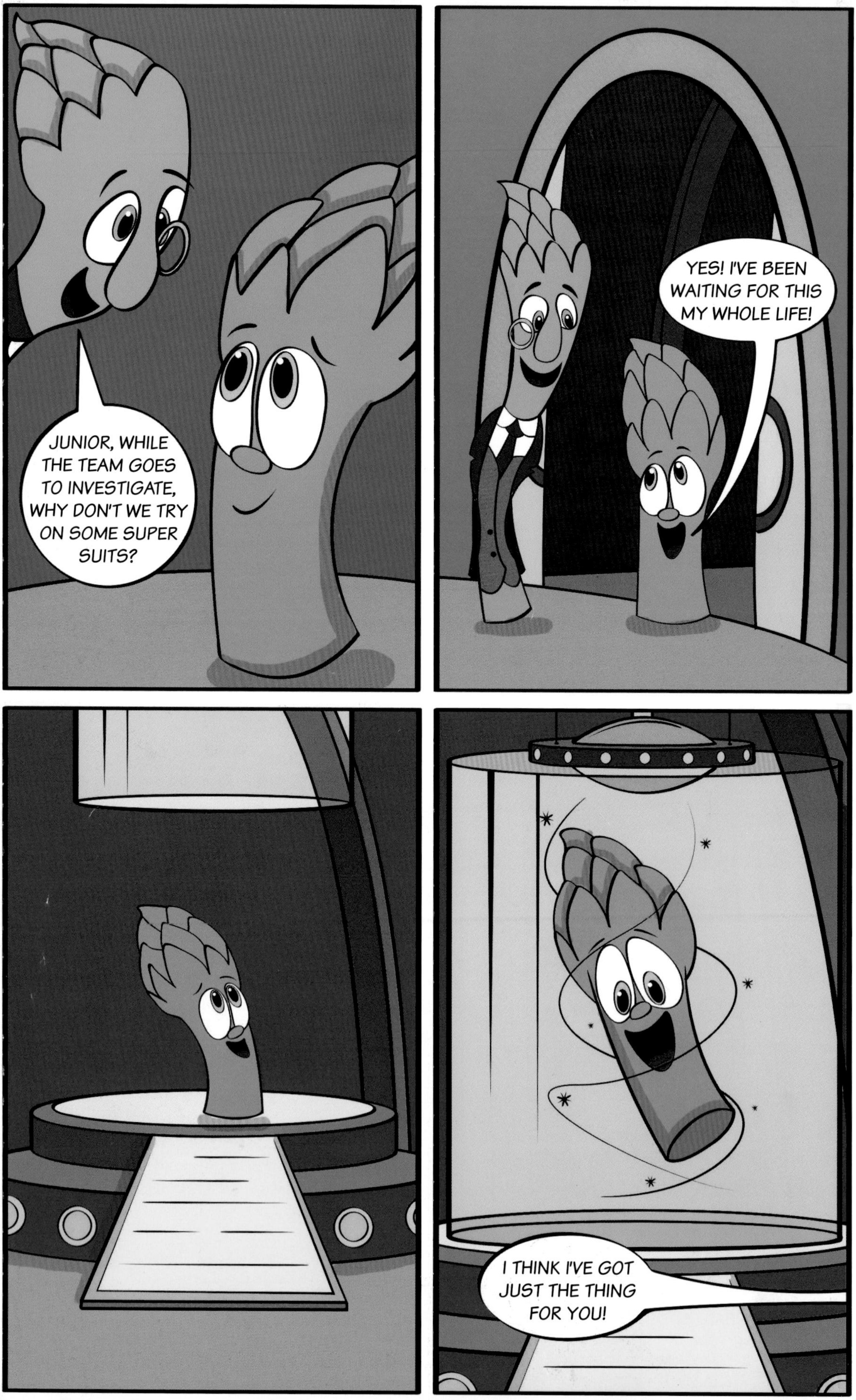
JUNIOR, WHILE THE TEAM GOES TO INVESTIGATE, WHY DON'T WE TRY ON SOME SUPER SUITS?
YES! I'VE BEEN WAITING FOR THIS MY WHOLE LIFE!
I THINK I'VE GOT JUST THE THING FOR YOU!

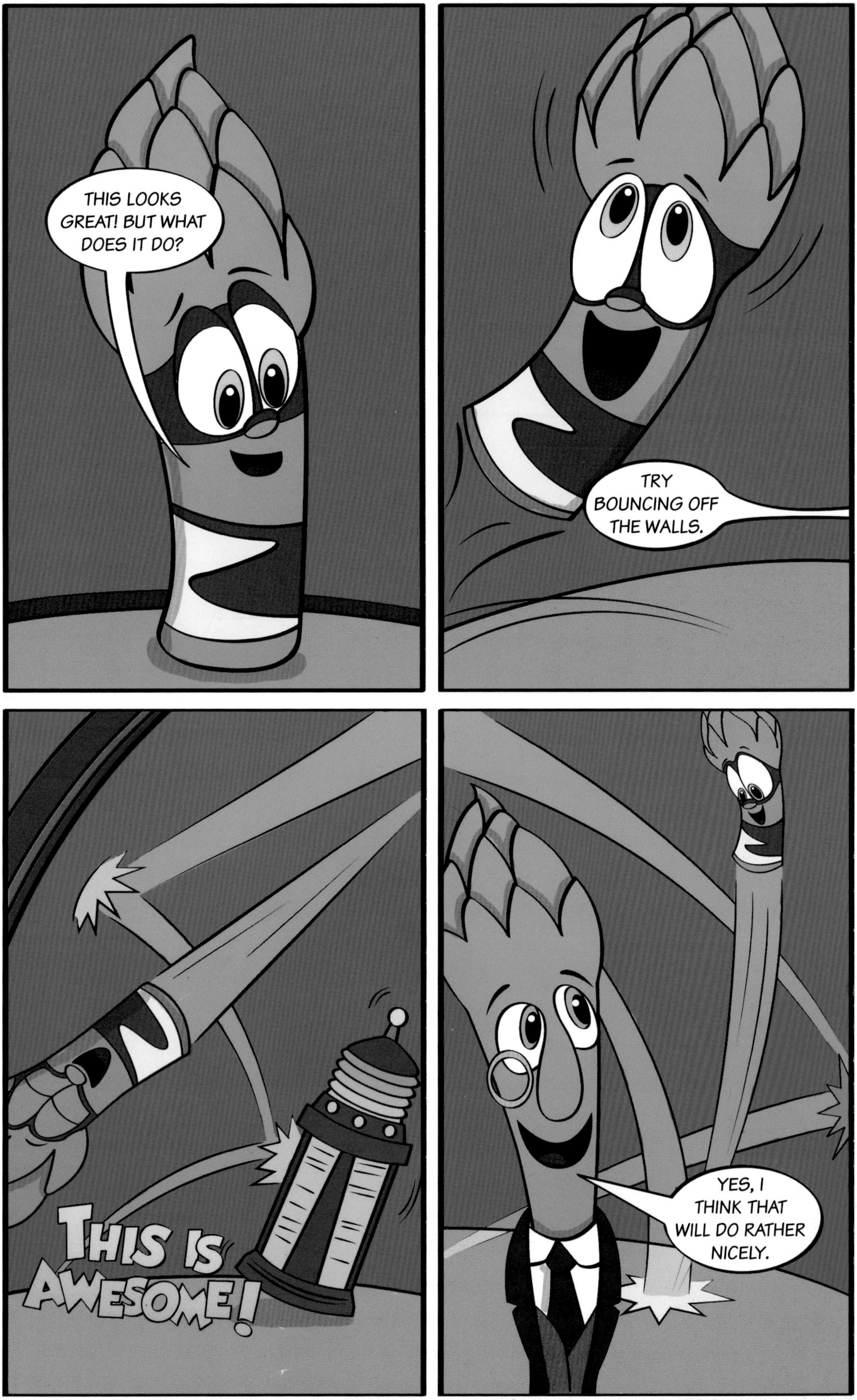
THIS LOOKS GREAT! BUT WHAT DOES IT DO?
TRY BOUNCING OFF THE WALLS.
THIS IS AWESOME!
YES, I THINK THAT WILL DO RATHER NICELY.

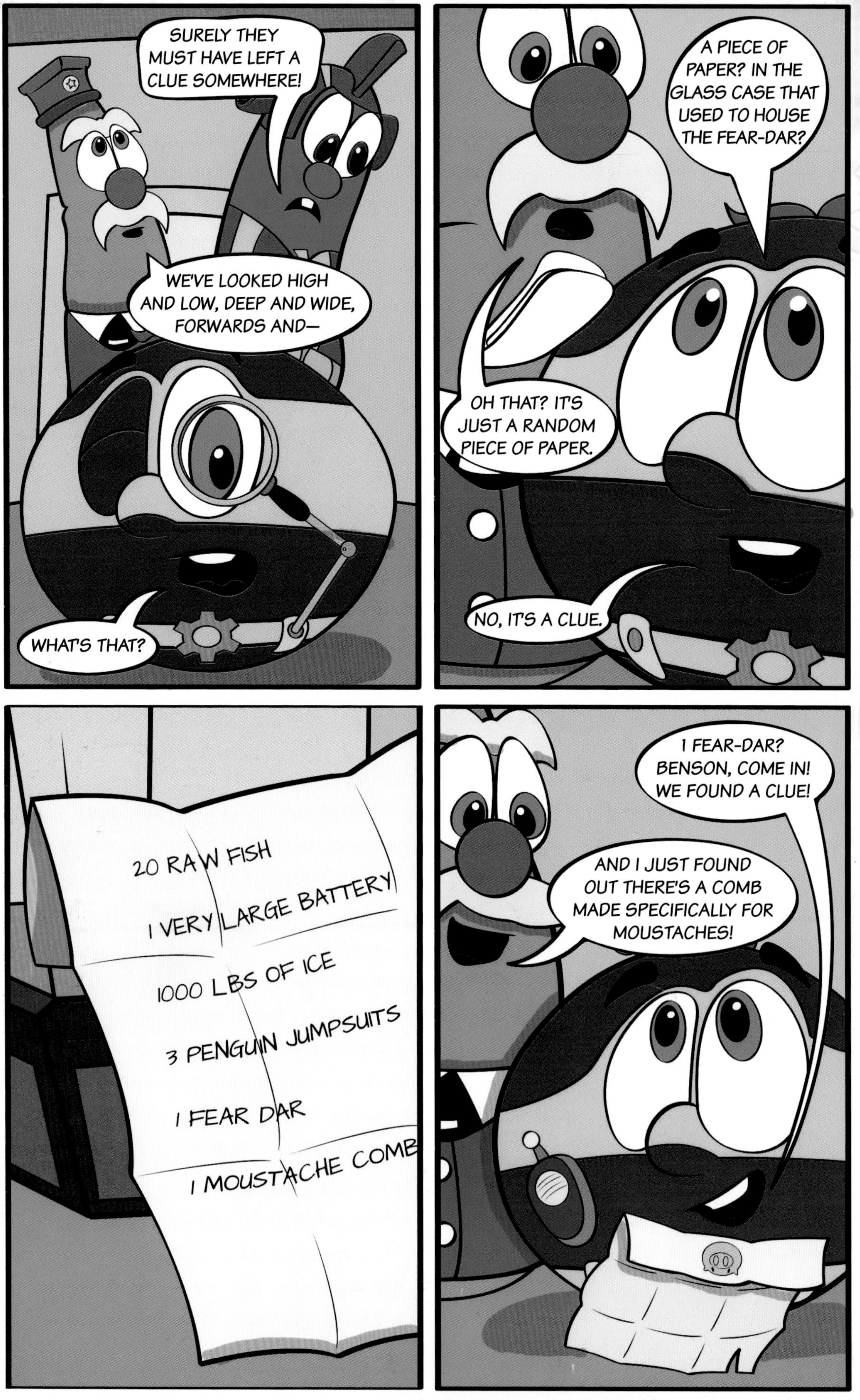
SURELY THEY MUST HAVE LEFT A CLUE SOMEWHERE!
WE'VE LOOKED HIGH AND LOW, DEEP AND WIDE, FORWARDS AND—
WHAT'S THAT?
A PIECE OF PAPER? IN THE GLASS CASE THAT USED TO HOUSE THE FEAR-DAR?
OH THAT? IT'S JUST A RANDOM PIECE OF PAPER.
NO, IT'S A CLUE.
20 RAW FISH
1 VERY LARGE BATTERY
1000 LBS OF ICE
3 PENGUIN JUMPSUITS
1 FEAR DAR
1 MOUSTACHE COMB
1 FEAR-DAR? BENSON, COME IN! WE FOUND A CLUE!
AND I JUST FOUND OUT THERE'S A COMB MADE SPECIFICALLY FOR MOUSTACHES!

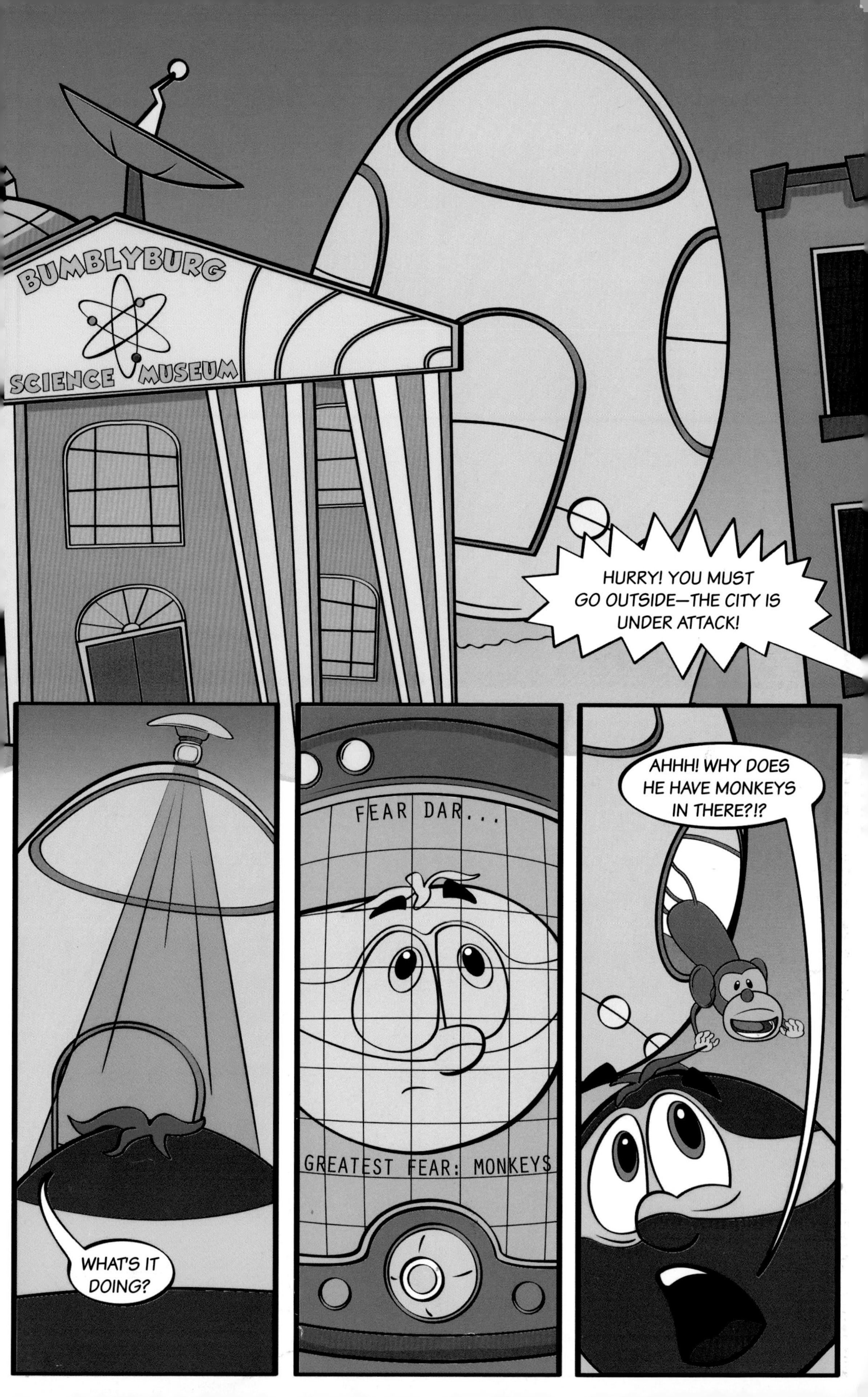
BUMBLYBURG
SCIENCE MUSEUM
HURRY! YOU MUST GO OUTSIDE—THE CITY IS UNDER ATTACK!
WHAT'S IT DOING?
FEAR DAR...
GREATEST FEAR: MONKEYS
AHHH! WHY DOES HE HAVE MONKEYS IN THERE?!?

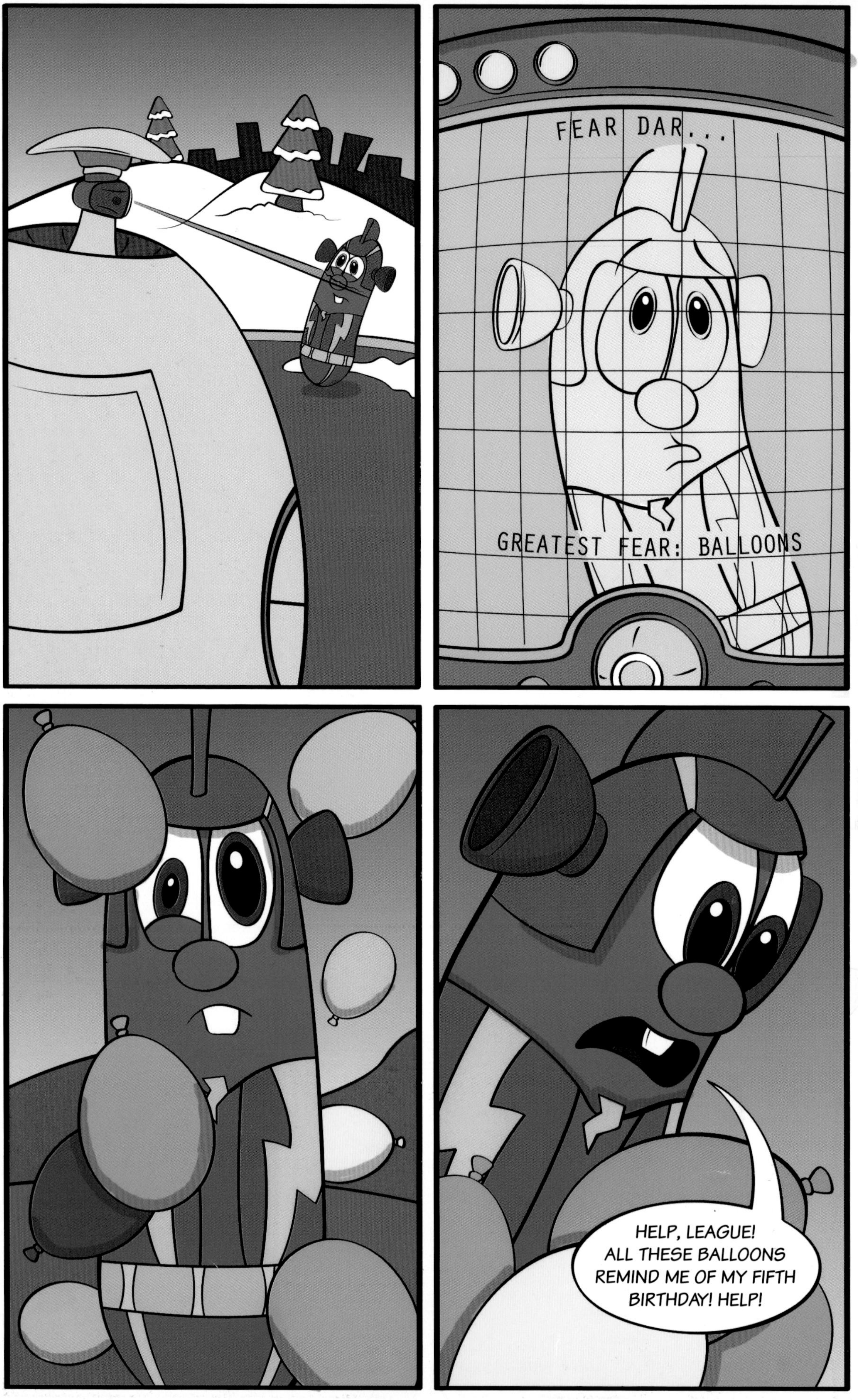
FEAR DAR...
GREATEST FEAR: BALLOONS
HELP, LEAGUE! ALL THESE BALLOONS REMIND ME OF MY FIFTH BIRTHDAY! HELP!

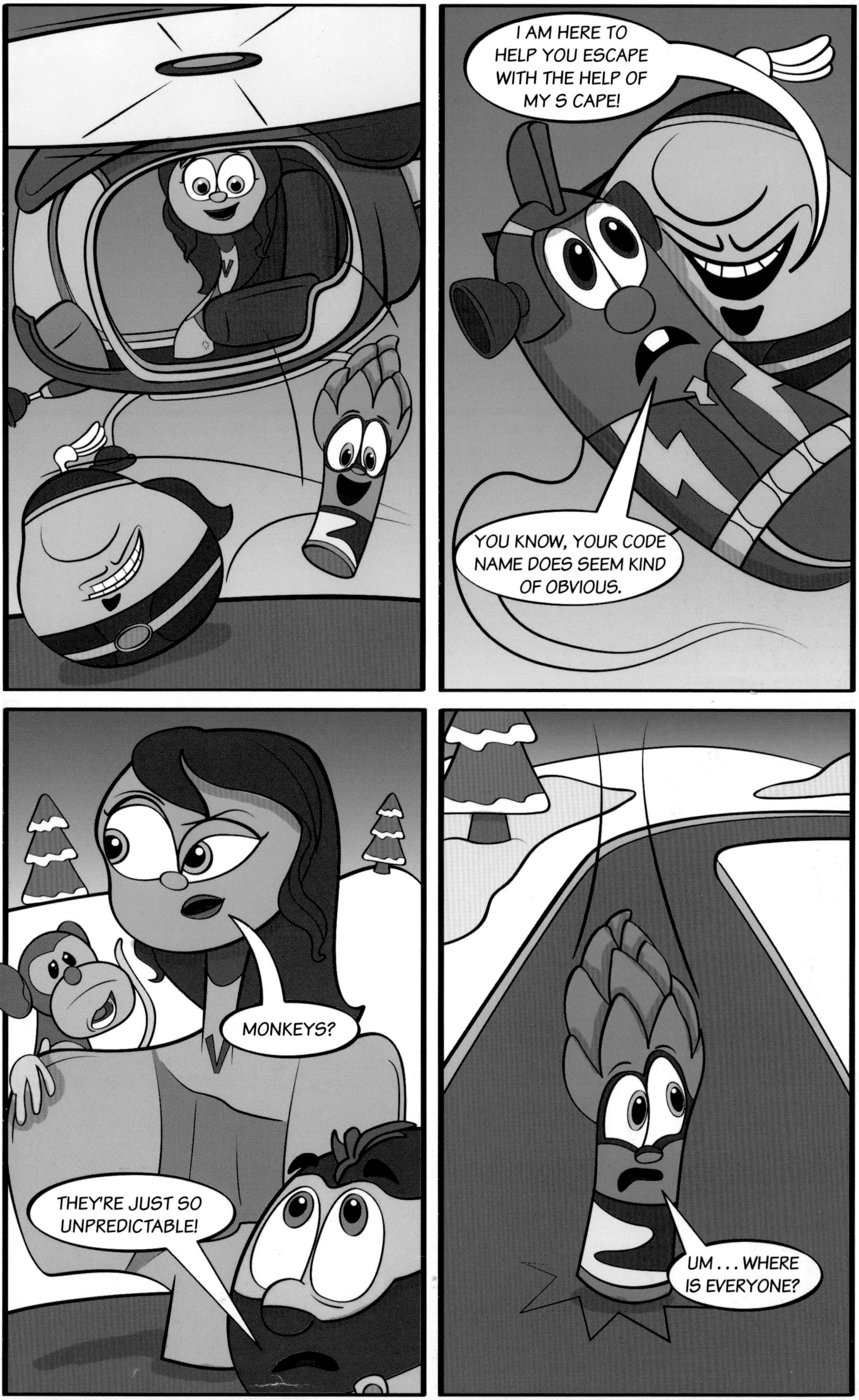
I AM HERE TO HELP YOU ESCAPE WITH THE HELP OF MY S CAPE!
YOU KNOW, YOUR CODE NAME DOES SEEM KIND OF OBVIOUS.
MONKEYS?
THEY'RE JUST SO UNPREDICTABLE!
UM . . . WHERE IS EVERYONE?

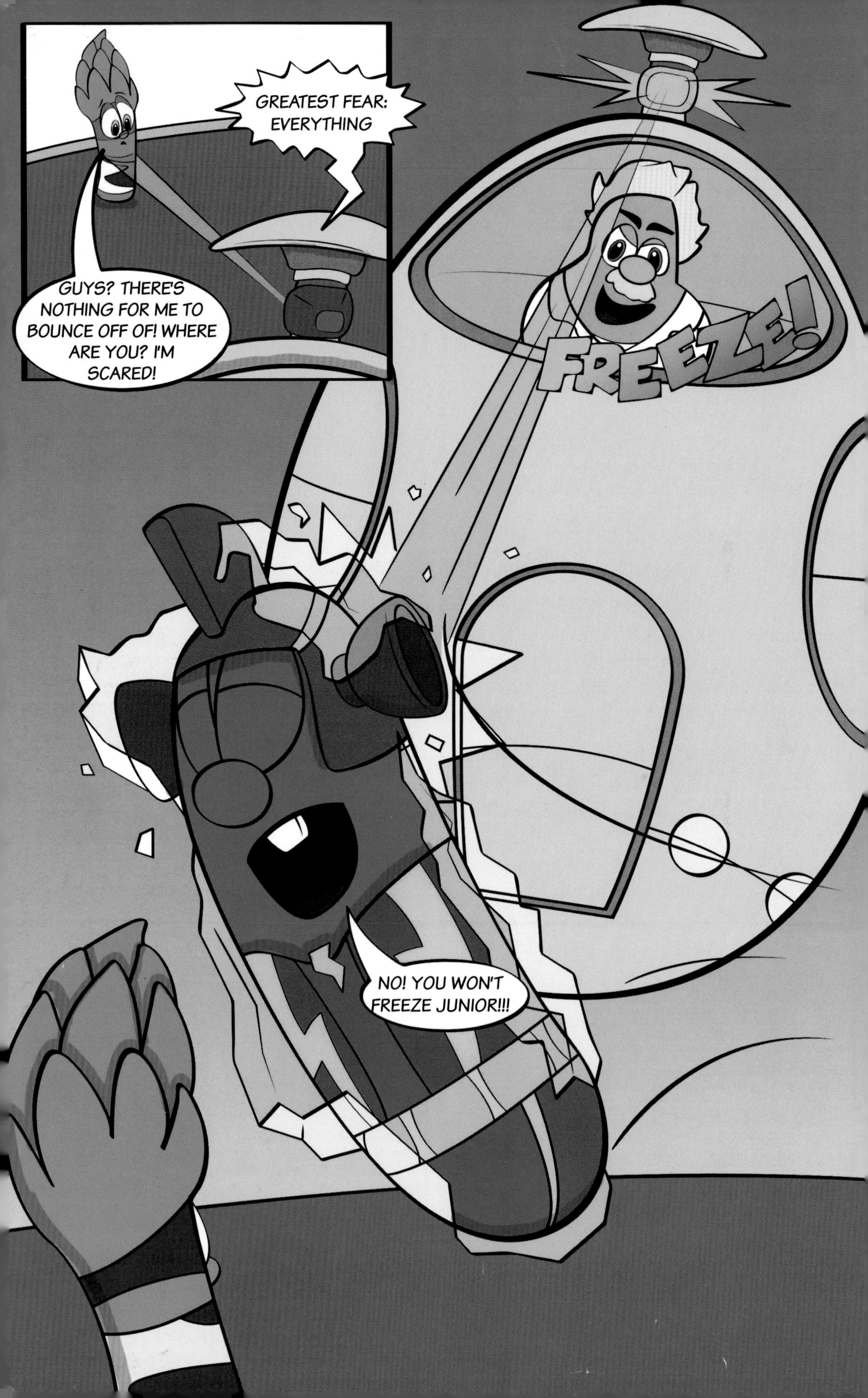
GREATEST FEAR: EVERYTHING
GUYS? THERE'S NOTHING FOR ME TO BOUNCE OFF OF! WHERE ARE YOU? I'M SCARED!
FREEZE!
NO! YOU WON'T FREEZE JUNIOR!!!

LARRYBOY?

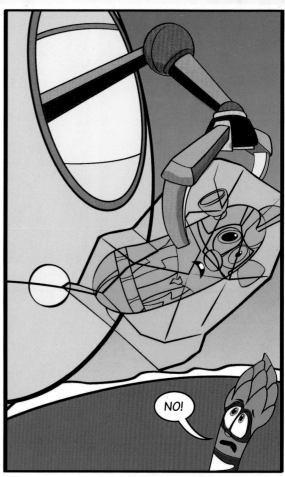

NO!

HURRY! TO THE LARRYCOPTER!

WE MUST RETREAT TO THE LARRYCAVE AND FIND A WAY TO SAVE LARRYBOY!

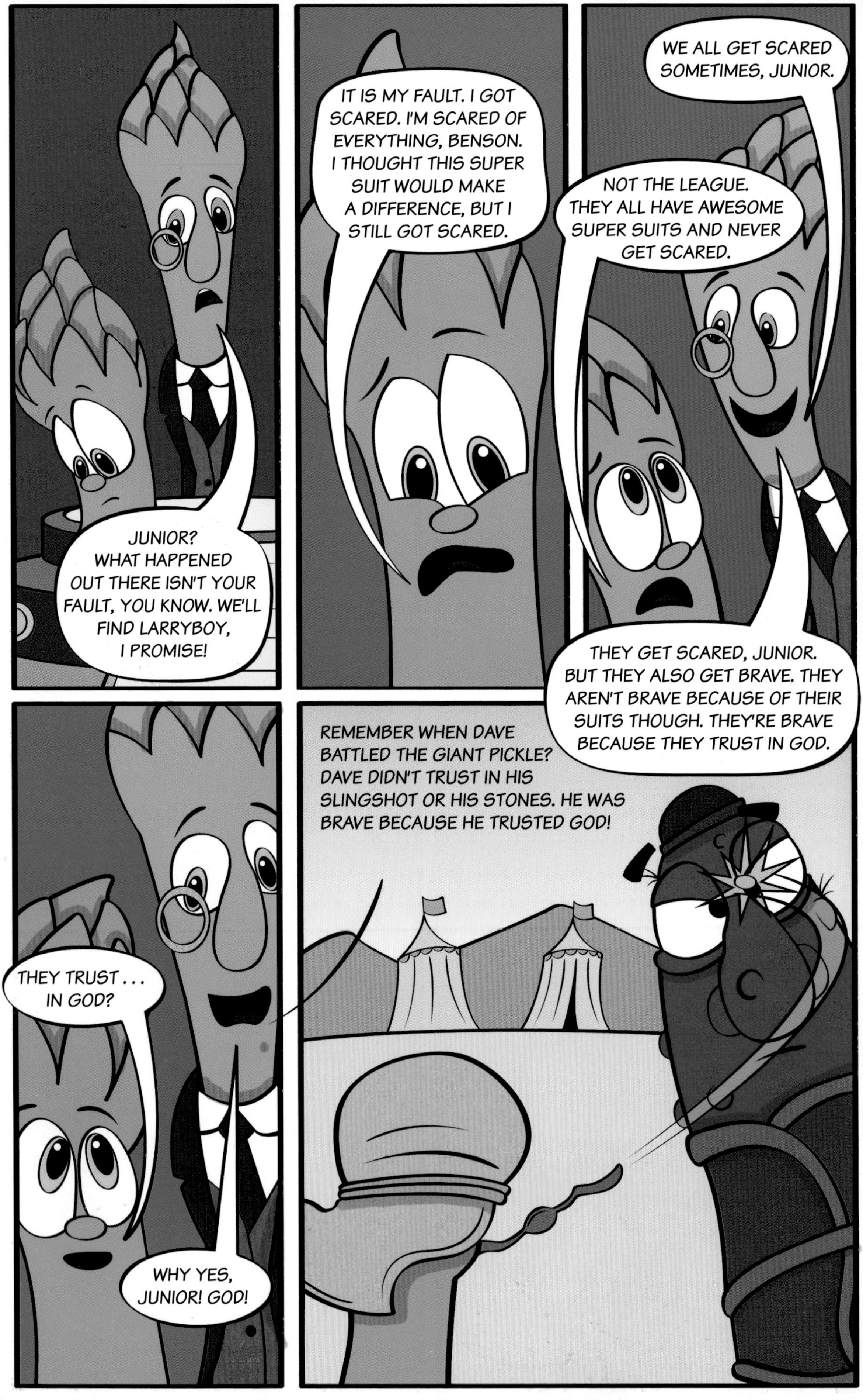
JUNIOR? WHAT HAPPENED OUT THERE ISN'T YOUR FAULT, YOU KNOW. WE'LL FIND LARRYBOY, I PROMISE!
IT IS MY FAULT. I GOT SCARED. I'M SCARED OF EVERYTHING, BENSON. I THOUGHT THIS SUPER SUIT WOULD MAKE A DIFFERENCE, BUT I STILL GOT SCARED.
WE ALL GET SCARED SOMETIMES, JUNIOR.
NOT THE LEAGUE. THEY ALL HAVE AWESOME SUPER SUITS AND NEVER GET SCARED.
THEY GET SCARED, JUNIOR. BUT THEY ALSO GET BRAVE. THEY AREN'T BRAVE BECAUSE OF THEIR SUITS THOUGH. THEY'RE BRAVE BECAUSE THEY TRUST IN GOD.
THEY TRUST . . . IN GOD?
WHY YES, JUNIOR! GOD!
REMEMBER WHEN DAVE BATTLED THE GIANT PICKLE? DAVE DIDN'T TRUST IN HIS SLINGSHOT OR HIS STONES. HE WAS BRAVE BECAUSE HE TRUSTED GOD!

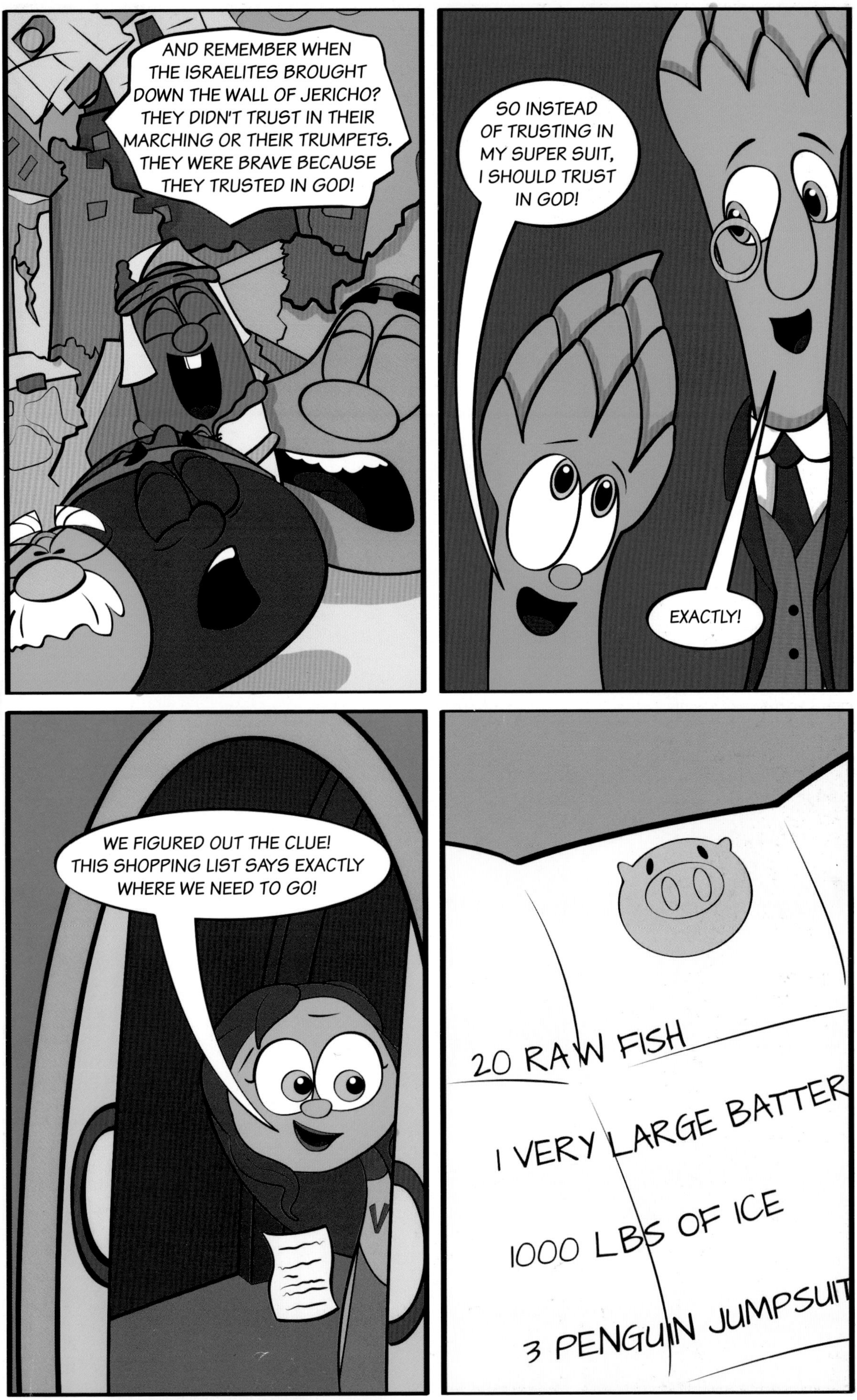
AND REMEMBER WHEN THE ISRAELITES BROUGHT DOWN THE WALL OF JERICHO? THEY DIDN'T TRUST IN THEIR MARCHING OR THEIR TRUMPETS. THEY WERE BRAVE BECAUSE THEY TRUSTED IN GOD!
SO INSTEAD OF TRUSTING IN MY SUPER SUIT, I SHOULD TRUST IN GOD!
EXACTLY!
WE FIGURED OUT THE CLUE! THIS SHOPPING LIST SAYS EXACTLY WHERE WE NEED TO GO!
20 RAW FISH
1 VERY LARGE BATTER
1000 LBS OF ICE
3 PENGUIN JUMPSUIT

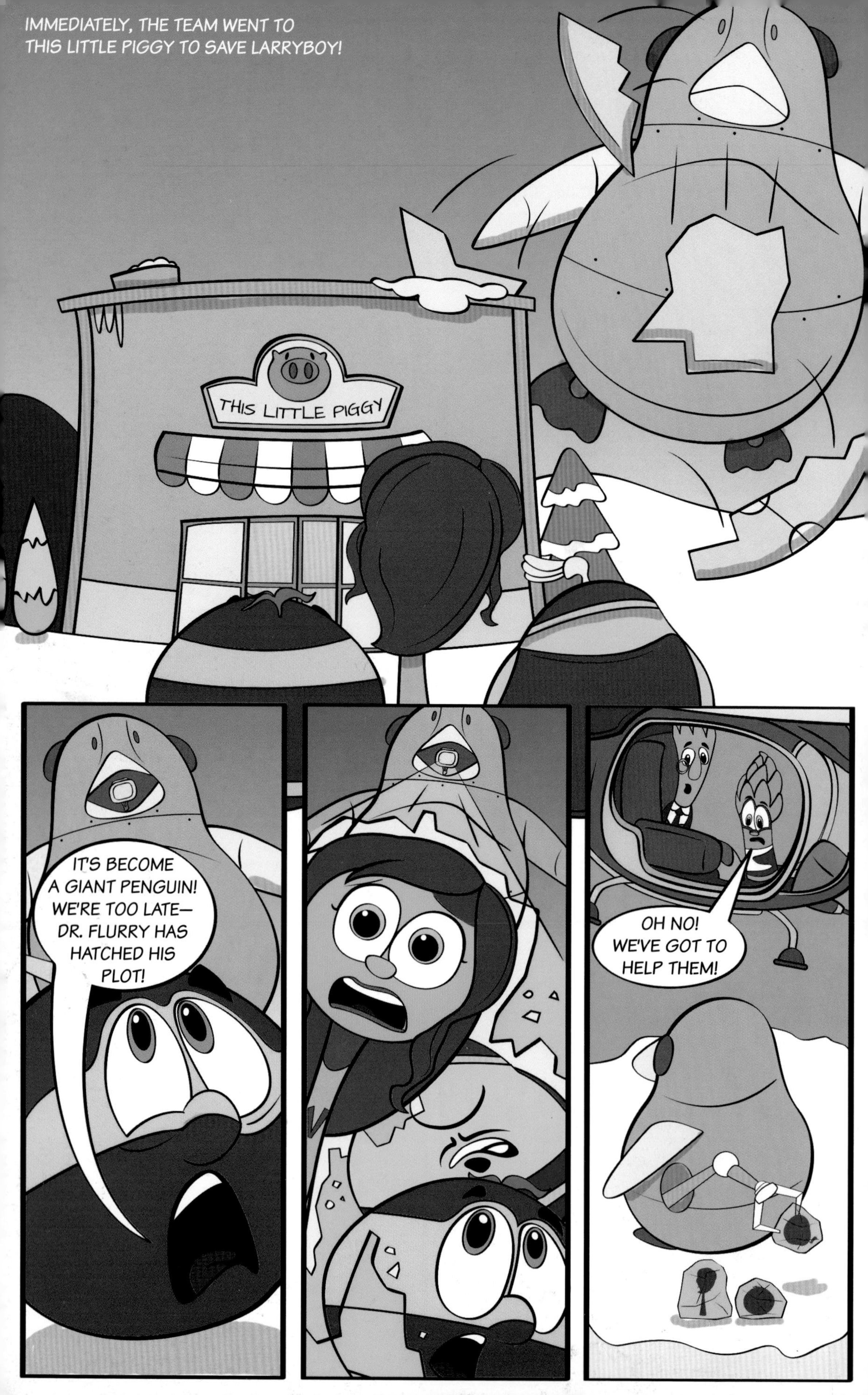
IMMEDIATELY, THE TEAM WENT TO THIS LITTLE PIGGY TO SAVE LARRYBOY!
THIS LITTLE PIGGY
IT'S BECOME A GIANT PENGUIN! WE'RE TOO LATE— DR. FLURRY HAS HATCHED HIS PLOT!
OH NO! WE'VE GOT TO HELP THEM!

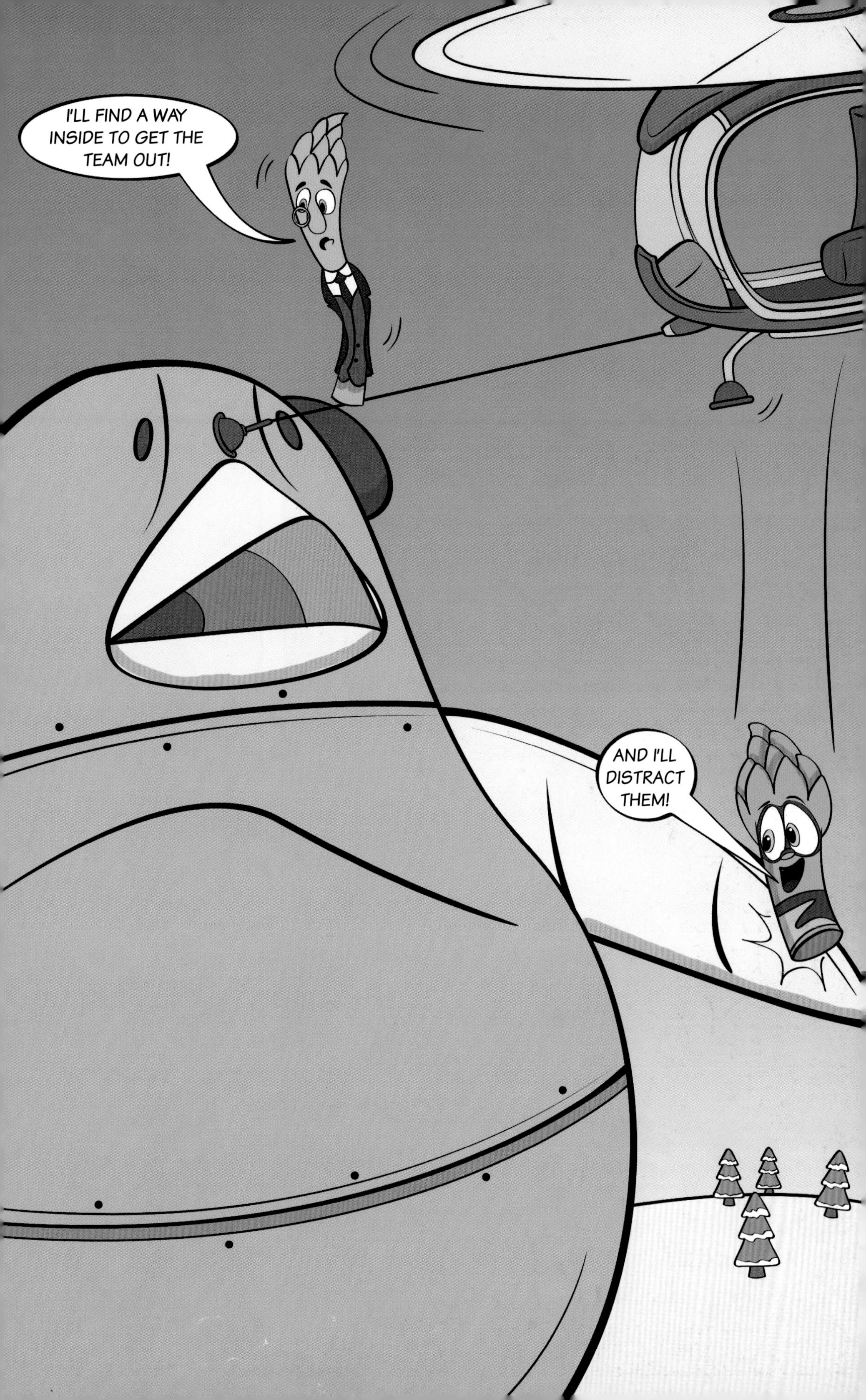
I'LL FIND A WAY INSIDE TO GET THE TEAM OUT!
AND I'LL DISTRACT THEM!

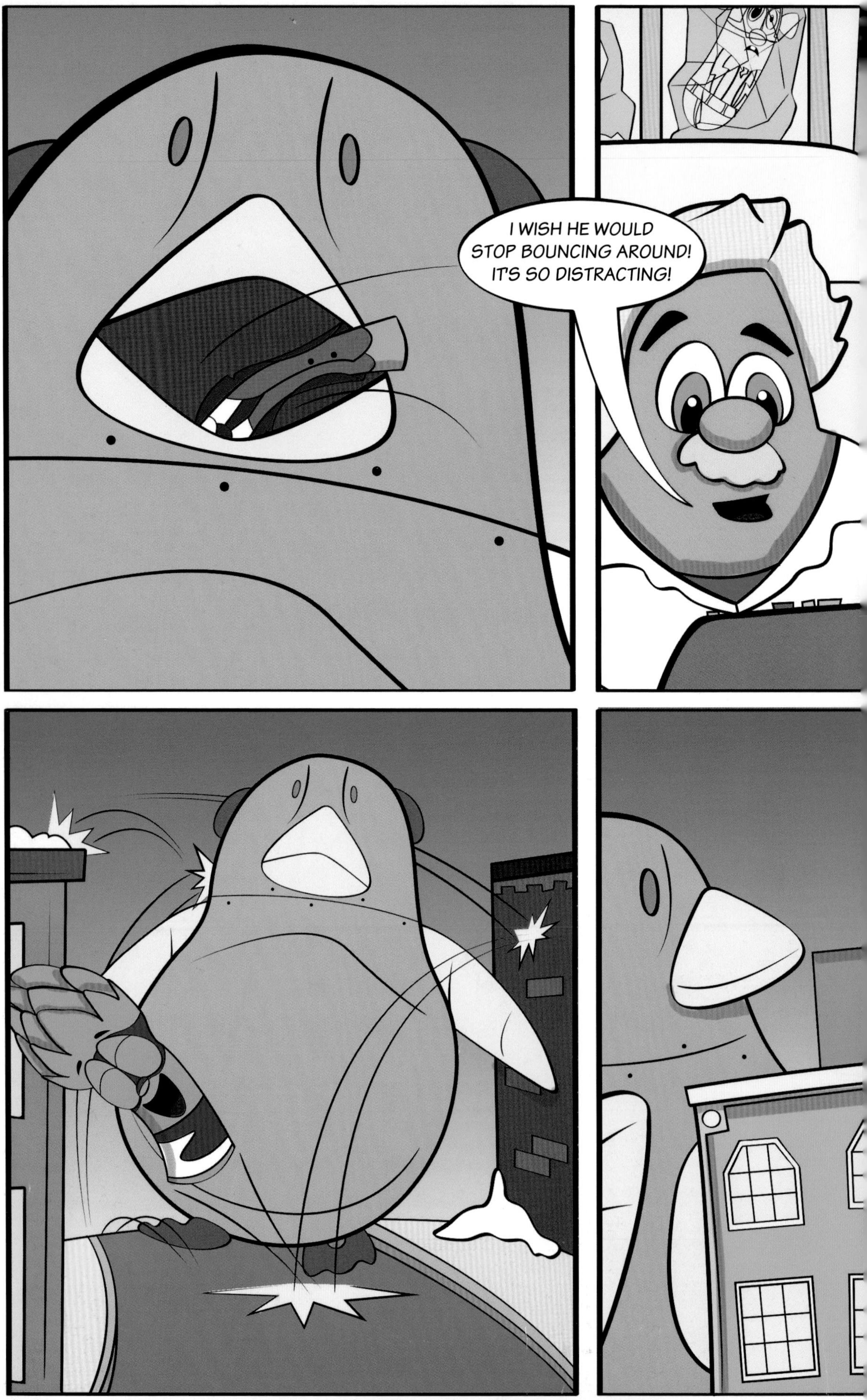
I WISH HE WOULD STOP BOUNCING AROUND! IT'S SO DISTRACTING!

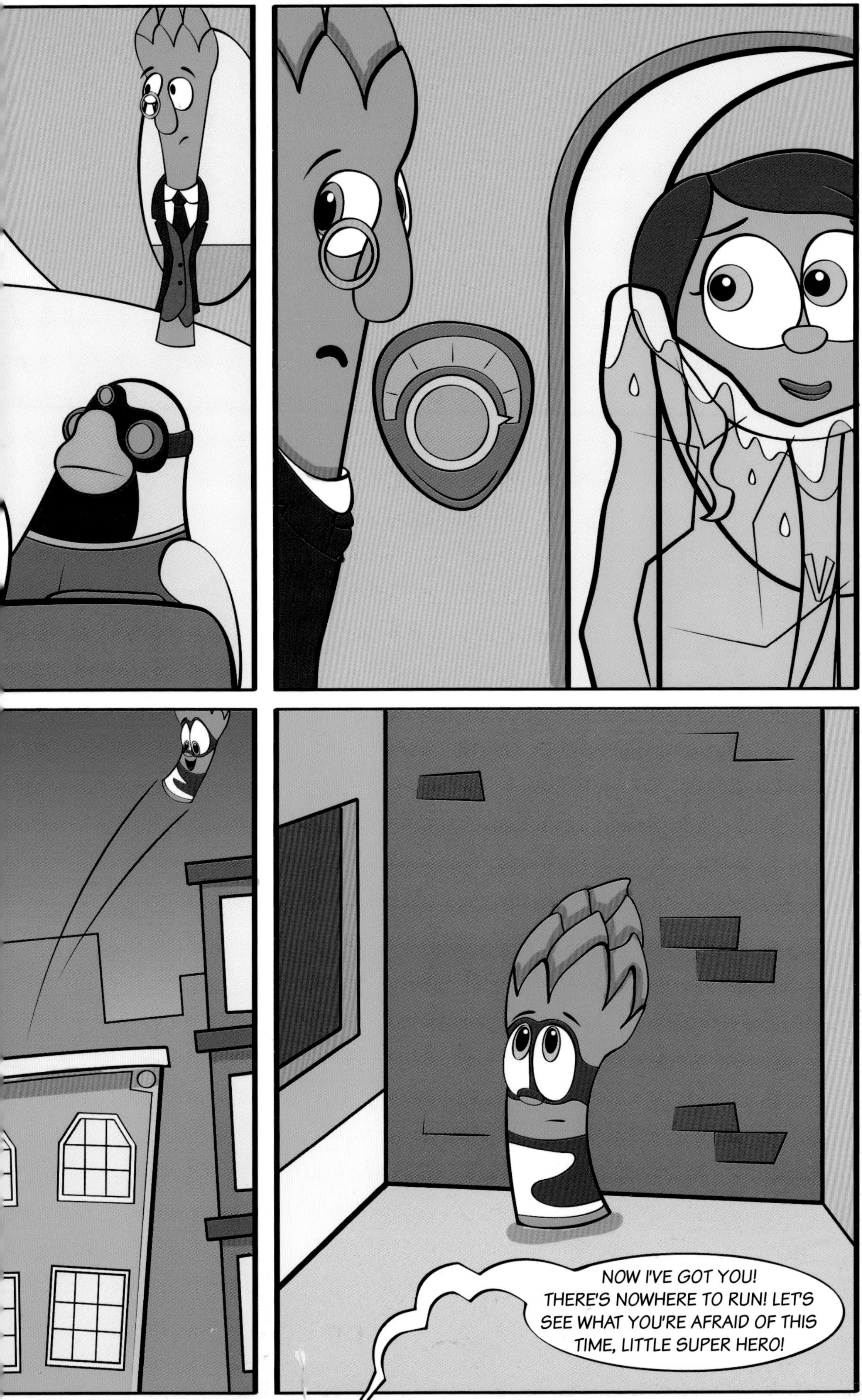
NOW I'VE GOT YOU! THERE'S NOWHERE TO RUN! LET'S SEE WHAT YOU'RE AFRAID OF THIS TIME, LITTLE SUPER HERO!

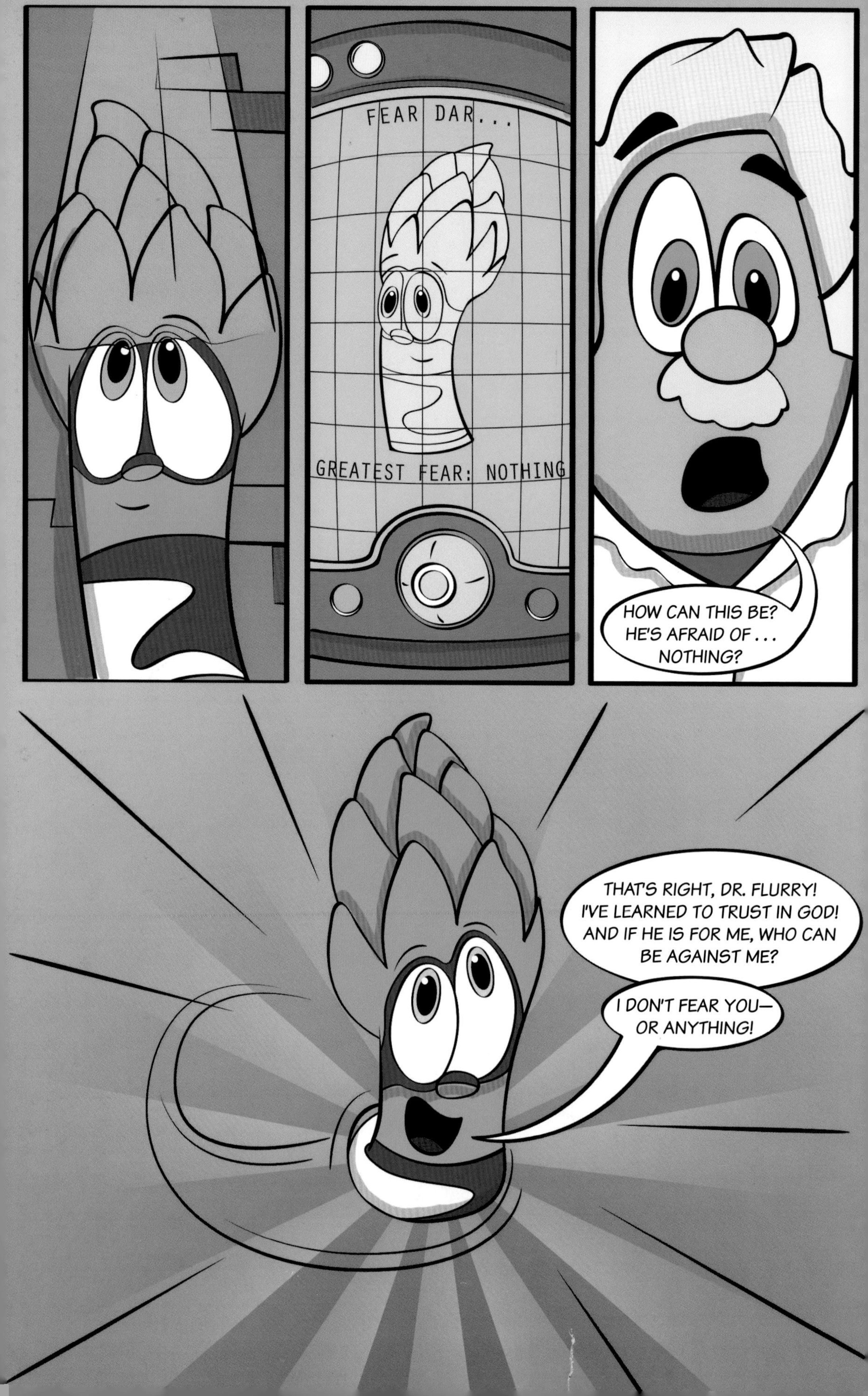
FEAR DAR...
GREATEST FEAR: NOTHING
HOW CAN THIS BE? HE'S AFRAID OF . . . NOTHING?
THAT'S RIGHT, DR. FLURRY! I'VE LEARNED TO TRUST IN GOD! AND IF HE IS FOR ME, WHO CAN BE AGAINST ME?
I DON'T FEAR YOU— OR ANYTHING!

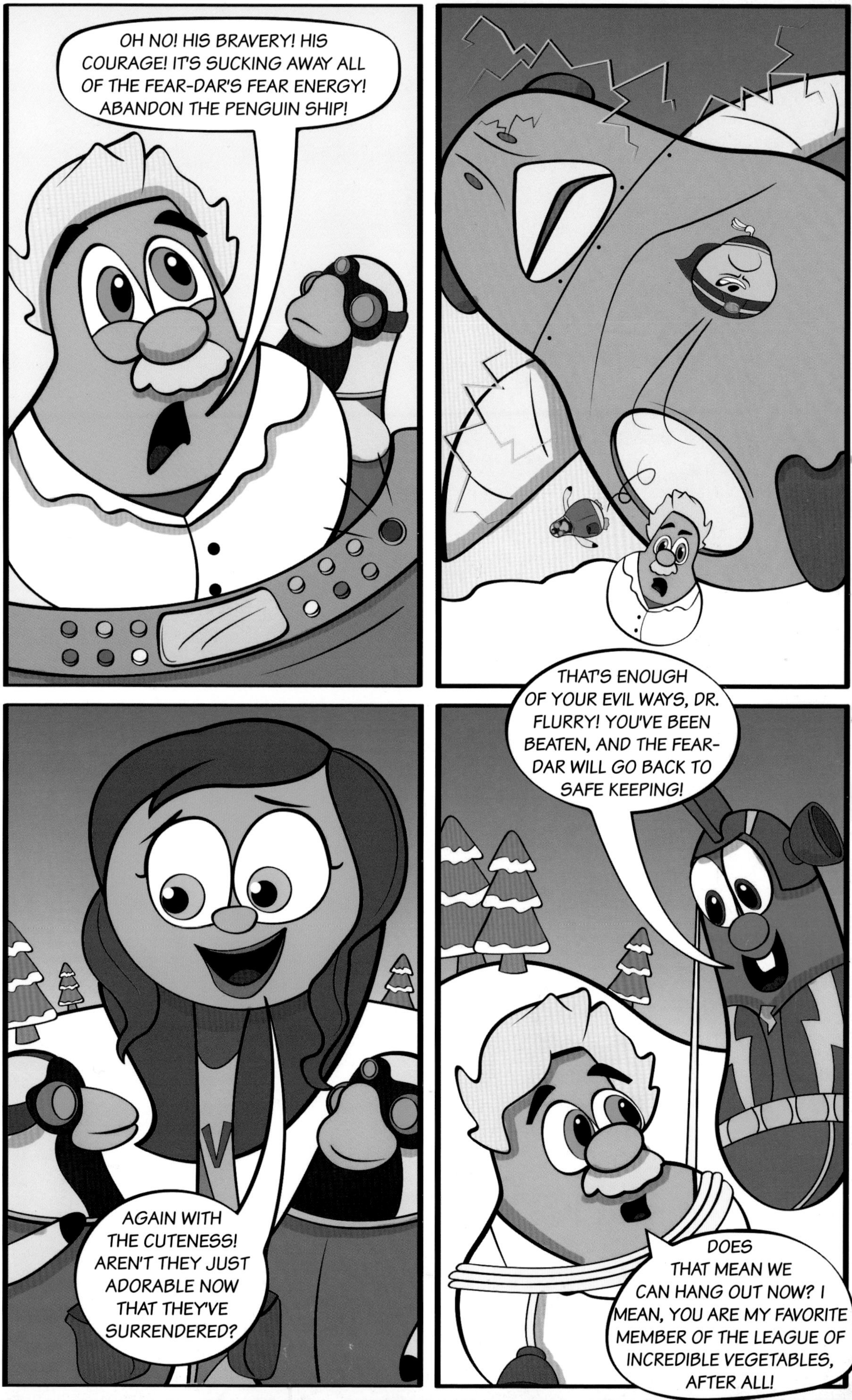
OH NO! HIS BRAVERY! HIS COURAGE! IT'S SUCKING AWAY ALL OF THE FEAR-DAR'S FEAR ENERGY! ABANDON THE PENGUIN SHIP!
AGAIN WITH THE CUTENESS! AREN'T THEY JUST ADORABLE NOW THAT THEY'VE SURRENDERED?
THAT'S ENOUGH OF YOUR EVIL WAYS, DR. FLURRY! YOU'VE BEEN BEATEN, AND THE FEAR-DAR WILL GO BACK TO SAFE KEEPING!
DOES THAT MEAN WE CAN HANG OUT NOW? I MEAN, YOU ARE MY FAVORITE MEMBER OF THE LEAGUE OF INCREDIBLE VEGETABLES, AFTER ALL!

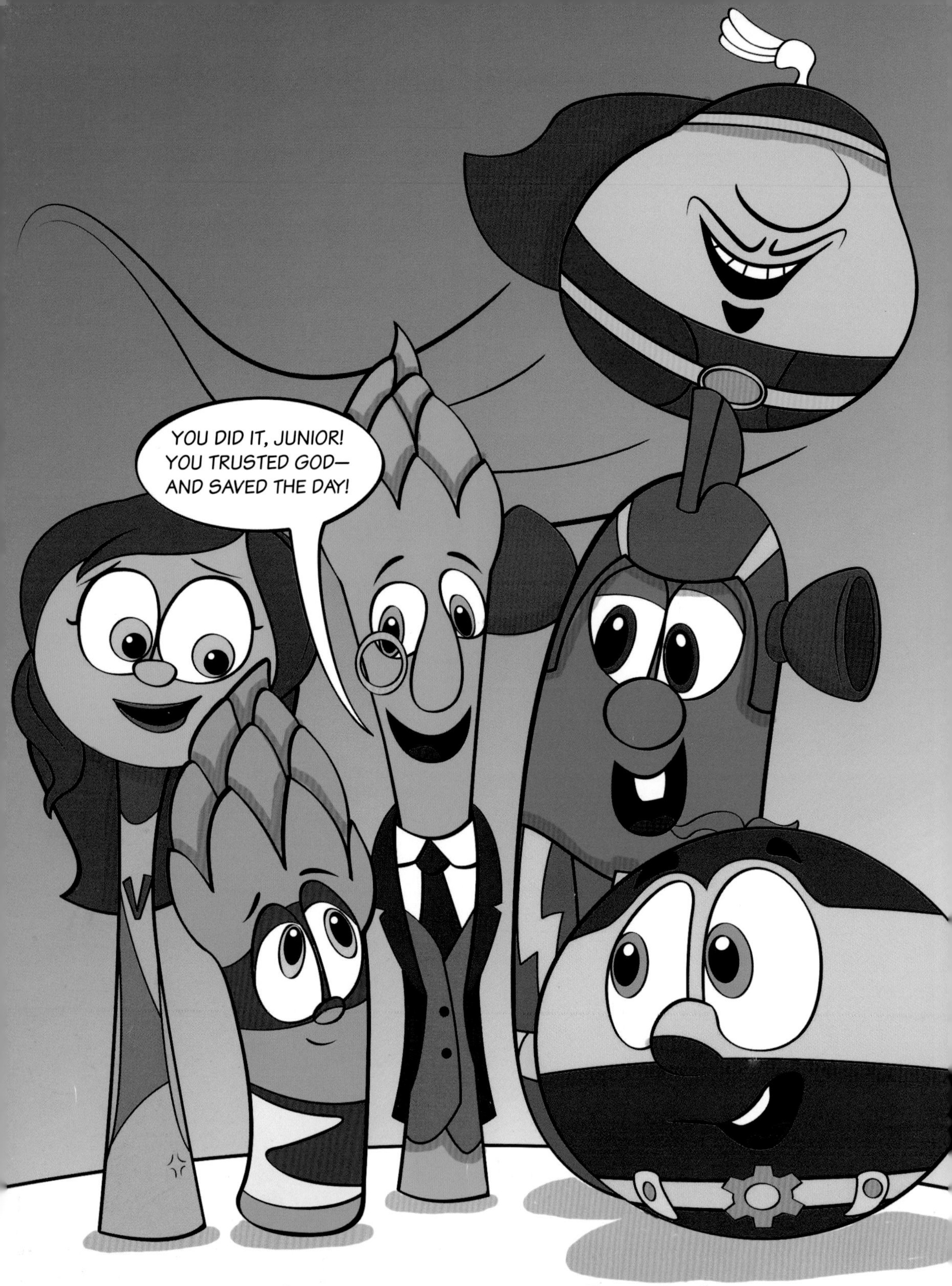
YOU DID IT, JUNIOR! YOU TRUSTED GOD— AND SAVED THE DAY!

When I am afraid,
I put my trust in you.

—PSALM 56:3 (NIV)

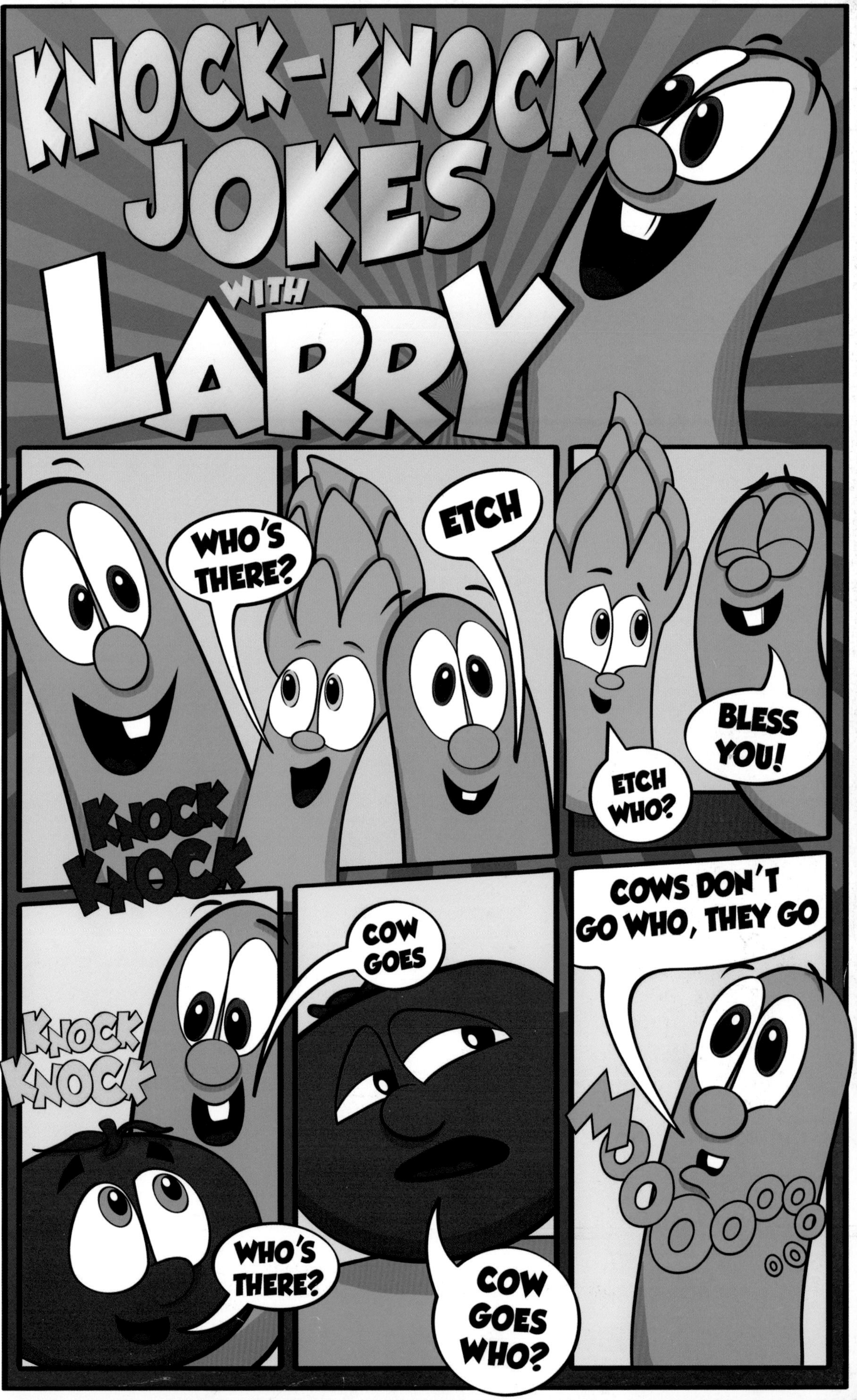
KNOCK-KNOCK JOKES WITH LARRY
KNOCK KNOCK
WHO'S THERE?
ETCH
ETCH WHO?
BLESS YOU!
KNOCK KNOCK
WHO'S THERE?
COW GOES
COW GOES WHO?
COWS DON'T GO WHO, THEY GO
MOOOOOOOOO

NETFLIX

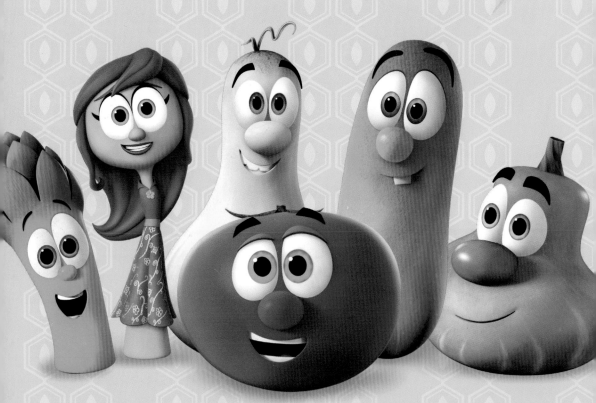

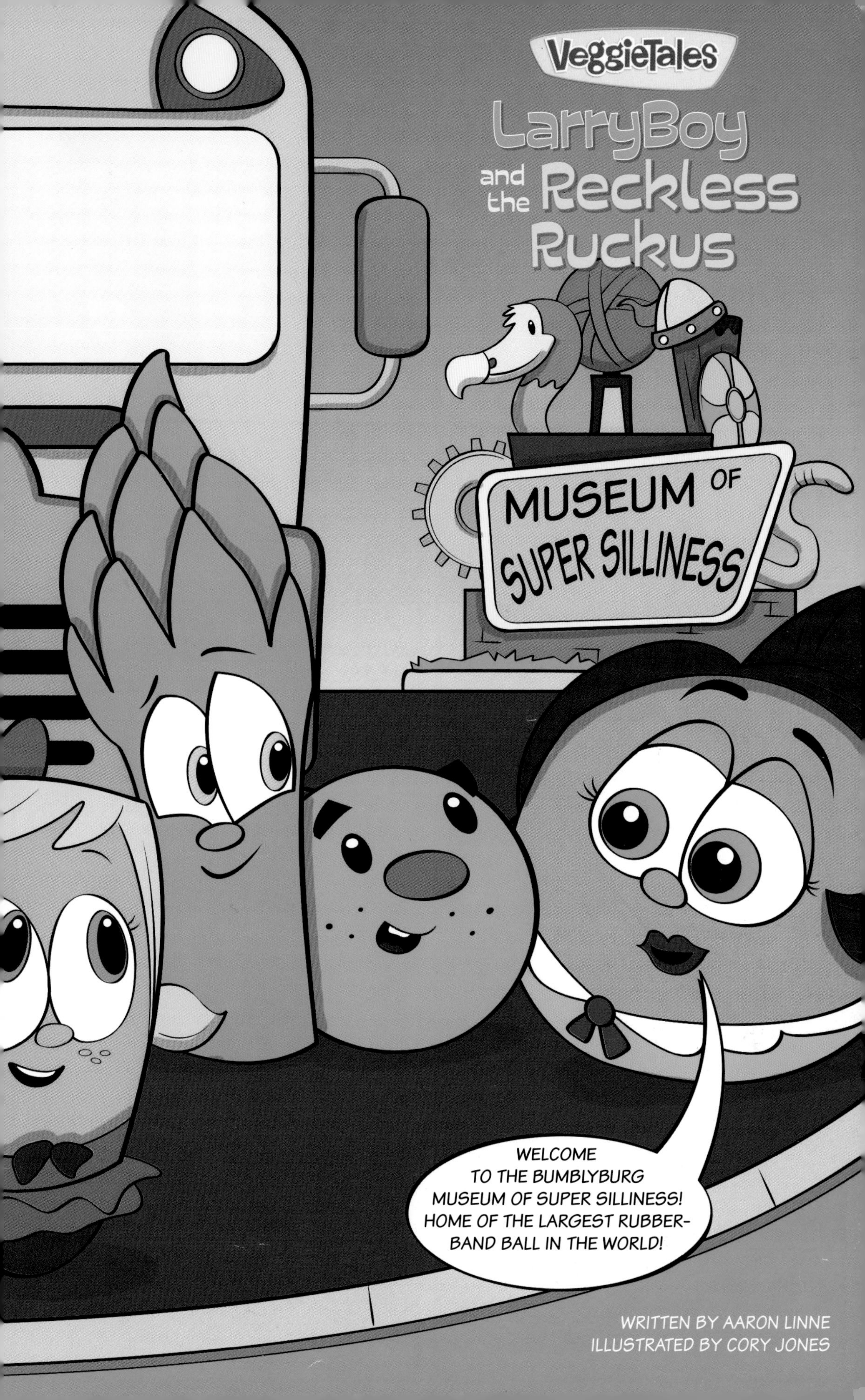
VeggieTales
LarryBoy and the Reckless Ruckus
MUSEUM OF SUPER SILLINESS
WELCOME TO THE BUMBLYBURG MUSEUM OF SUPER SILLINESS! HOME OF THE LARGEST RUBBER-BAND BALL IN THE WORLD!
WRITTEN BY AARON LINNE
ILLUSTRATED BY CORY JONES

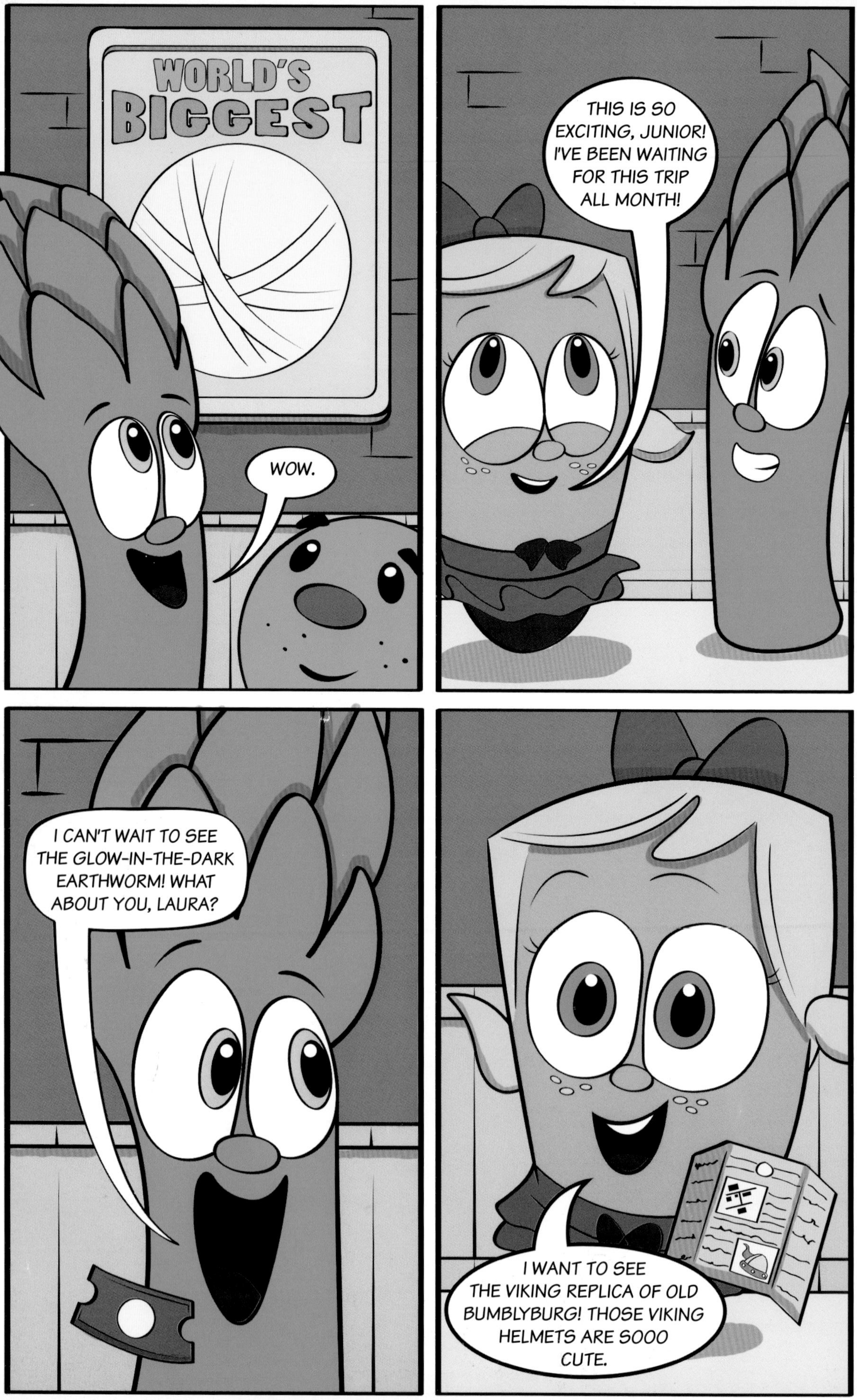
WORLD'S BIGGEST
WOW.
THIS IS SO EXCITING, JUNIOR! I'VE BEEN WAITING FOR THIS TRIP ALL MONTH!
I CAN'T WAIT TO SEE THE GLOW-IN-THE-DARK EARTHWORM! WHAT ABOUT YOU, LAURA?
I WANT TO SEE THE VIKING REPLICA OF OLD BUMBLYBURG! THOSE VIKING HELMETS ARE SOOO CUTE.

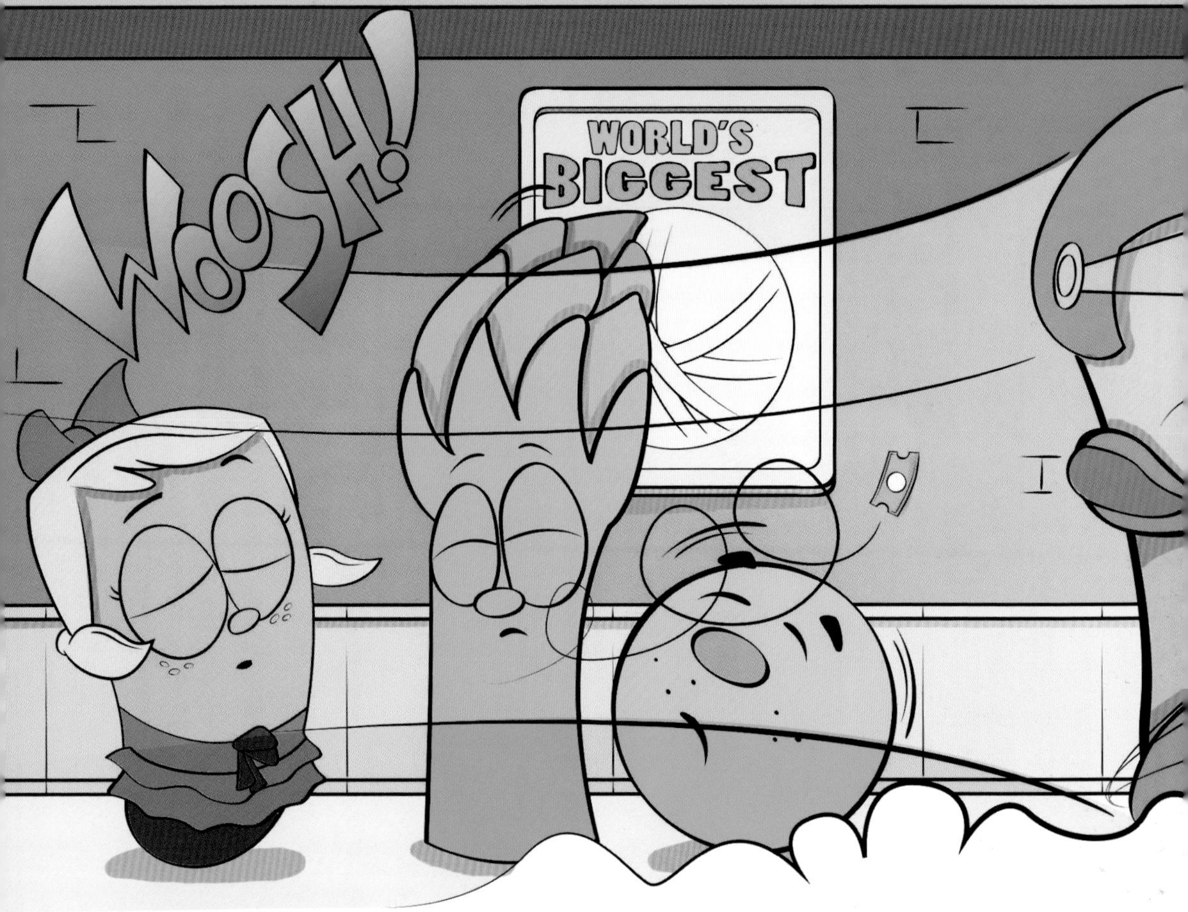
WOOSH!!
WORLD'S BIGGEST

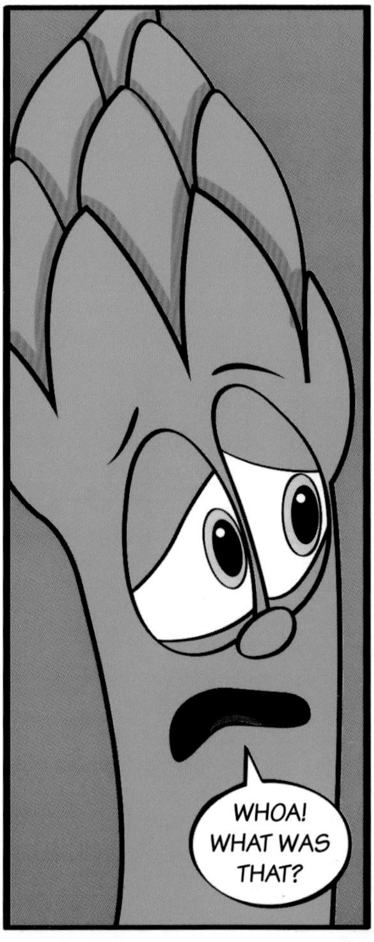
WHOA! WHAT WAS THAT?

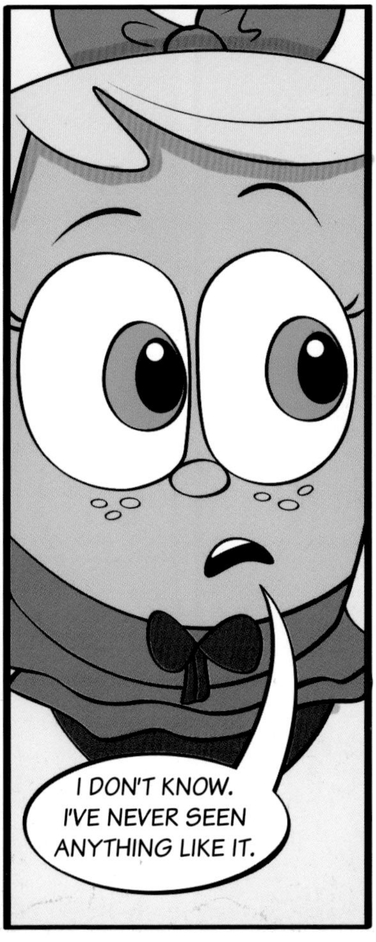
I DON'T KNOW. I'VE NEVER SEEN ANYTHING LIKE IT.

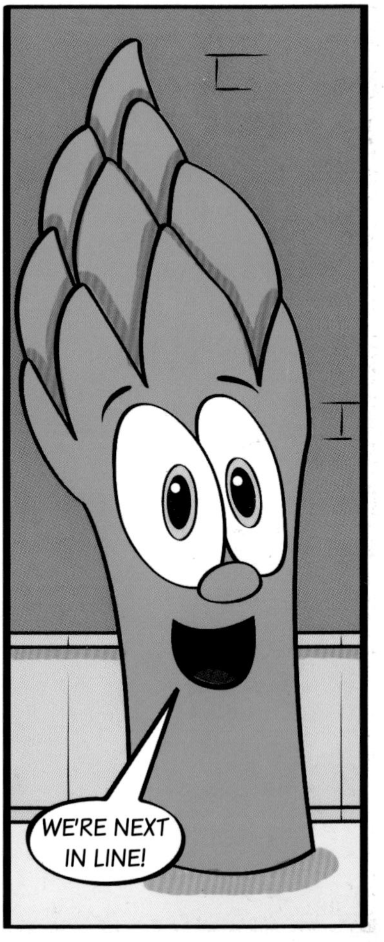
WE'RE NEXT IN LINE!

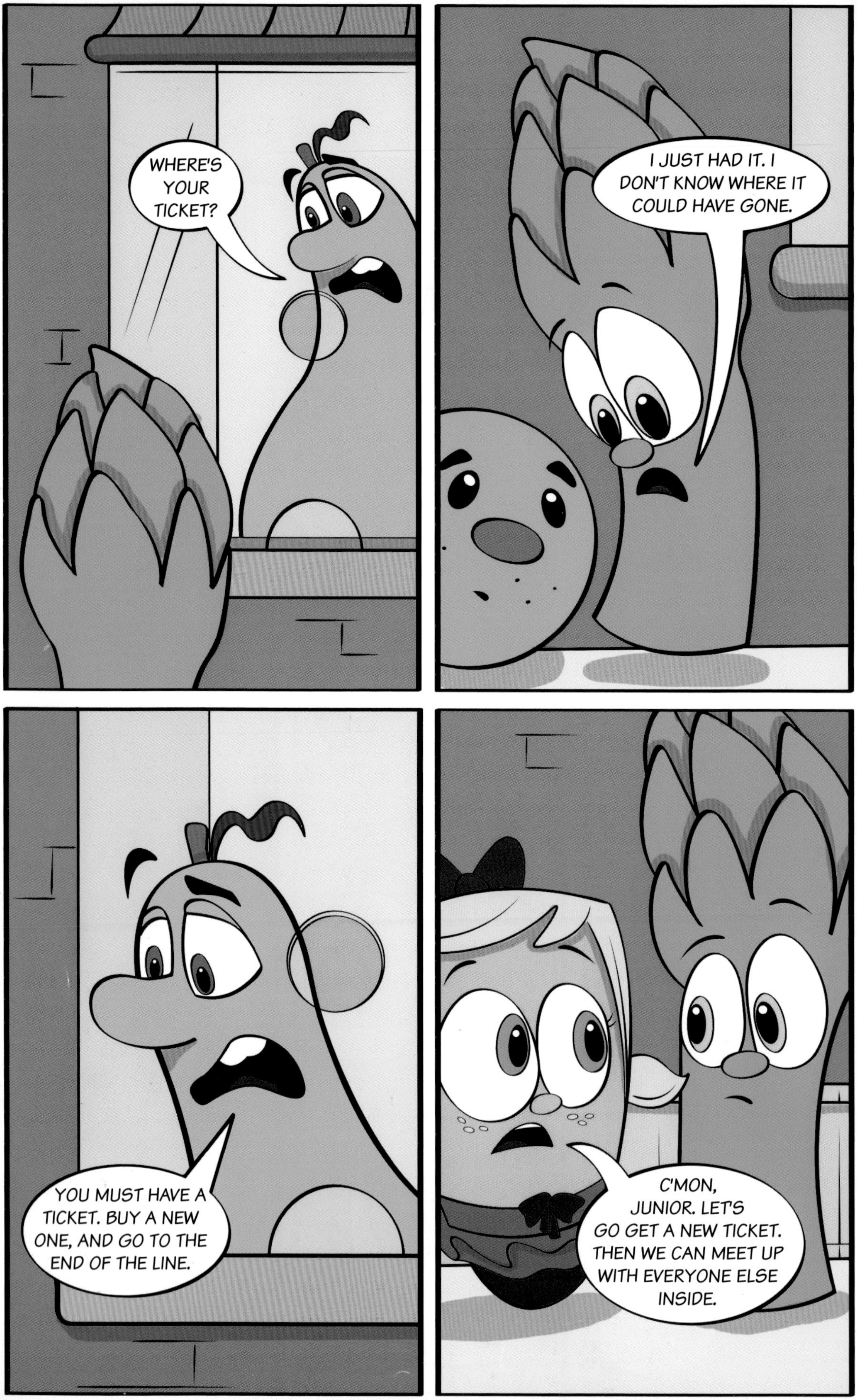
WHERE'S YOUR TICKET?
I JUST HAD IT. I DON'T KNOW WHERE IT COULD HAVE GONE.
YOU MUST HAVE A TICKET. BUY A NEW ONE, AND GO TO THE END OF THE LINE.
C'MON, JUNIOR. LET'S GO GET A NEW TICKET. THEN WE CAN MEET UP WITH EVERYONE ELSE INSIDE.

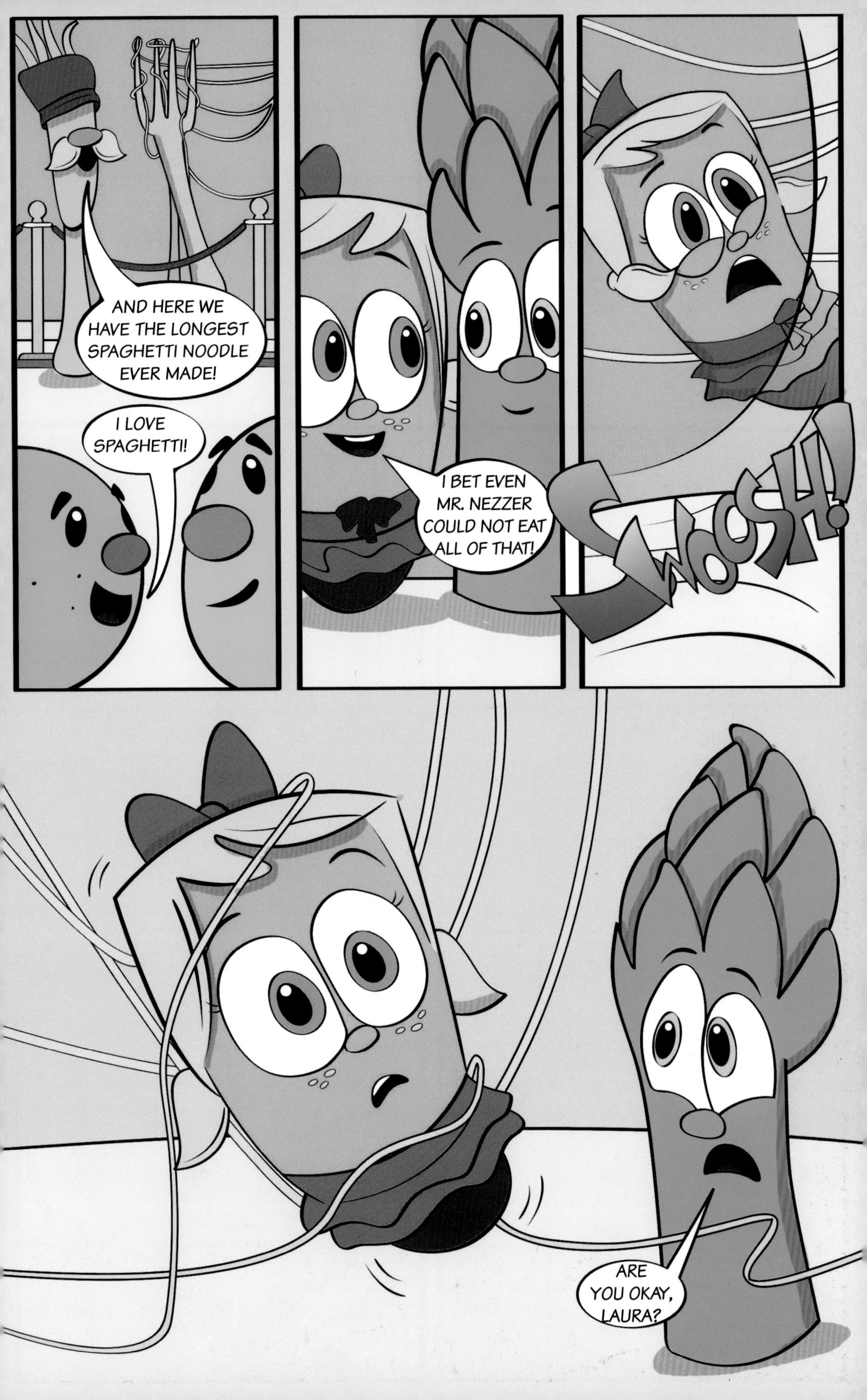
AND HERE WE HAVE THE LONGEST SPAGHETTI NOODLE EVER MADE!
I LOVE SPAGHETTI!
I BET EVEN MR. NEZZER COULD NOT EAT ALL OF THAT!
SWOOSH!
ARE YOU OKAY, LAURA?

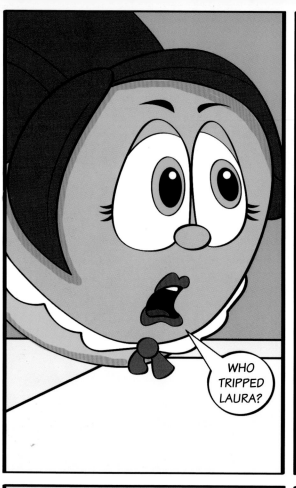

WHO TRIPPED LAURA?

I SAW DAVIS DO IT!

I DID NOT! I WOULD HAVE JUMPED IN AND EATEN SOME MYSELF IF I KNEW WE WERE ALLOWED!

WHO SAID THEY SAW DAVIS DO IT?

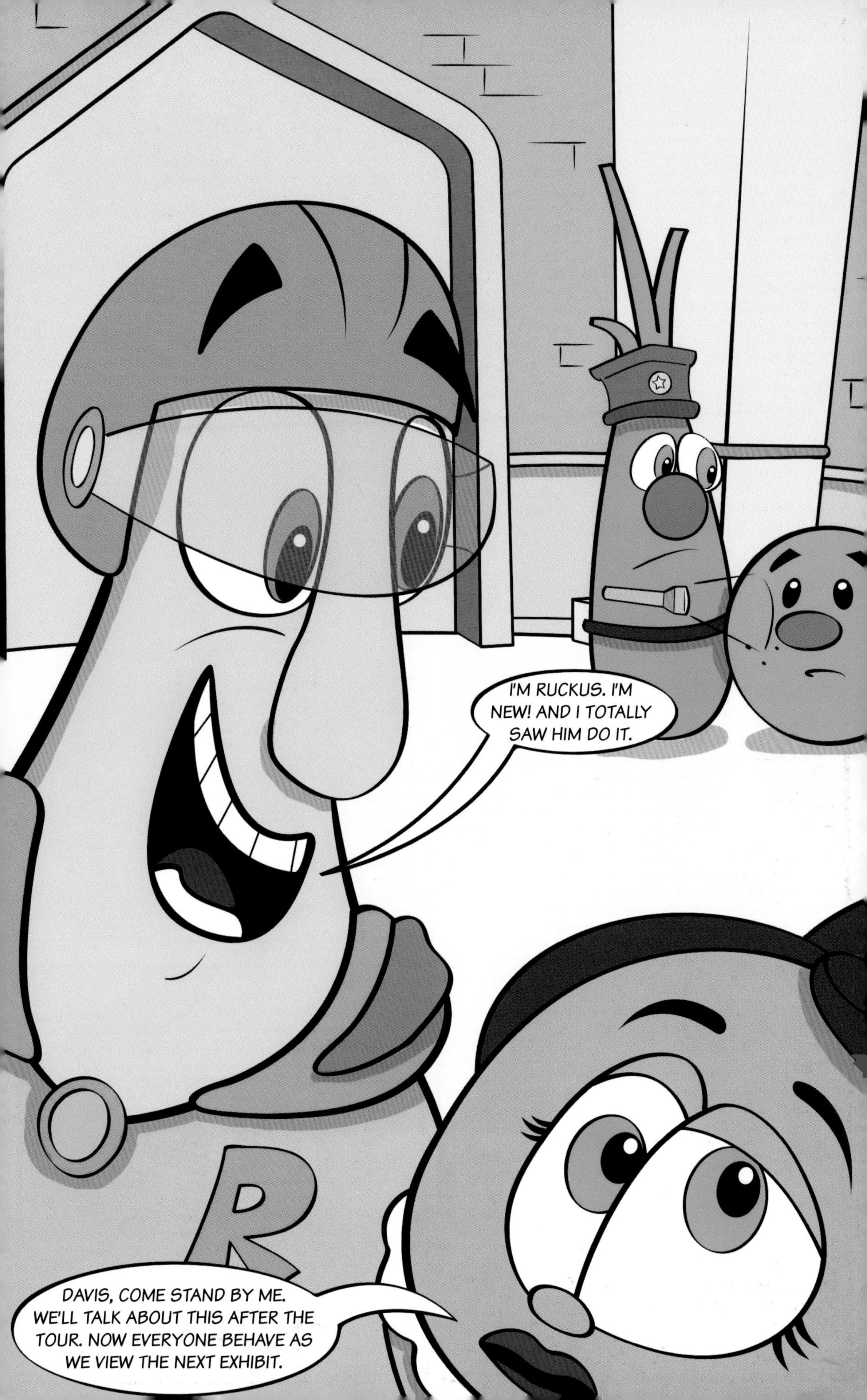
I'M RUCKUS. I'M NEW! AND I TOTALLY SAW HIM DO IT.
DAVIS, COME STAND BY ME. WE'LL TALK ABOUT THIS AFTER THE TOUR. NOW EVERYONE BEHAVE AS WE VIEW THE NEXT EXHIBIT.

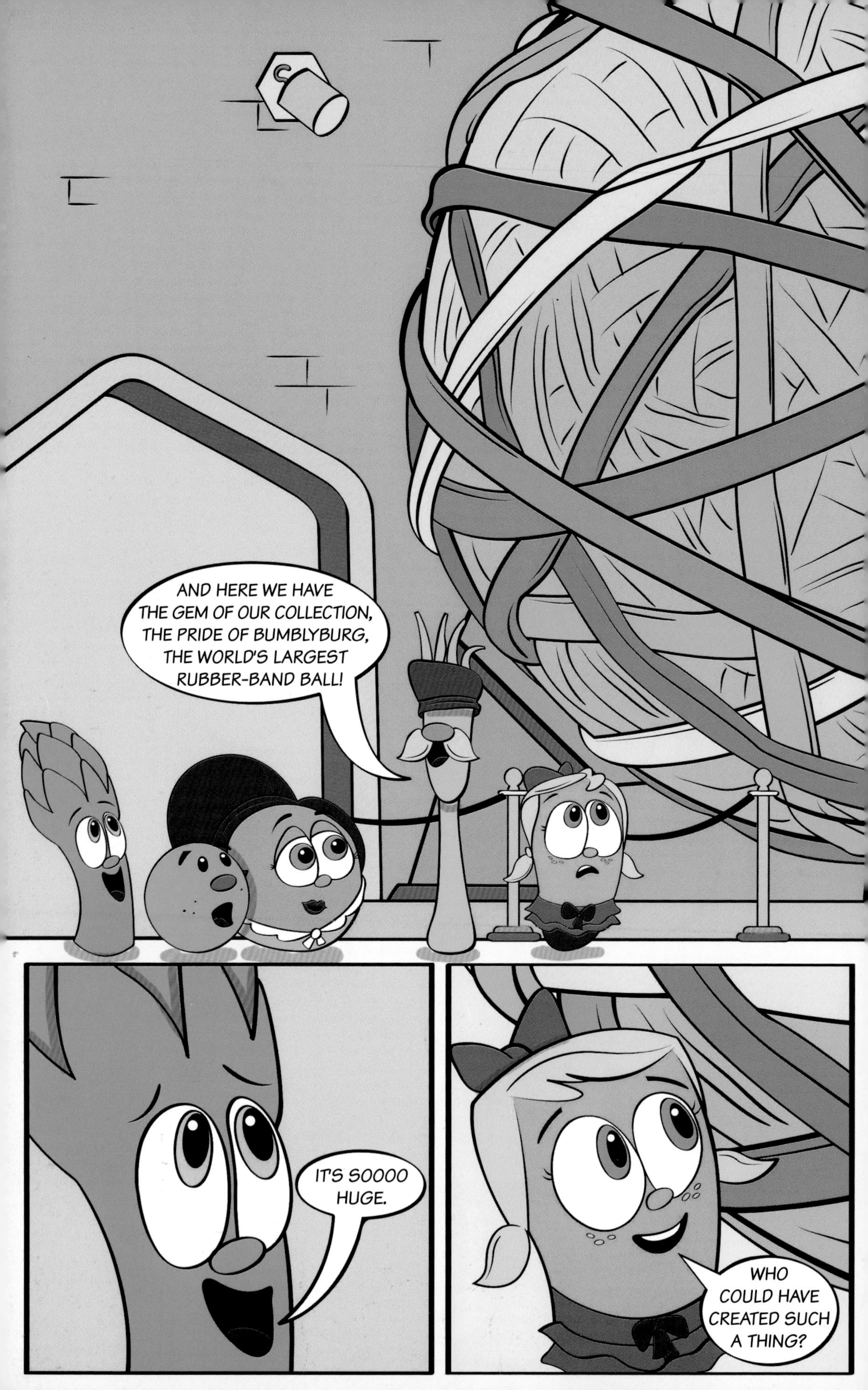
AND HERE WE HAVE THE GEM OF OUR COLLECTION, THE PRIDE OF BUMBLYBURG, THE WORLD'S LARGEST RUBBER-BAND BALL!
IT'S SOOOO HUGE.
WHO COULD HAVE CREATED SUCH A THING?

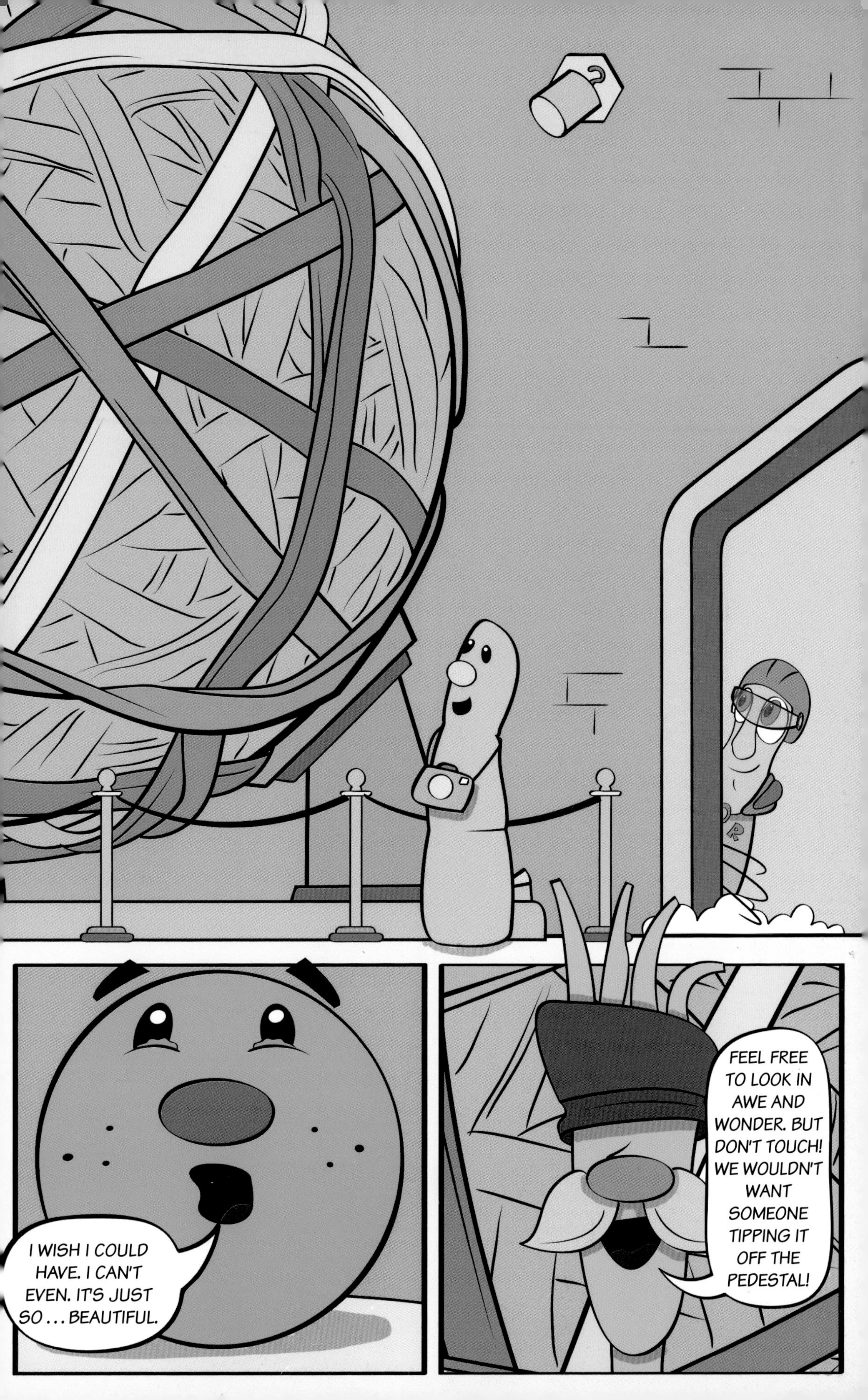
I WISH I COULD HAVE. I CAN'T EVEN. IT'S JUST SO . . . BEAUTIFUL.
FEEL FREE TO LOOK IN AWE AND WONDER. BUT DON'T TOUCH! WE WOULDN'T WANT SOMEONE TIPPING IT OFF THE PEDESTAL!

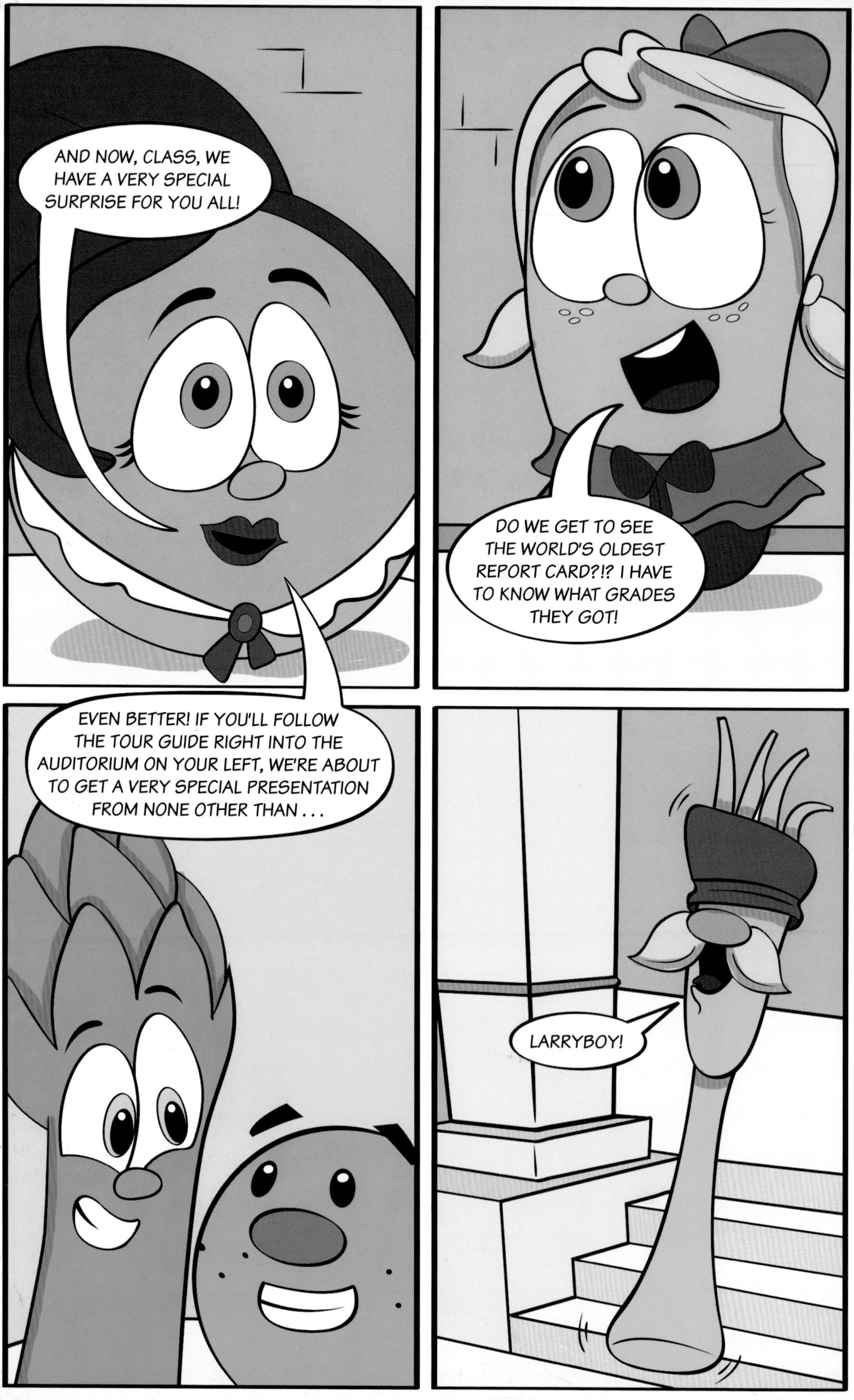
AND NOW, CLASS, WE HAVE A VERY SPECIAL SURPRISE FOR YOU ALL!
DO WE GET TO SEE THE WORLD'S OLDEST REPORT CARD?!? I HAVE TO KNOW WHAT GRADES THEY GOT!
EVEN BETTER! IF YOU'LL FOLLOW THE TOUR GUIDE RIGHT INTO THE AUDITORIUM ON YOUR LEFT, WE'RE ABOUT TO GET A VERY SPECIAL PRESENTATION FROM NONE OTHER THAN . . .
LARRYBOY!

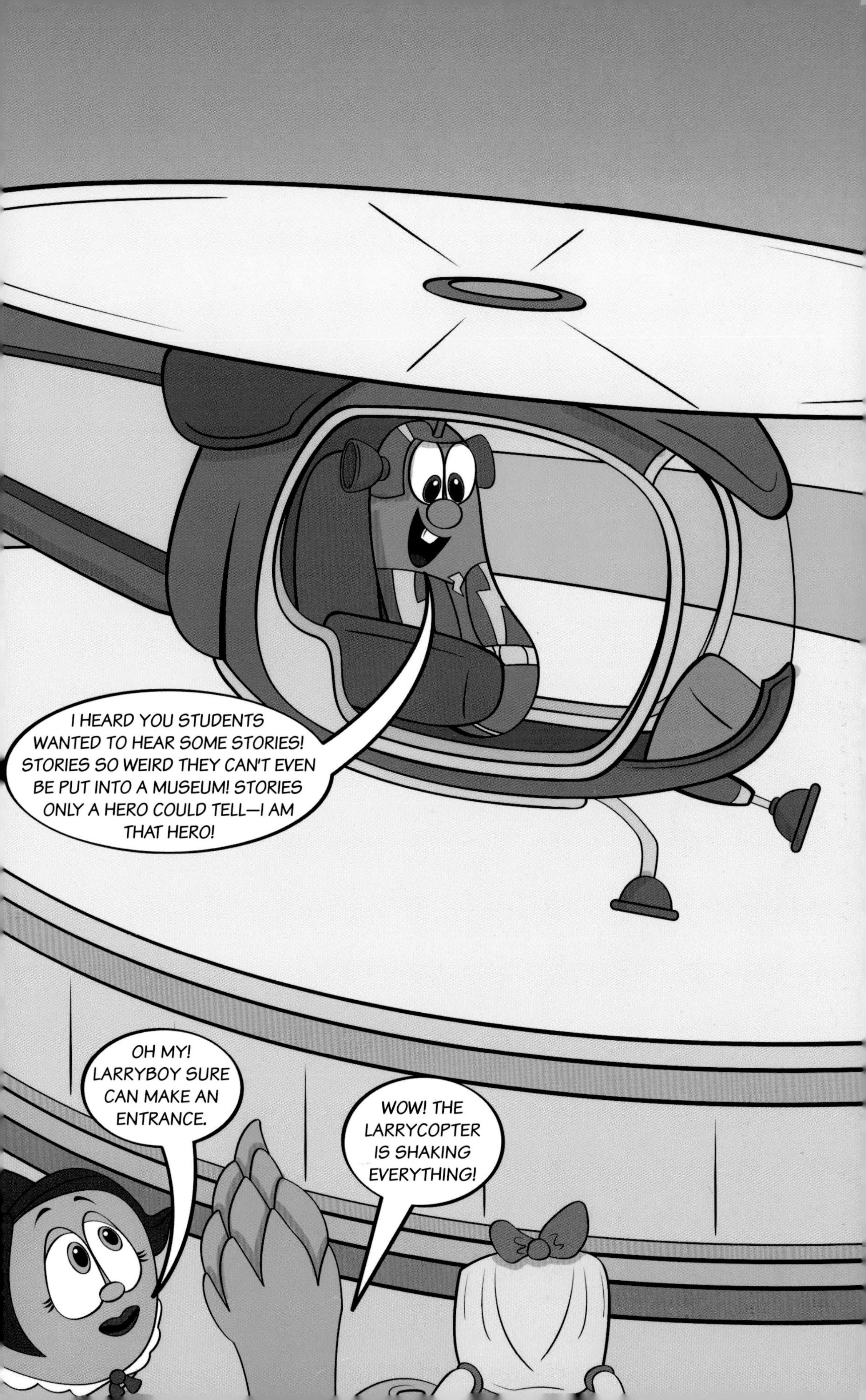
I HEARD YOU STUDENTS WANTED TO HEAR SOME STORIES! STORIES SO WEIRD THEY CAN'T EVEN BE PUT INTO A MUSEUM! STORIES ONLY A HERO COULD TELL—I AM THAT HERO!
OH MY! LARRYBOY SURE CAN MAKE AN ENTRANCE.
WOW! THE LARRYCOPTER IS SHAKING EVERYTHING!

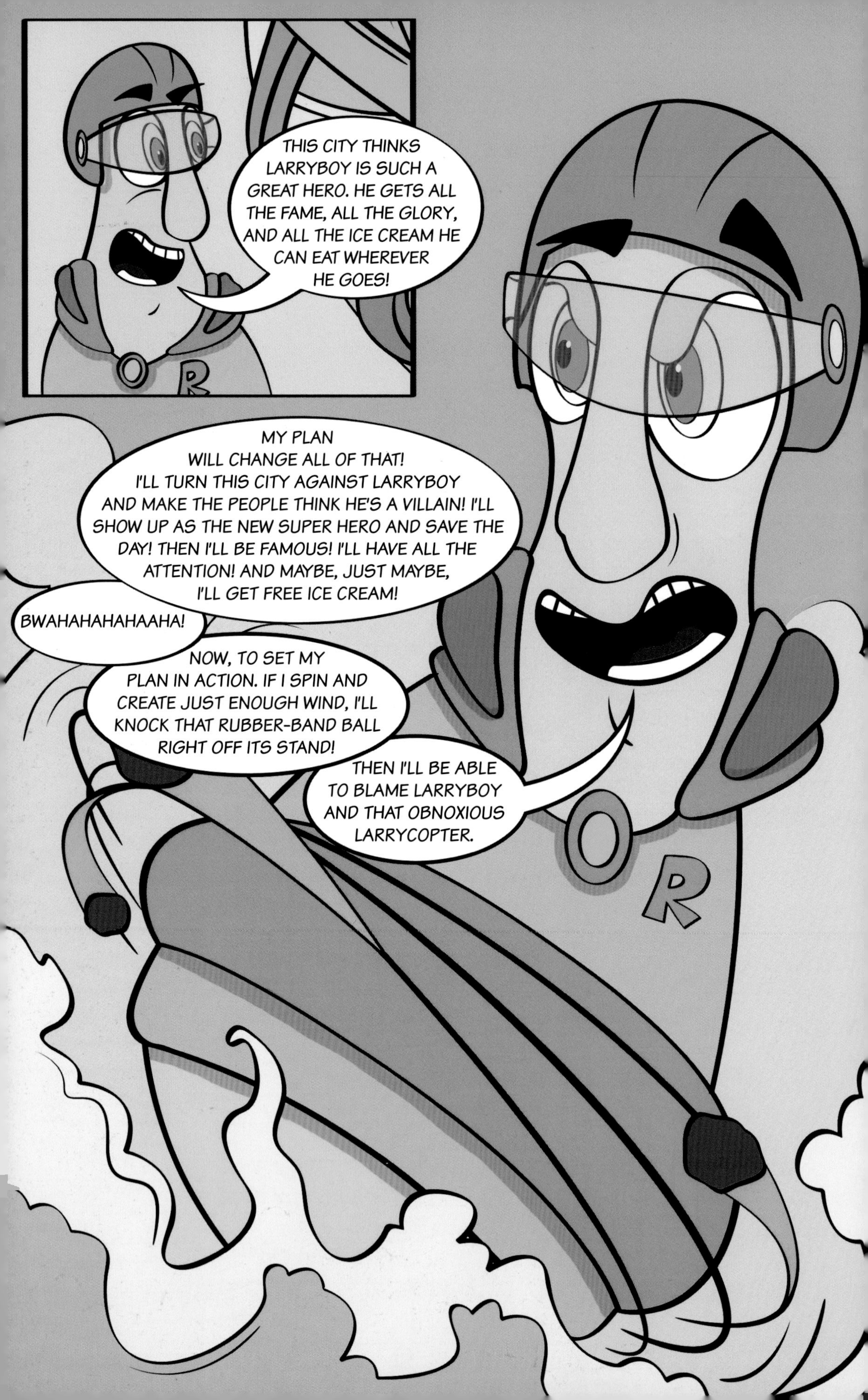
THIS CITY THINKS LARRYBOY IS SUCH A GREAT HERO. HE GETS ALL THE FAME, ALL THE GLORY, AND ALL THE ICE CREAM HE CAN EAT WHEREVER HE GOES!
MY PLAN WILL CHANGE ALL OF THAT! I'LL TURN THIS CITY AGAINST LARRYBOY AND MAKE THE PEOPLE THINK HE'S A VILLAIN! I'LL SHOW UP AS THE NEW SUPER HERO AND SAVE THE DAY! THEN I'LL BE FAMOUS! I'LL HAVE ALL THE ATTENTION! AND MAYBE, JUST MAYBE, I'LL GET FREE ICE CREAM!
BWAHAHAHAHAAHA!
NOW, TO SET MY PLAN IN ACTION. IF I SPIN AND CREATE JUST ENOUGH WIND, I'LL KNOCK THAT RUBBER-BAND BALL RIGHT OFF ITS STAND!
THEN I'LL BE ABLE TO BLAME LARRYBOY AND THAT OBNOXIOUS LARRYCOPTER.

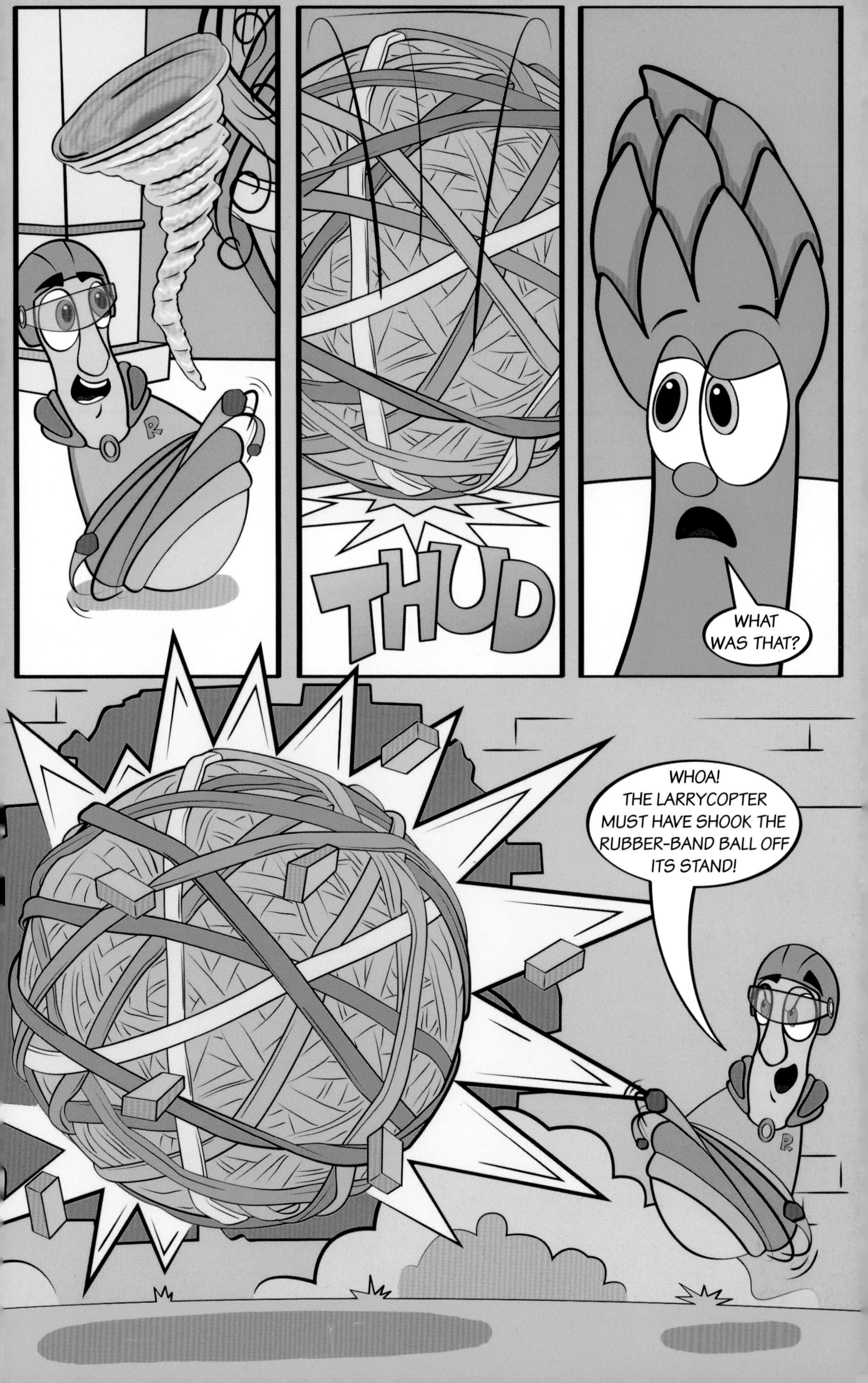
THUD
WHAT WAS THAT?
WHOA! THE LARRYCOPTER MUST HAVE SHOOK THE RUBBER-BAND BALL OFF ITS STAND!

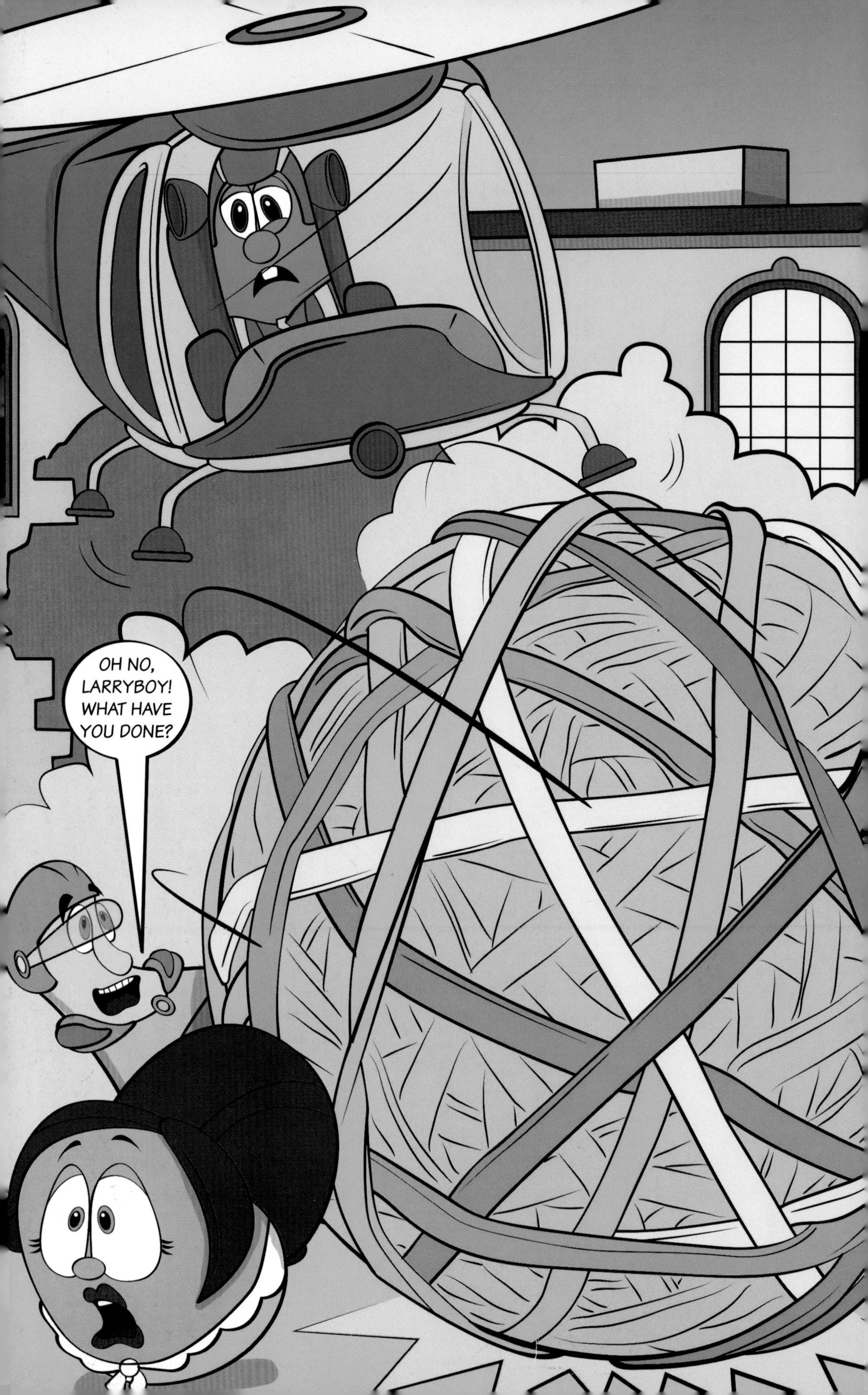
OH NO, LARRYBOY! WHAT HAVE YOU DONE?

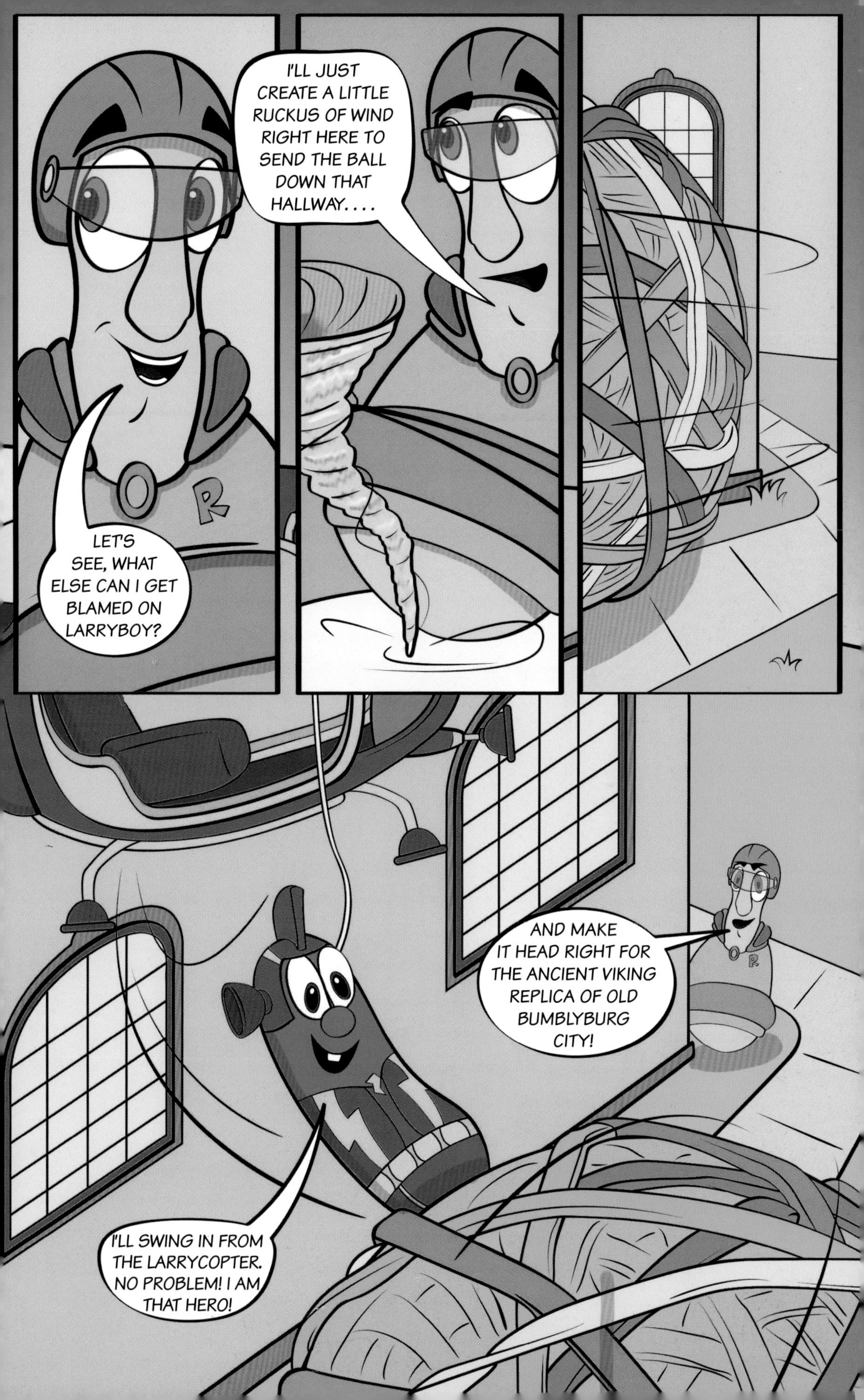
LET'S SEE, WHAT ELSE CAN I GET BLAMED ON LARRYBOY?
I'LL JUST CREATE A LITTLE RUCKUS OF WIND RIGHT HERE TO SEND THE BALL DOWN THAT HALLWAY. . . .
AND MAKE IT HEAD RIGHT FOR THE ANCIENT VIKING REPLICA OF OLD BUMBLYBURG CITY!
I'LL SWING IN FROM THE LARRYCOPTER. NO PROBLEM! I AM THAT HERO!

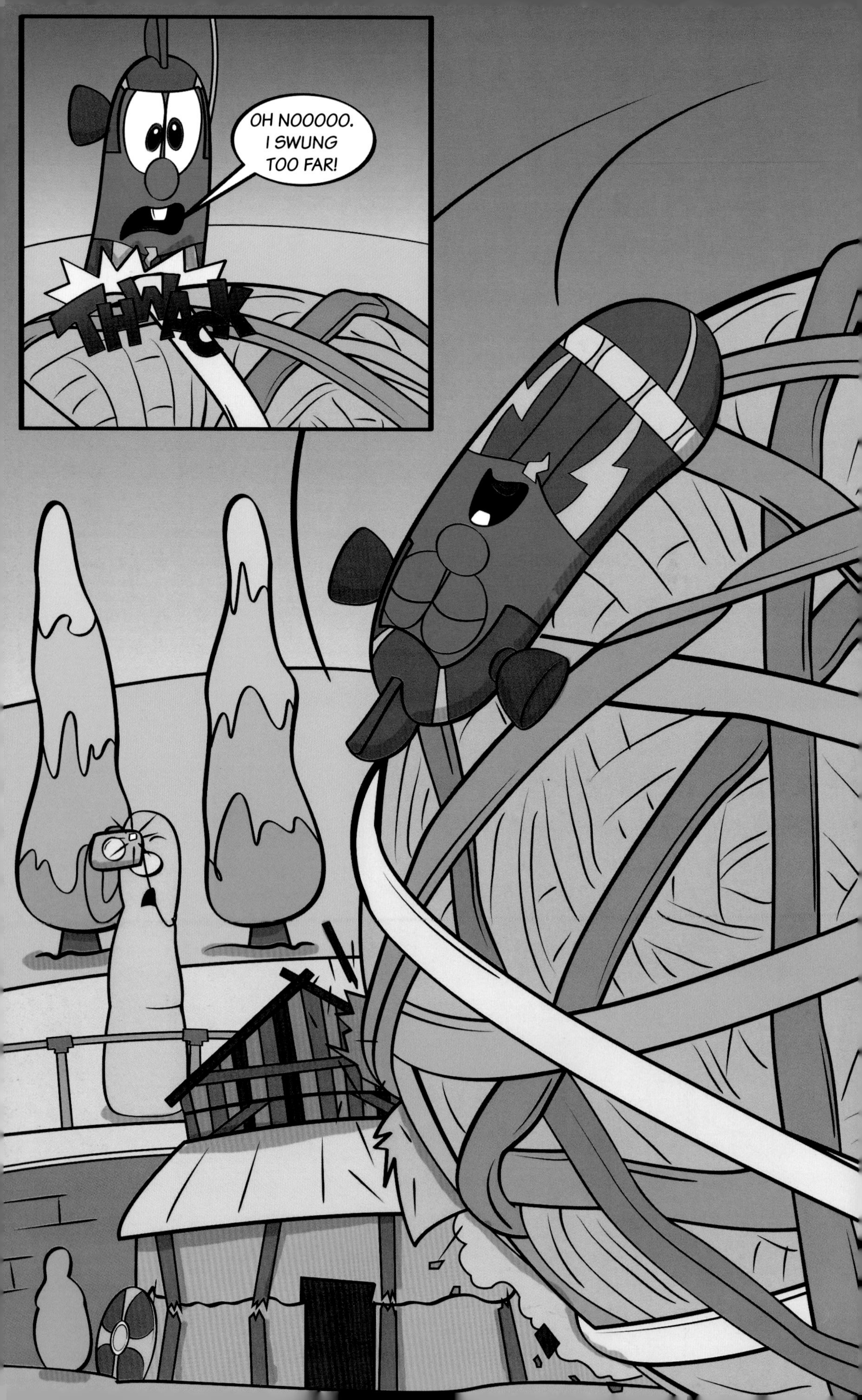
OH NOOOOO. I SWUNG TOO FAR!
THWACK

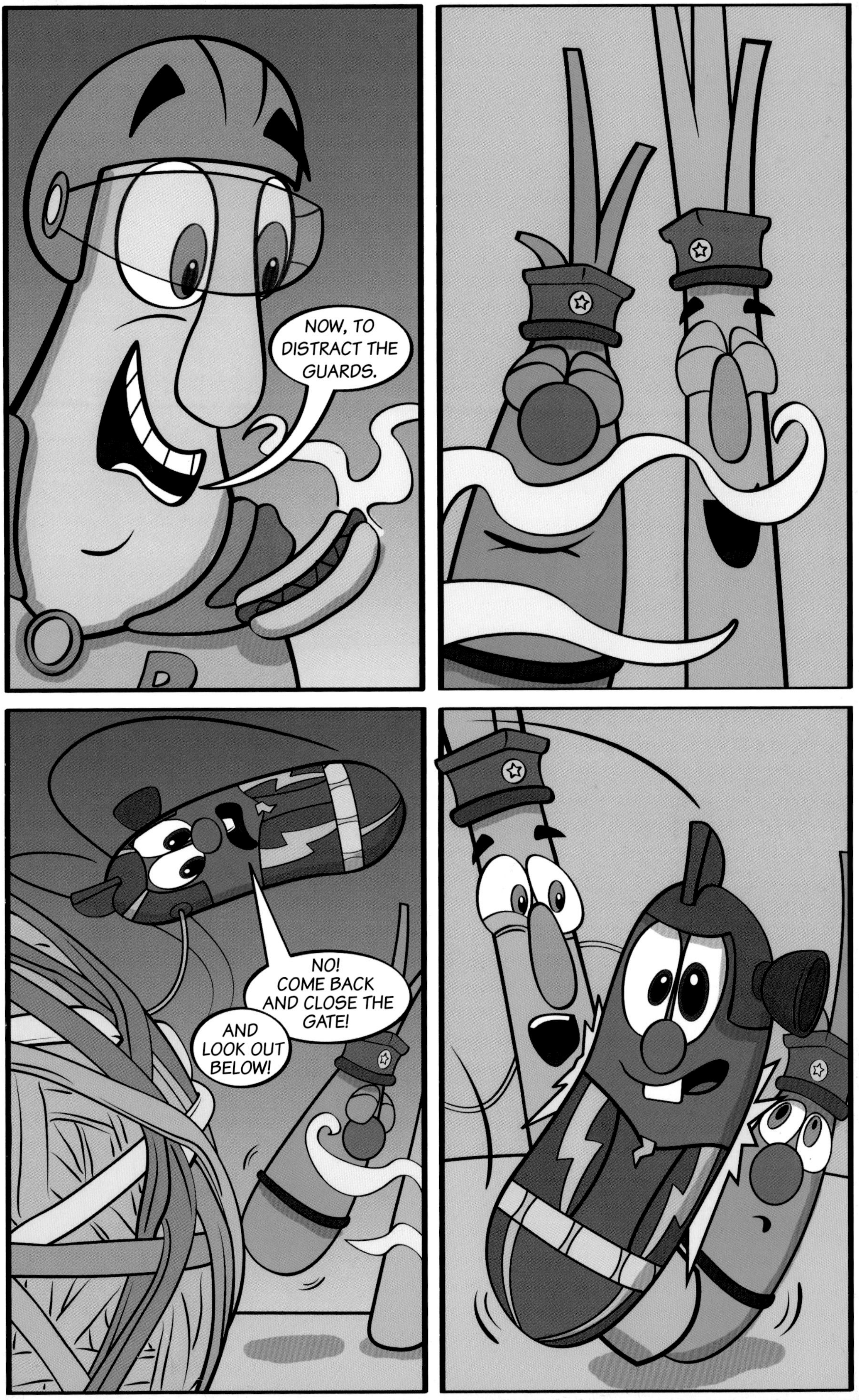
NOW, TO DISTRACT THE GUARDS.
NO! COME BACK AND CLOSE THE GATE!
AND LOOK OUT BELOW!

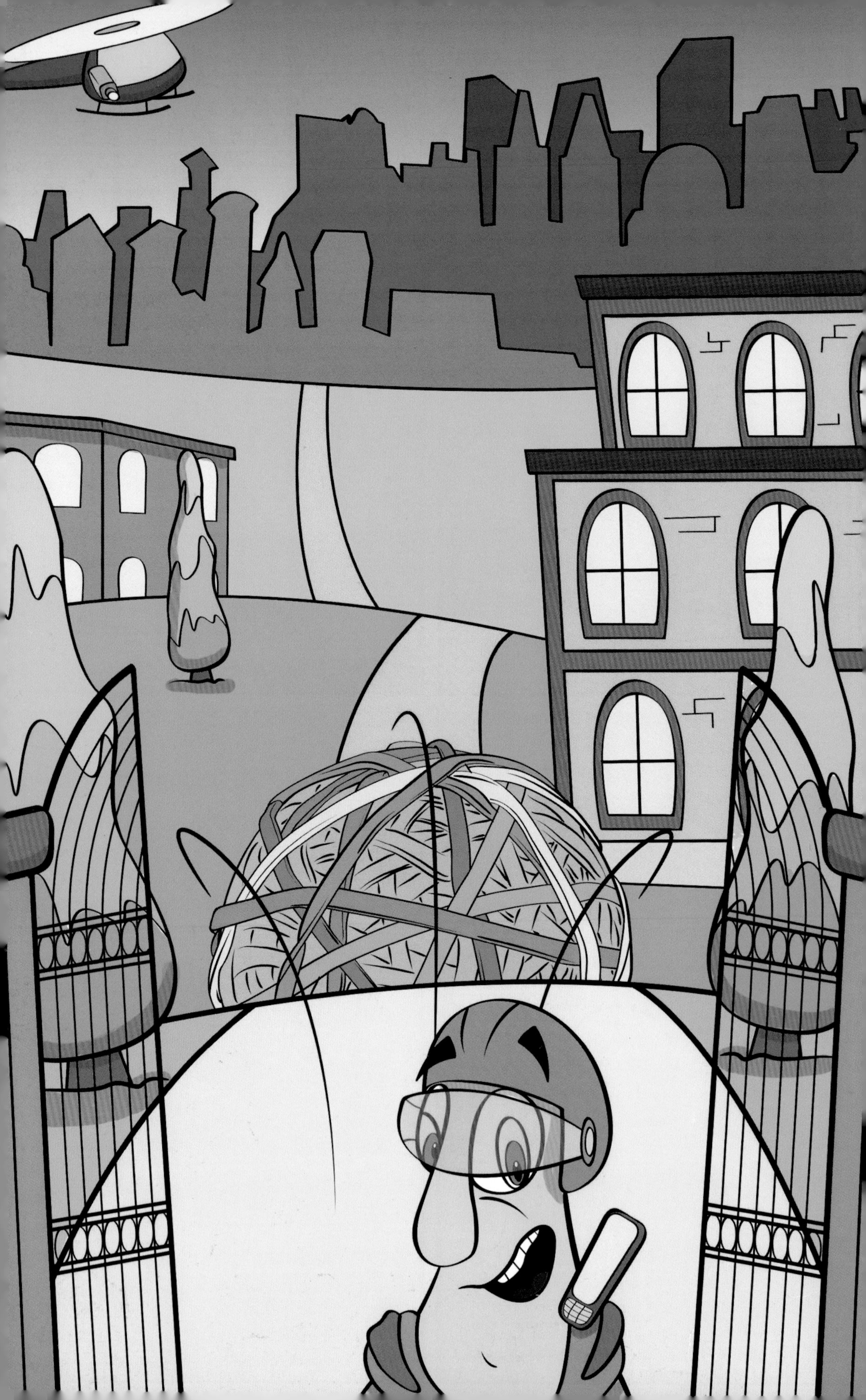

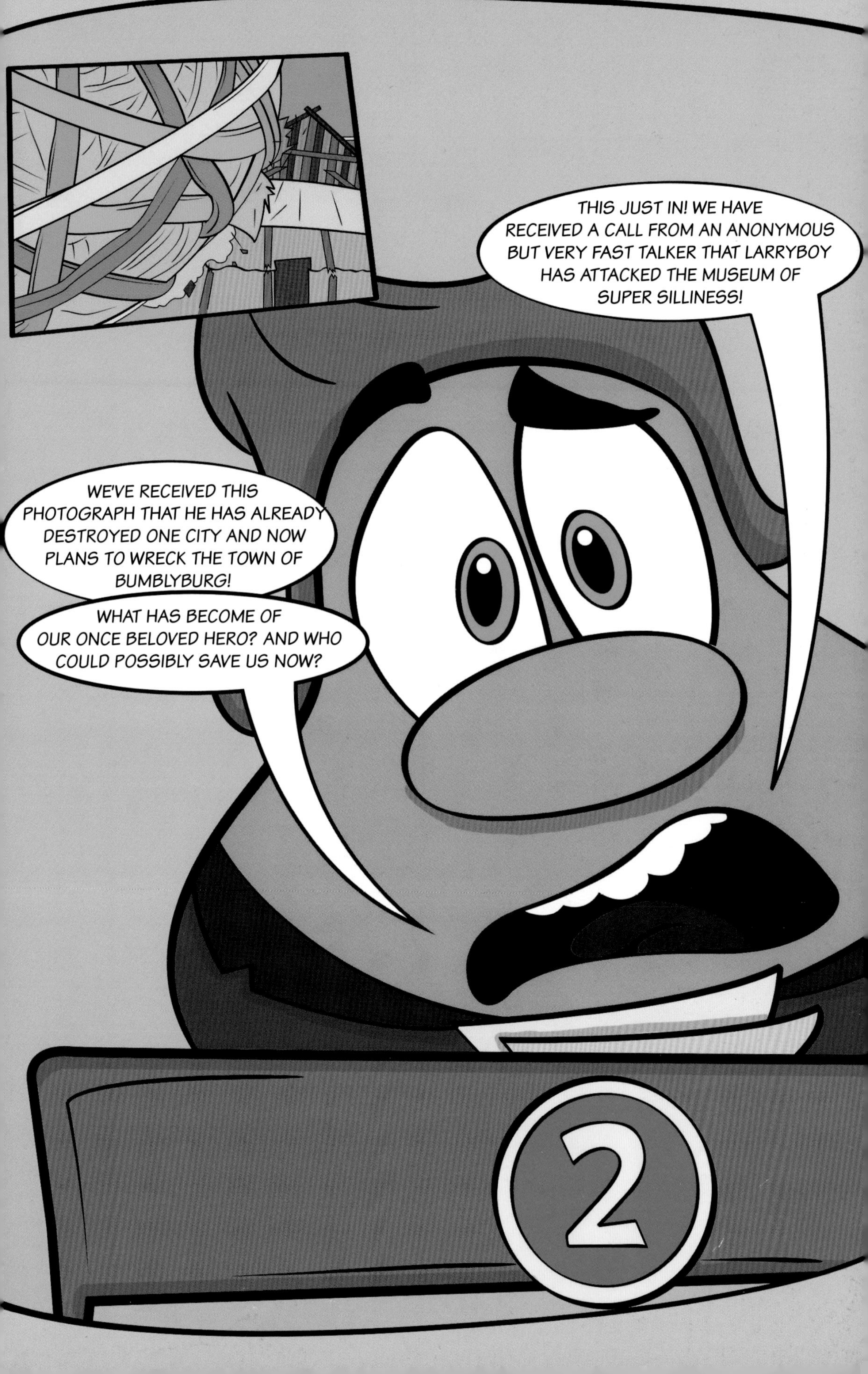
THIS JUST IN! WE HAVE RECEIVED A CALL FROM AN ANONYMOUS BUT VERY FAST TALKER THAT LARRYBOY HAS ATTACKED THE MUSEUM OF SUPER SILLINESS!
WE'VE RECEIVED THIS PHOTOGRAPH THAT HE HAS ALREADY DESTROYED ONE CITY AND NOW PLANS TO WRECK THE TOWN OF BUMBLYBURG!
WHAT HAS BECOME OF OUR ONCE BELOVED HERO? AND WHO COULD POSSIBLY SAVE US NOW?
2

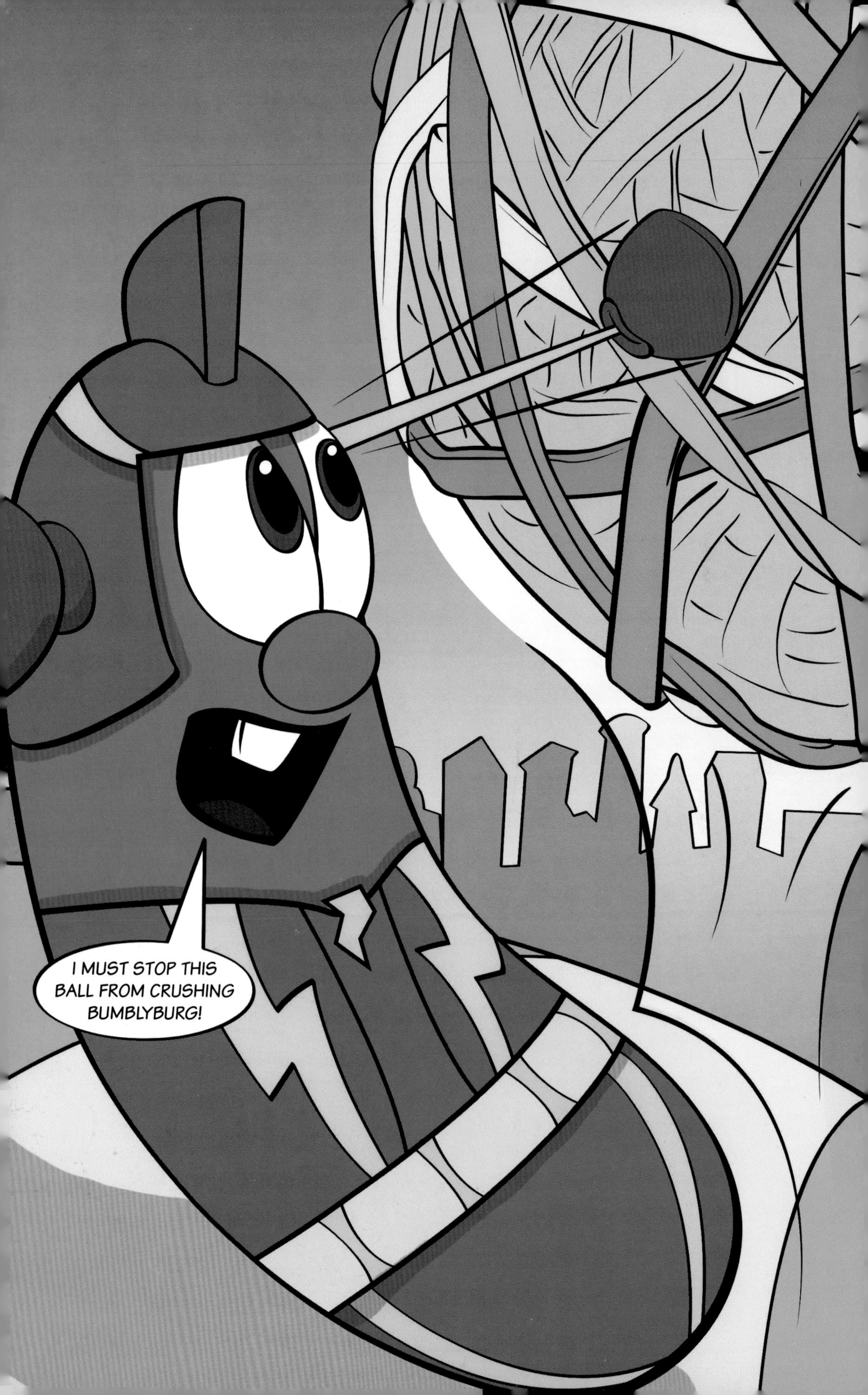
I MUST STOP THIS BALL FROM CRUSHING BUMBLYBURG!

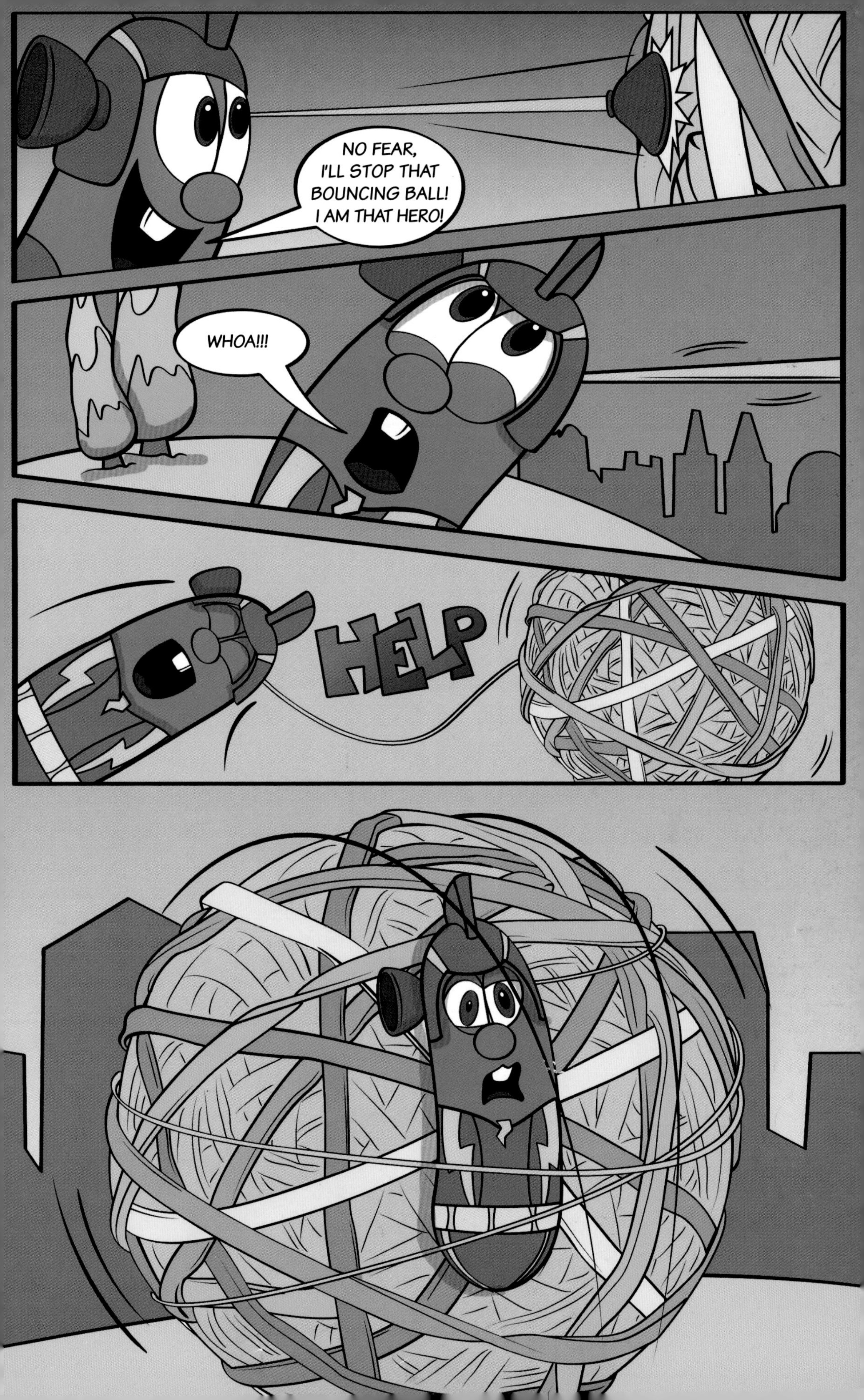
NO FEAR,
I'LL STOP THAT
BOUNCING BALL!
I AM THAT HERO!
WHOA!!!
HELP

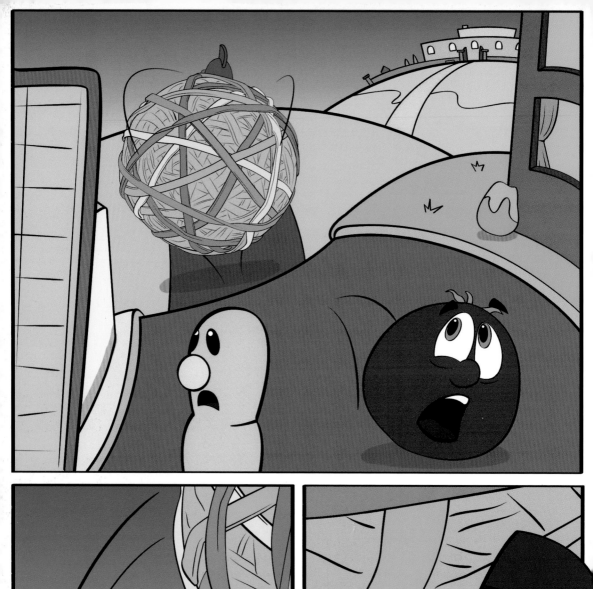

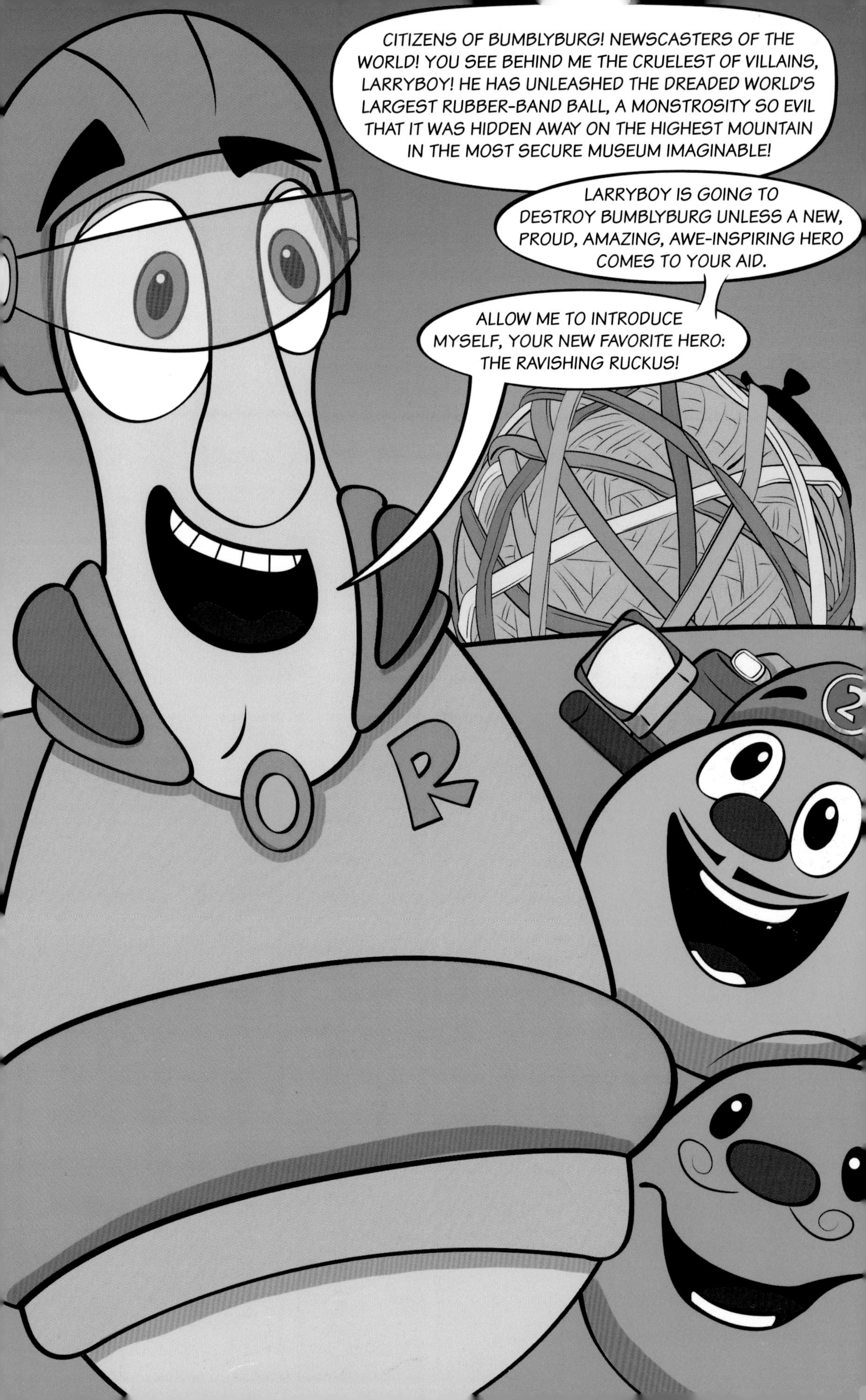
CITIZENS OF BUMBLYBURG! NEWSCASTERS OF THE WORLD! YOU SEE BEHIND ME THE CRUELEST OF VILLAINS, LARRYBOY! HE HAS UNLEASHED THE DREADED WORLD'S LARGEST RUBBER-BAND BALL, A MONSTROSITY SO EVIL THAT IT WAS HIDDEN AWAY ON THE HIGHEST MOUNTAIN IN THE MOST SECURE MUSEUM IMAGINABLE!
LARRYBOY IS GOING TO DESTROY BUMBLYBURG UNLESS A NEW, PROUD, AMAZING, AWE-INSPIRING HERO COMES TO YOUR AID.
ALLOW ME TO INTRODUCE MYSELF, YOUR NEW FAVORITE HERO: THE RAVISHING RUCKUS!

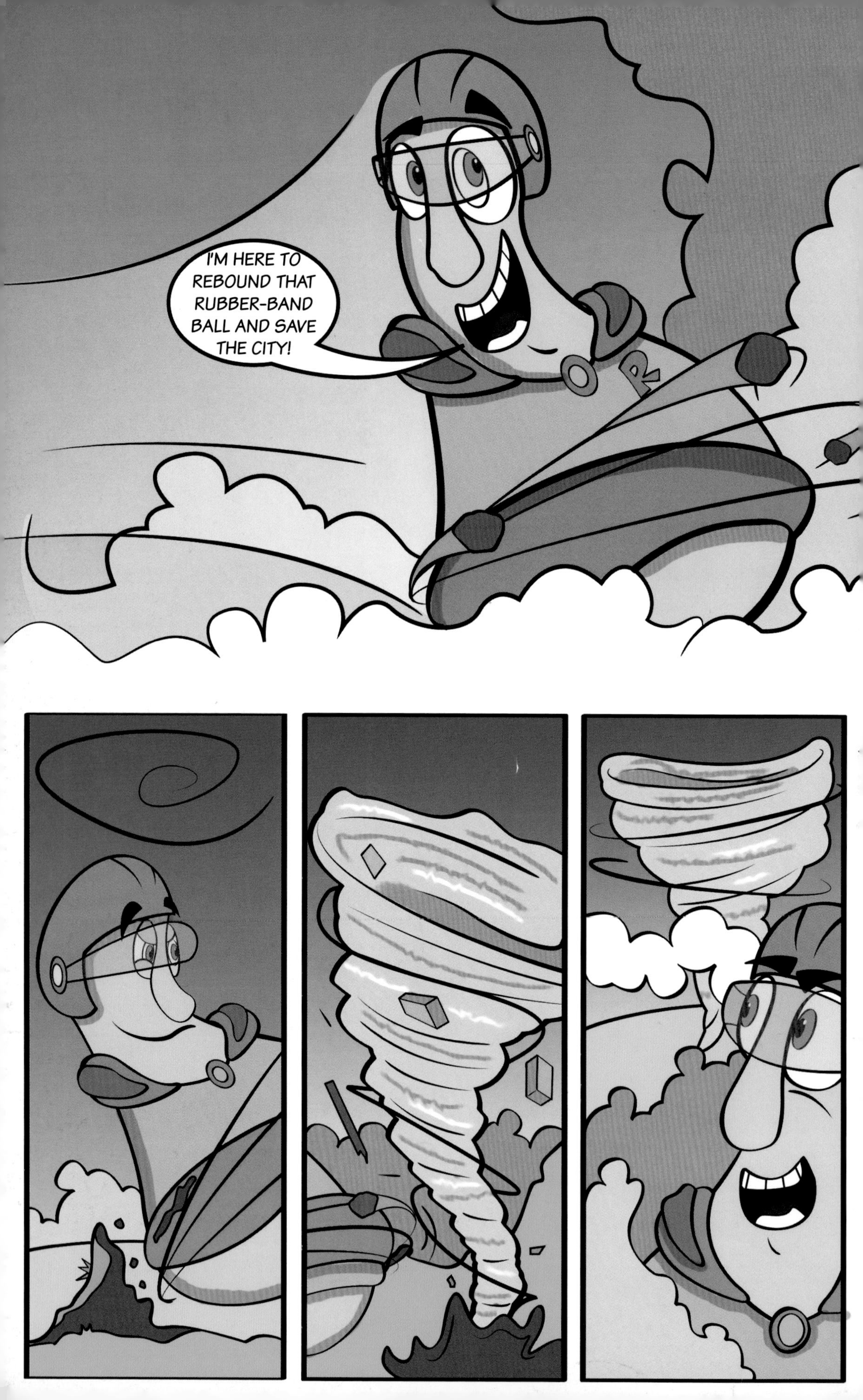
I'M HERE TO REBOUND THAT RUBBER-BAND BALL AND SAVE THE CITY!

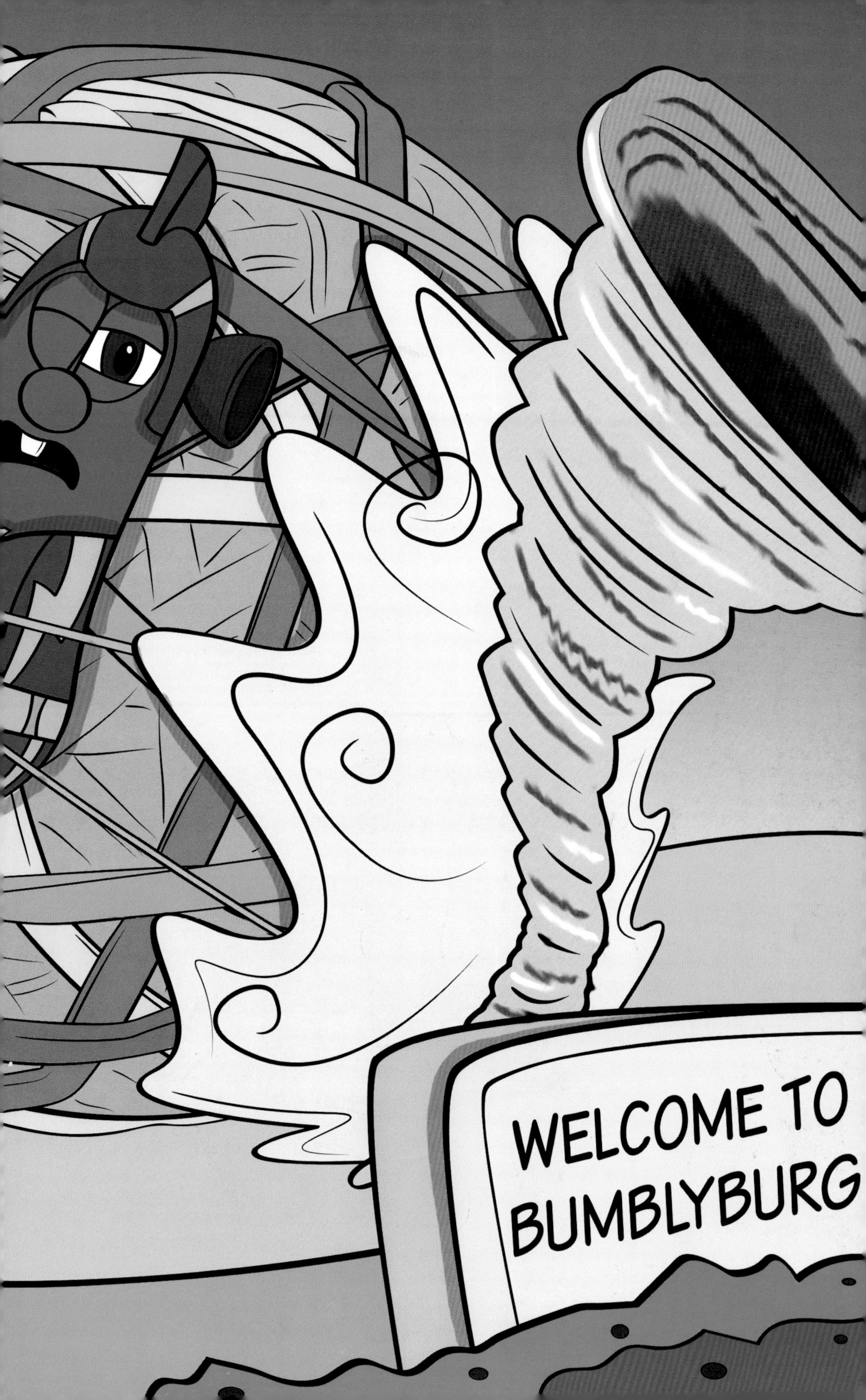
WELCOME TO
BUMBLYBURG

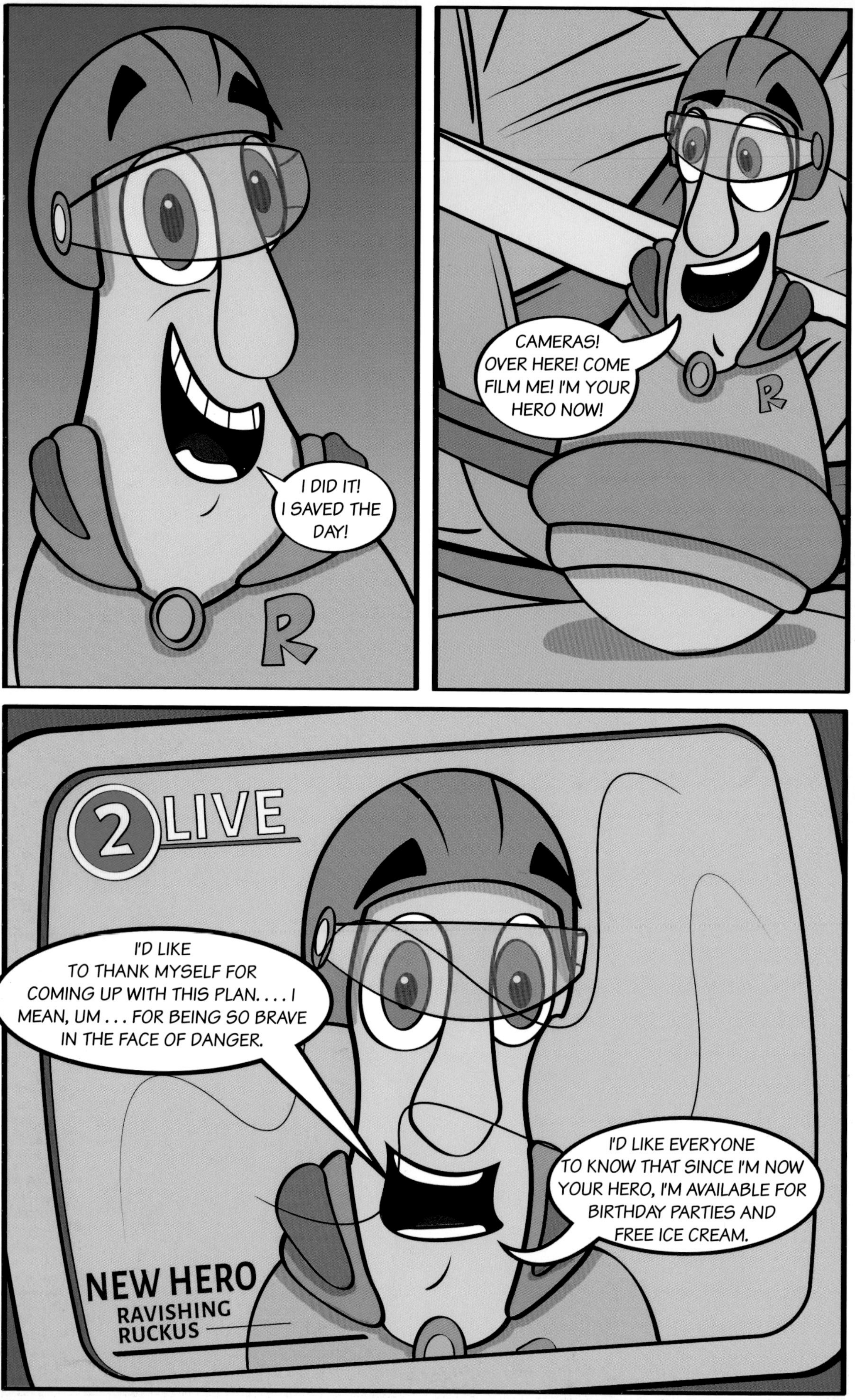
I DID IT! I SAVED THE DAY!
CAMERAS! OVER HERE! COME FILM ME! I'M YOUR HERO NOW!
2 LIVE
I'D LIKE TO THANK MYSELF FOR COMING UP WITH THIS PLAN. . . . I MEAN, UM . . . FOR BEING SO BRAVE IN THE FACE OF DANGER.
I'D LIKE EVERYONE TO KNOW THAT SINCE I'M NOW YOUR HERO, I'M AVAILABLE FOR BIRTHDAY PARTIES AND FREE ICE CREAM.
NEW HERO
RAVISHING RUCKUS

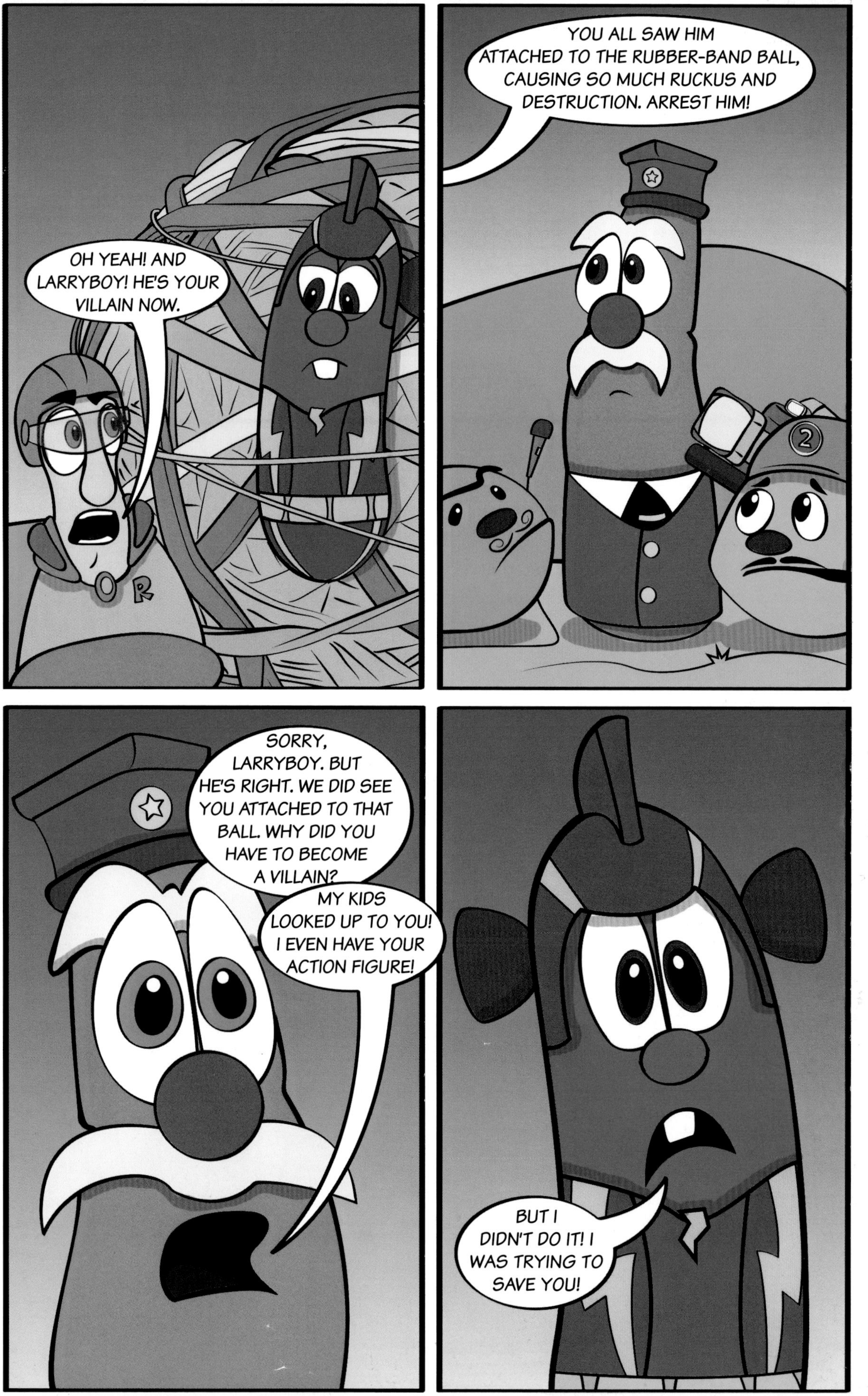
OH YEAH! AND LARRYBOY! HE'S YOUR VILLAIN NOW.
YOU ALL SAW HIM ATTACHED TO THE RUBBER-BAND BALL, CAUSING SO MUCH RUCKUS AND DESTRUCTION. ARREST HIM!
SORRY, LARRYBOY. BUT HE'S RIGHT. WE DID SEE YOU ATTACHED TO THAT BALL. WHY DID YOU HAVE TO BECOME A VILLAIN?
MY KIDS LOOKED UP TO YOU! I EVEN HAVE YOUR ACTION FIGURE!
BUT I DIDN'T DO IT! I WAS TRYING TO SAVE YOU!

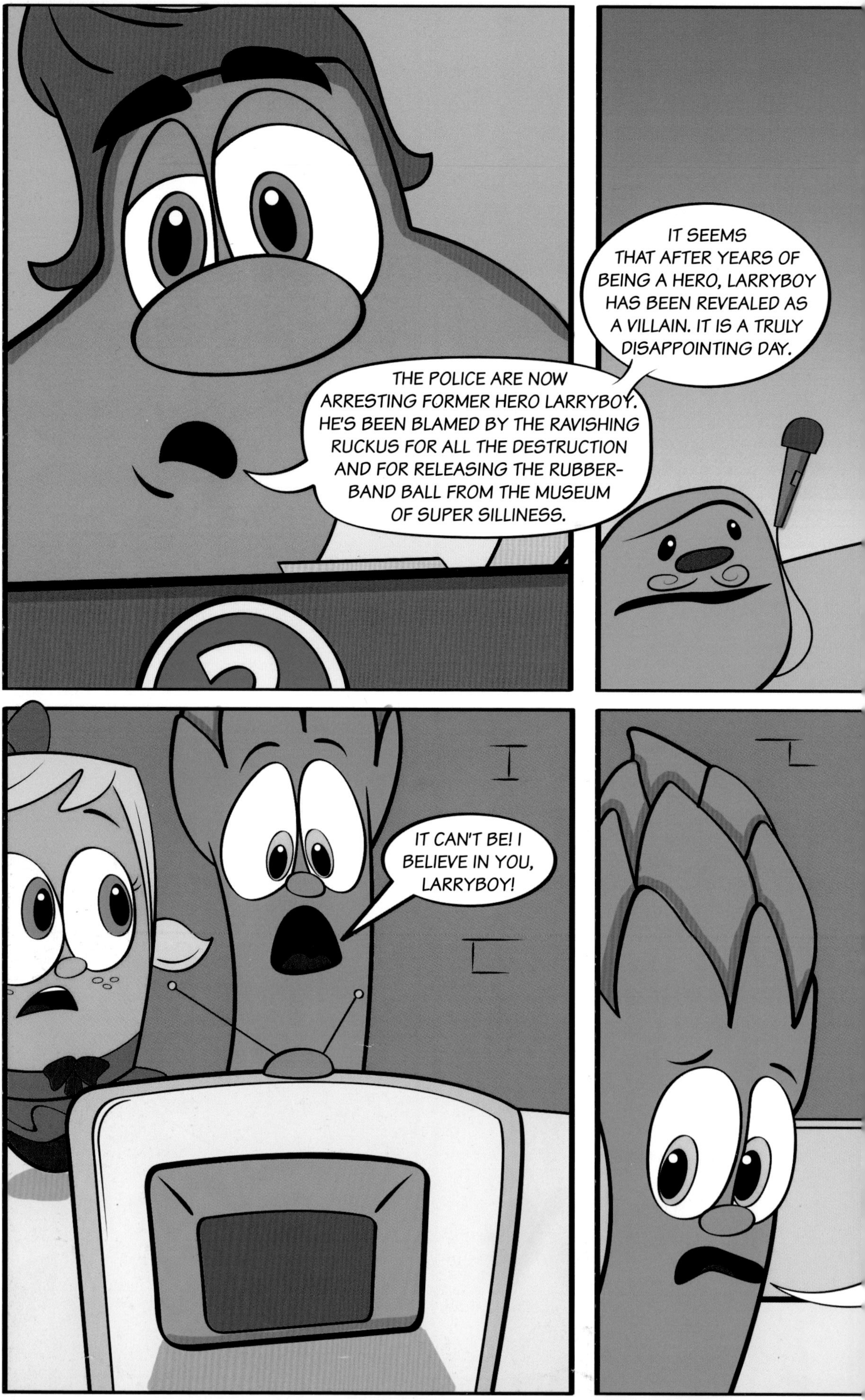
THE POLICE ARE NOW ARRESTING FORMER HERO LARRYBOY. HE'S BEEN BLAMED BY THE RAVISHING RUCKUS FOR ALL THE DESTRUCTION AND FOR RELEASING THE RUBBER-BAND BALL FROM THE MUSEUM OF SUPER SILLINESS.
IT SEEMS THAT AFTER YEARS OF BEING A HERO, LARRYBOY HAS BEEN REVEALED AS A VILLAIN. IT IS A TRULY DISAPPOINTING DAY.
IT CAN'T BE! I BELIEVE IN YOU, LARRYBOY!

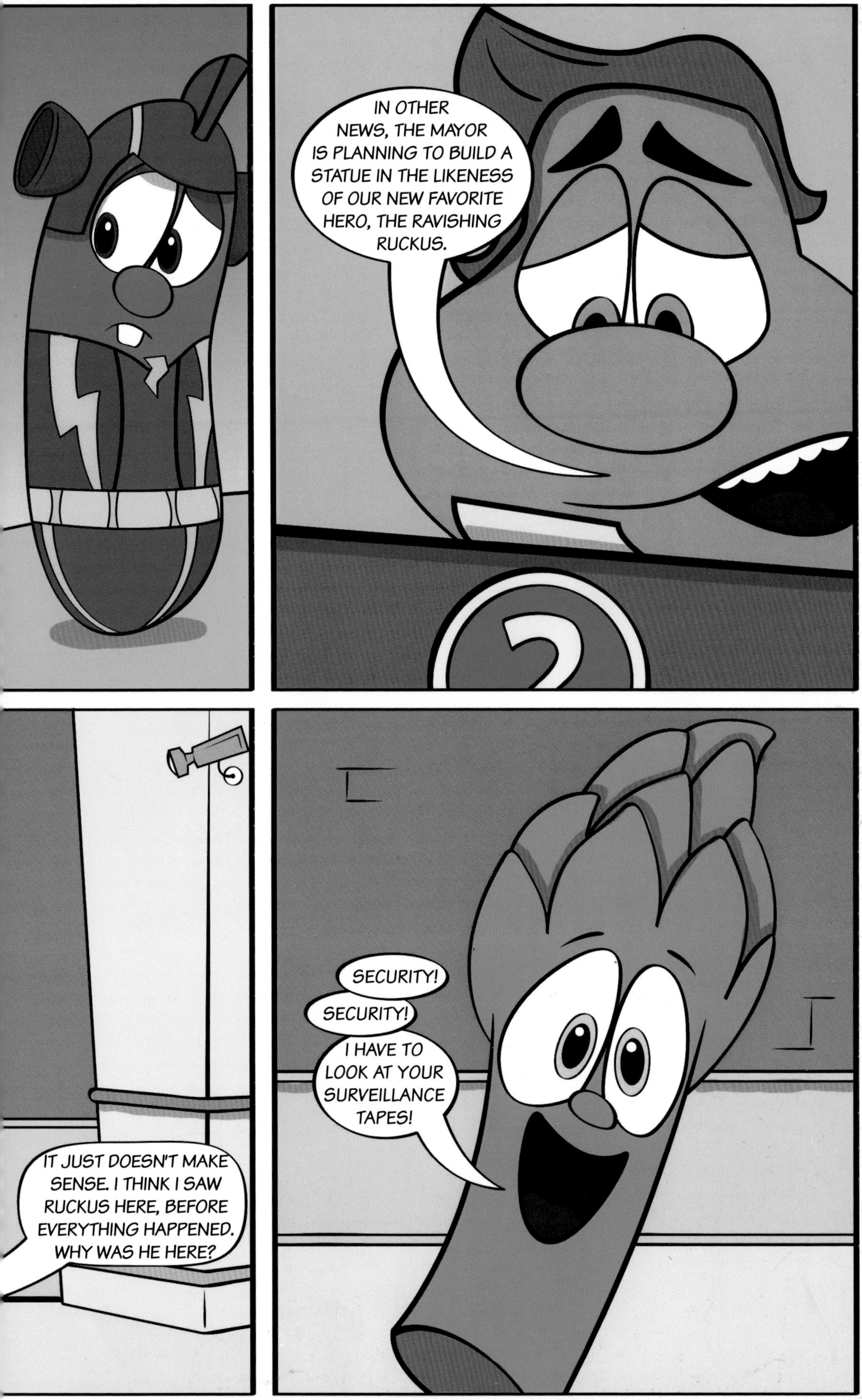
IN OTHER NEWS, THE MAYOR IS PLANNING TO BUILD A STATUE IN THE LIKENESS OF OUR NEW FAVORITE HERO, THE RAVISHING RUCKUS.
IT JUST DOESN'T MAKE SENSE. I THINK I SAW RUCKUS HERE, BEFORE EVERYTHING HAPPENED. WHY WAS HE HERE?
SECURITY!
SECURITY!
I HAVE TO LOOK AT YOUR SURVEILLANCE TAPES!

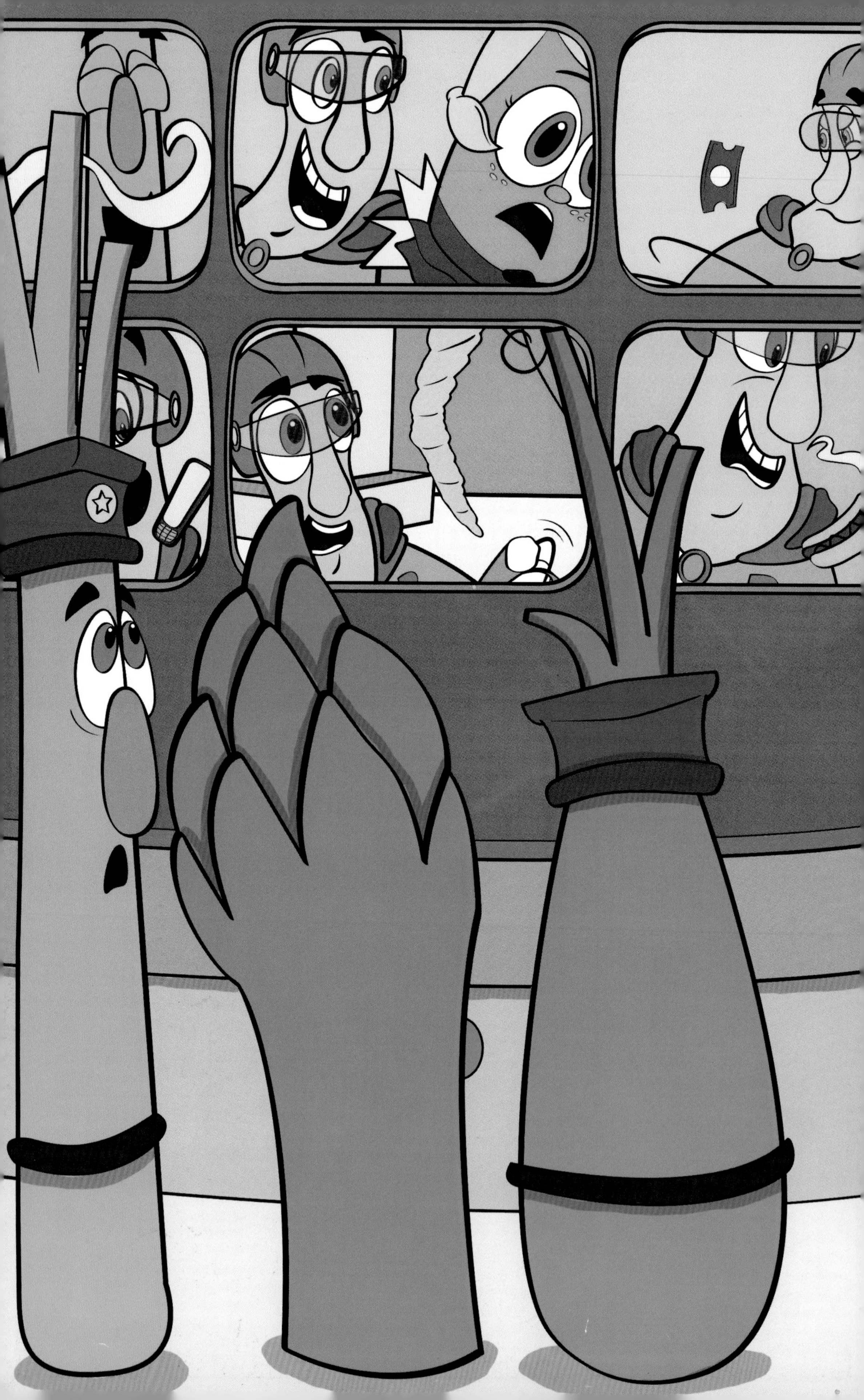

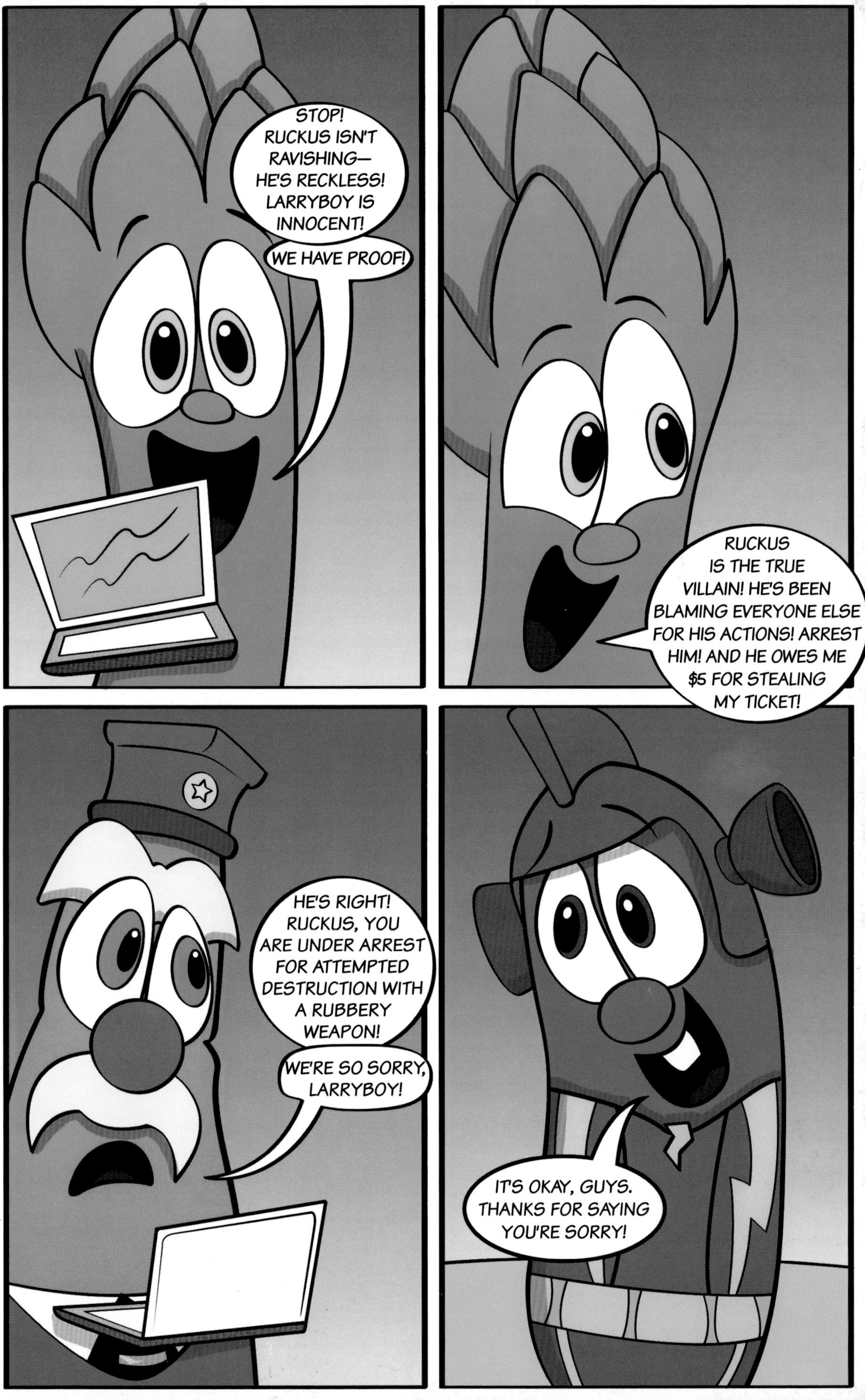
STOP! RUCKUS ISN'T RAVISHING— HE'S RECKLESS! LARRYBOY IS INNOCENT!
WE HAVE PROOF!
RUCKUS IS THE TRUE VILLAIN! HE'S BEEN BLAMING EVERYONE ELSE FOR HIS ACTIONS! ARREST HIM! AND HE OWES ME $5 FOR STEALING MY TICKET!
HE'S RIGHT! RUCKUS, YOU ARE UNDER ARREST FOR ATTEMPTED DESTRUCTION WITH A RUBBERY WEAPON!
WE'RE SO SORRY, LARRYBOY!
IT'S OKAY, GUYS. THANKS FOR SAYING YOU'RE SORRY!

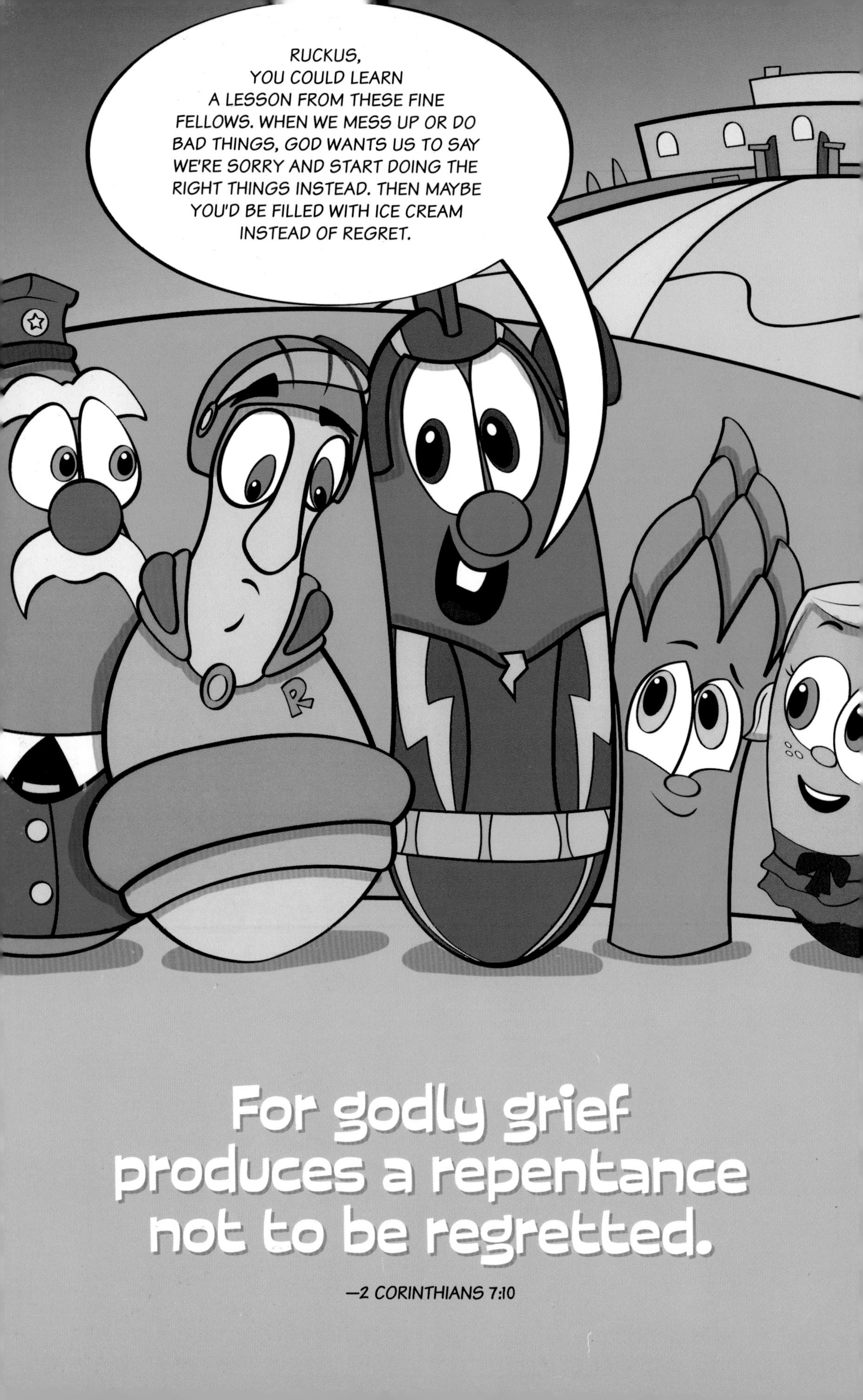
RUCKUS, YOU COULD LEARN A LESSON FROM THESE FINE FELLOWS. WHEN WE MESS UP OR DO BAD THINGS, GOD WANTS US TO SAY WE'RE SORRY AND START DOING THE RIGHT THINGS INSTEAD. THEN MAYBE YOU'D BE FILLED WITH ICE CREAM INSTEAD OF REGRET.
R

For godly grief produces a repentance not to be regretted.

—2 CORINTHIANS 7:10

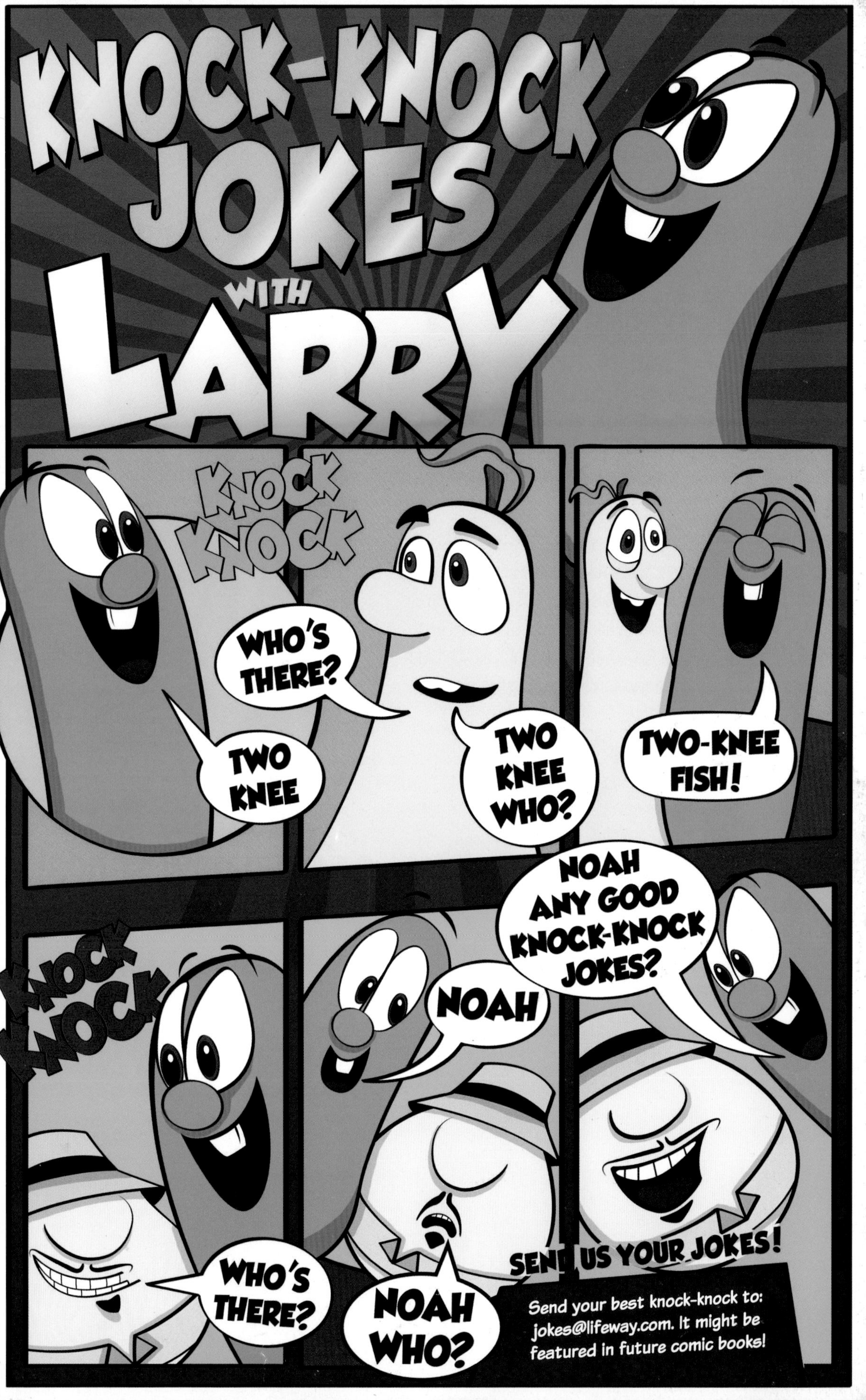
KNOCK-KNOCK JOKES
WITH LARRY
KNOCK KNOCK
WHO'S THERE?
TWO KNEE
TWO KNEE WHO?
TWO-KNEE FISH!
KNOCK KNOCK
WHO'S THERE?
NOAH
NOAH WHO?
NOAH ANY GOOD KNOCK-KNOCK JOKES?
SEND US YOUR JOKES!
Send your best knock-knock to: jokes@lifeway.com. It might be featured in future comic books!

VeggieTales

Noah's Ark

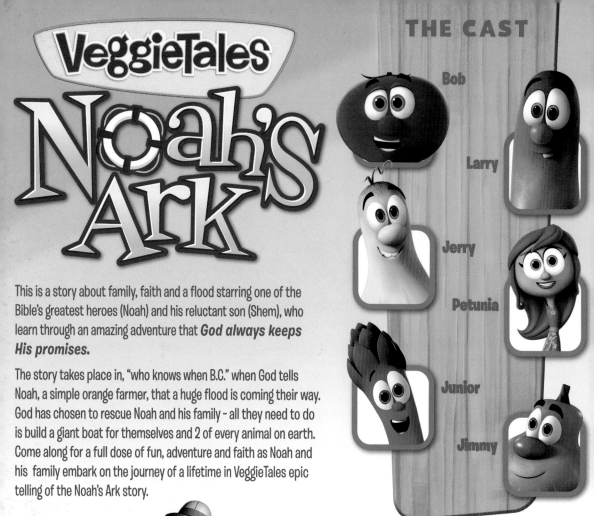

THE CAST

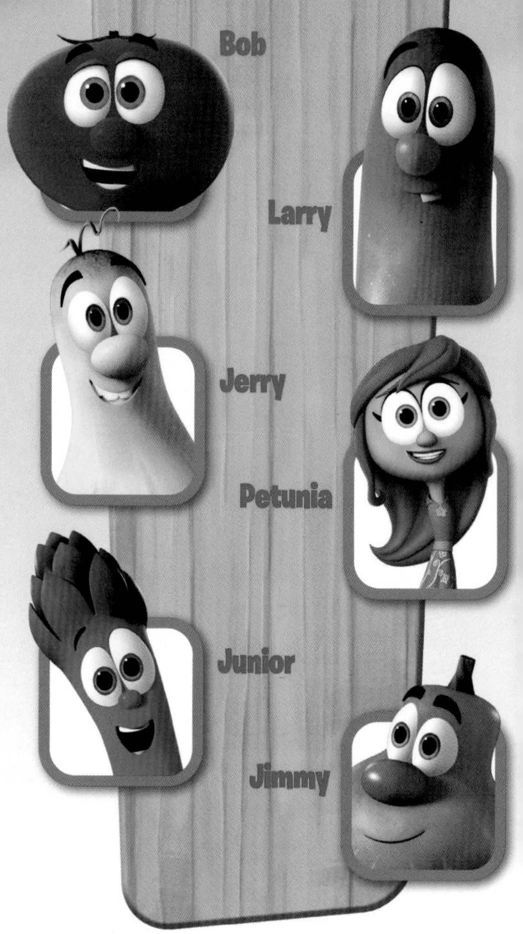
Bob
Larry
Jerry
Petunia
Junior
Jimmy

This is a story about family, faith and a flood starring one of the Bible's greatest heroes (Noah) and his reluctant son (Shem), who learn through an amazing adventure that ***God always keeps His promises.***

The story takes place in, "who knows when B.C." when God tells Noah, a simple orange farmer, that a huge flood is coming their way. God has chosen to rescue Noah and his family - all they need to do is build a giant boat for themselves and 2 of every animal on earth. Come along for a full dose of fun, adventure and faith as Noah and his family embark on the journey of a lifetime in VeggieTales epic telling of the Noah's Ark story.

Featuring the all-new Silly Song MY GOLDEN EGG

Includes 7 original new songs!

Noah's Ark DVD coming to a store near you Spring 2015!

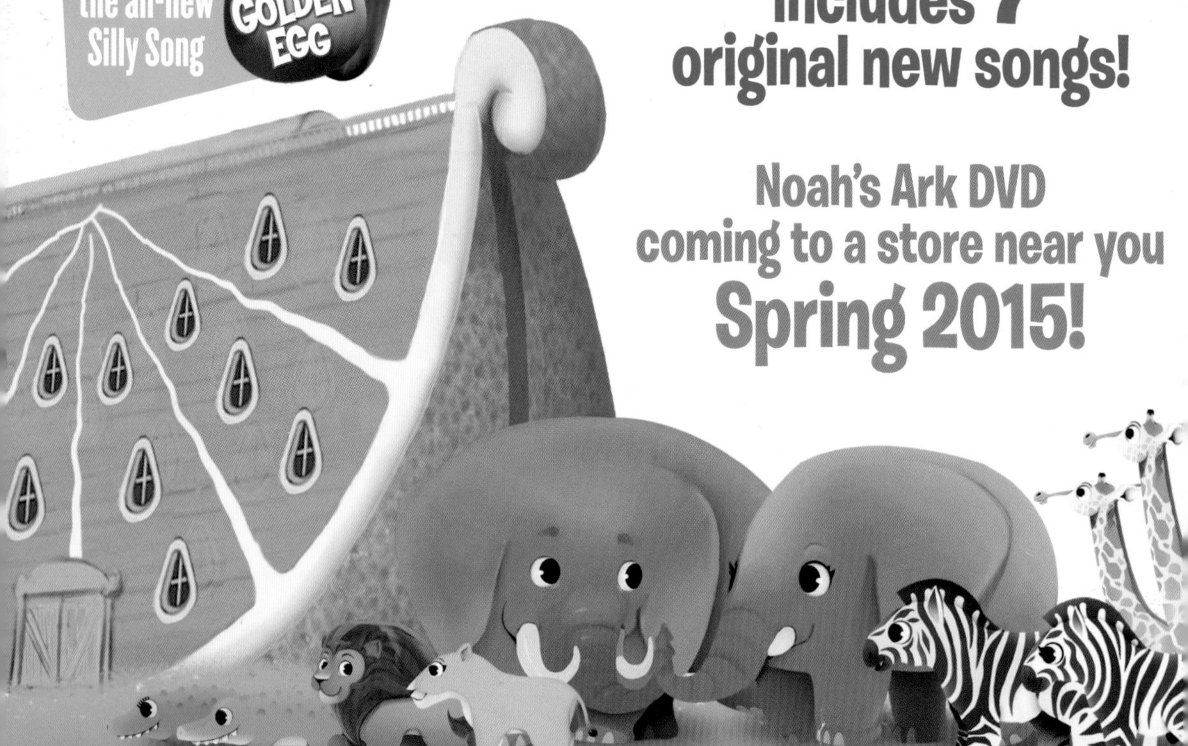

VeggieTales

Josh and the Big Wall

COMIC ADAPTATION BY
AARON LINNE
ILLUSTRATED BY
CORY JONES

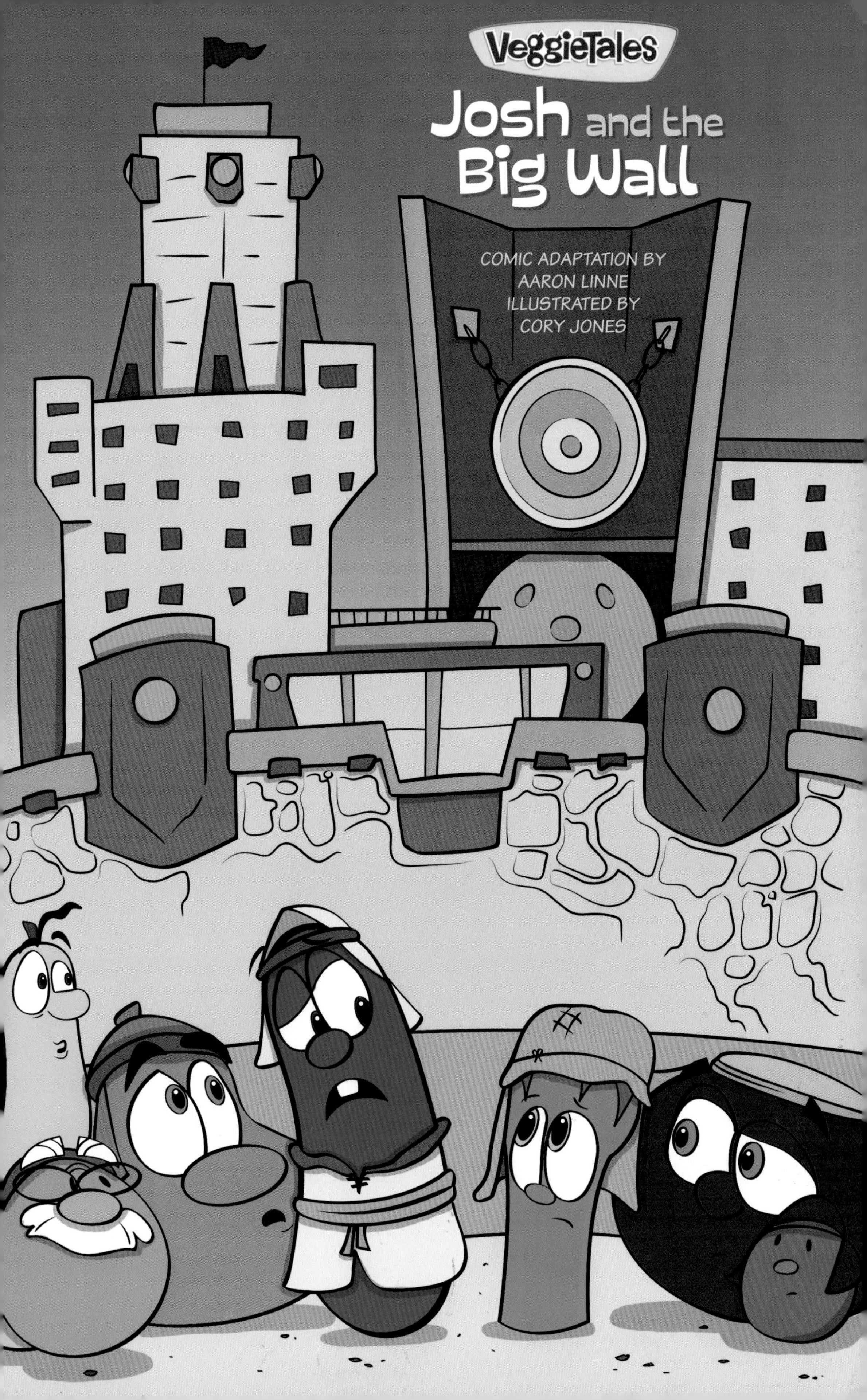

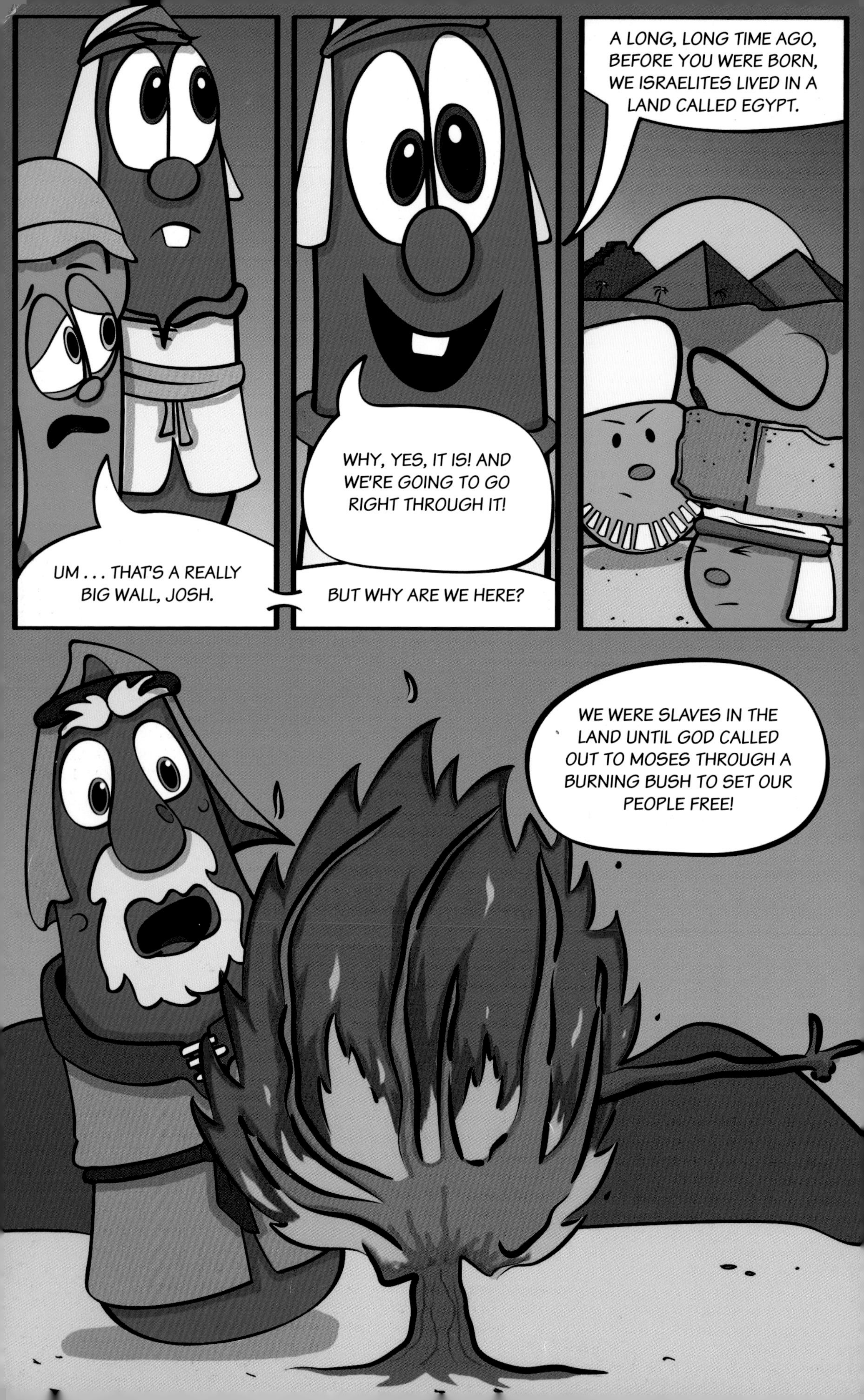
UM . . . THAT'S A REALLY BIG WALL, JOSH.
WHY, YES, IT IS! AND WE'RE GOING TO GO RIGHT THROUGH IT!
BUT WHY ARE WE HERE?
A LONG, LONG TIME AGO, BEFORE YOU WERE BORN, WE ISRAELITES LIVED IN A LAND CALLED EGYPT.
WE WERE SLAVES IN THE LAND UNTIL GOD CALLED OUT TO MOSES THROUGH A BURNING BUSH TO SET OUR PEOPLE FREE!

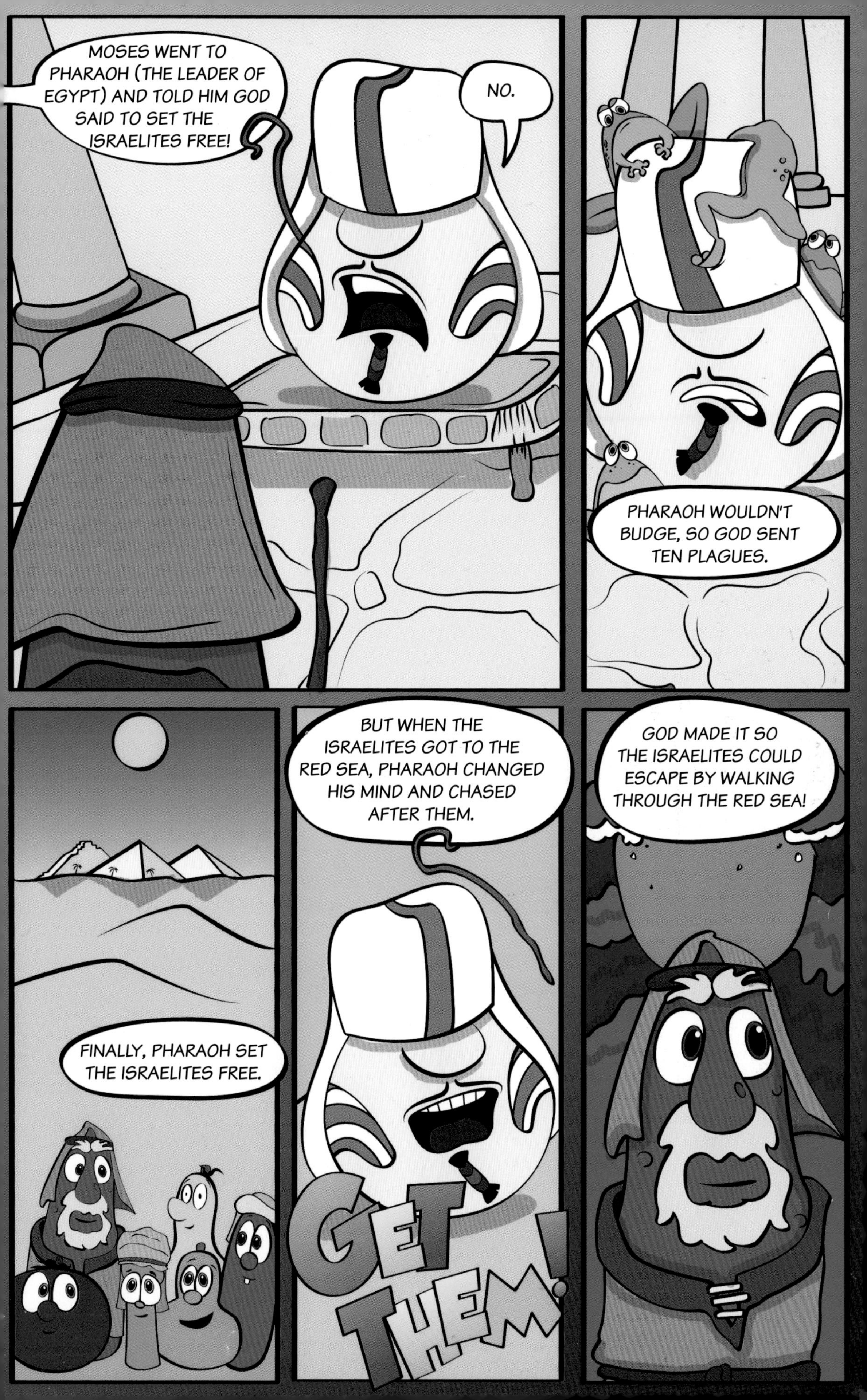
MOSES WENT TO PHARAOH (THE LEADER OF EGYPT) AND TOLD HIM GOD SAID TO SET THE ISRAELITES FREE!
NO.
PHARAOH WOULDN'T BUDGE, SO GOD SENT TEN PLAGUES.
FINALLY, PHARAOH SET THE ISRAELITES FREE.
BUT WHEN THE ISRAELITES GOT TO THE RED SEA, PHARAOH CHANGED HIS MIND AND CHASED AFTER THEM.
GET THEM!
GOD MADE IT SO THE ISRAELITES COULD ESCAPE BY WALKING THROUGH THE RED SEA!

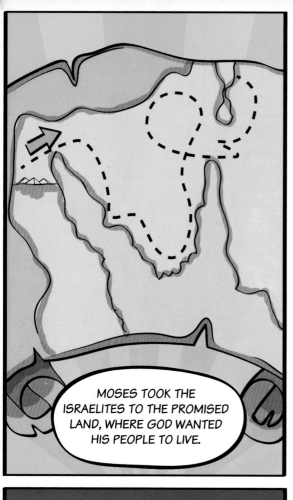

MOSES TOOK THE ISRAELITES TO THE PROMISED LAND, WHERE GOD WANTED HIS PEOPLE TO LIVE.

THEY SENT SPIES TO THE LAND AND DISCOVERED THAT THE PEOPLE WHO LIVED THERE WERE STRONG AND SCARY!

OUR PEOPLE WERE SO SCARED THAT INSTEAD OF TAKING THE LAND LIKE GOD HAD PROMISED, WE LEFT.

THAT WAS FORTY YEARS AGO. AND NOW IT'S TIME FOR US TO GO TO THE PROMISED LAND. AND IT'S ON THE OTHER SIDE OF THAT WALL.

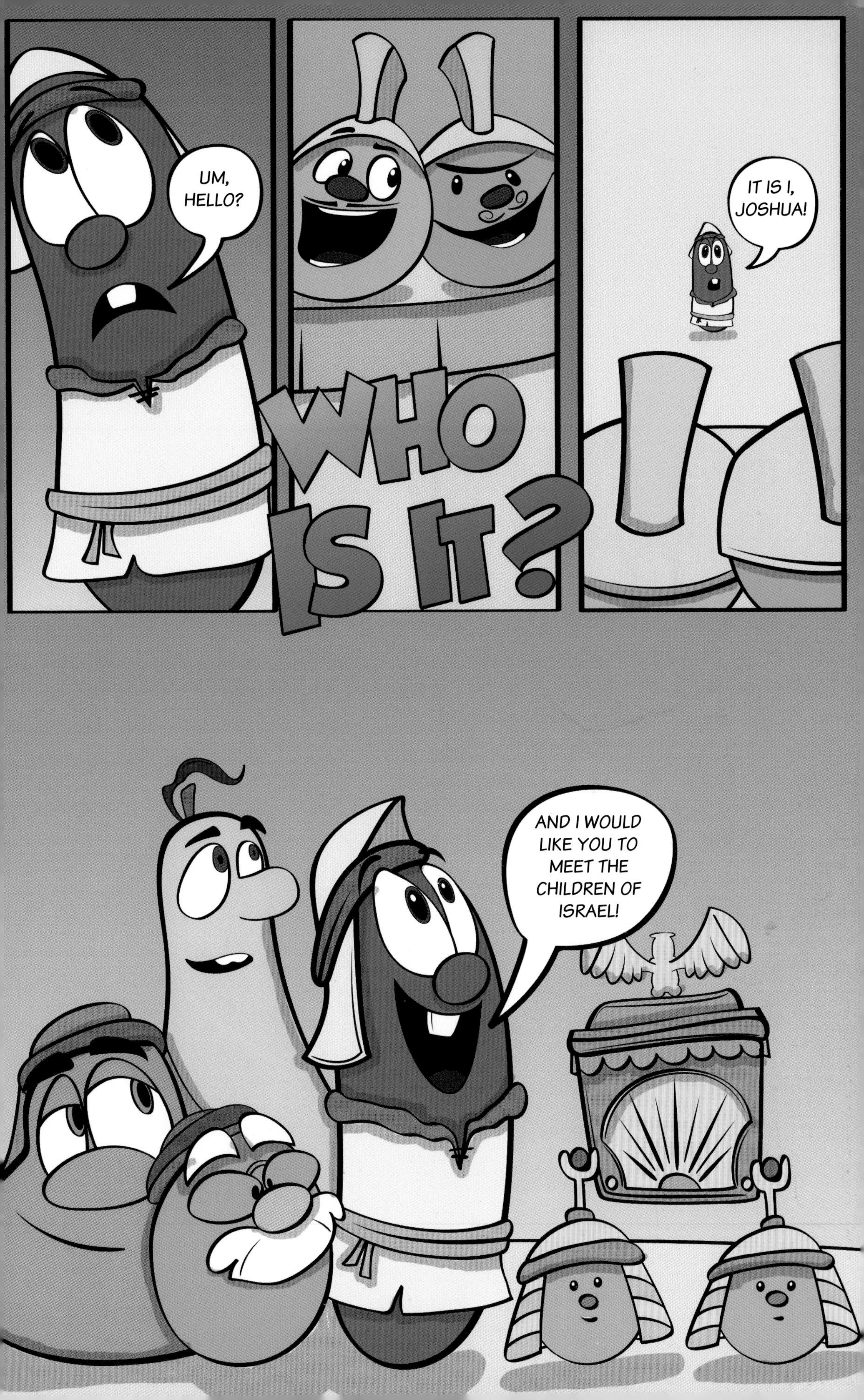
UM,
HELLO?
WHO IS IT?
IT IS I,
JOSHUA!
AND I WOULD LIKE YOU TO MEET THE CHILDREN OF ISRAEL!

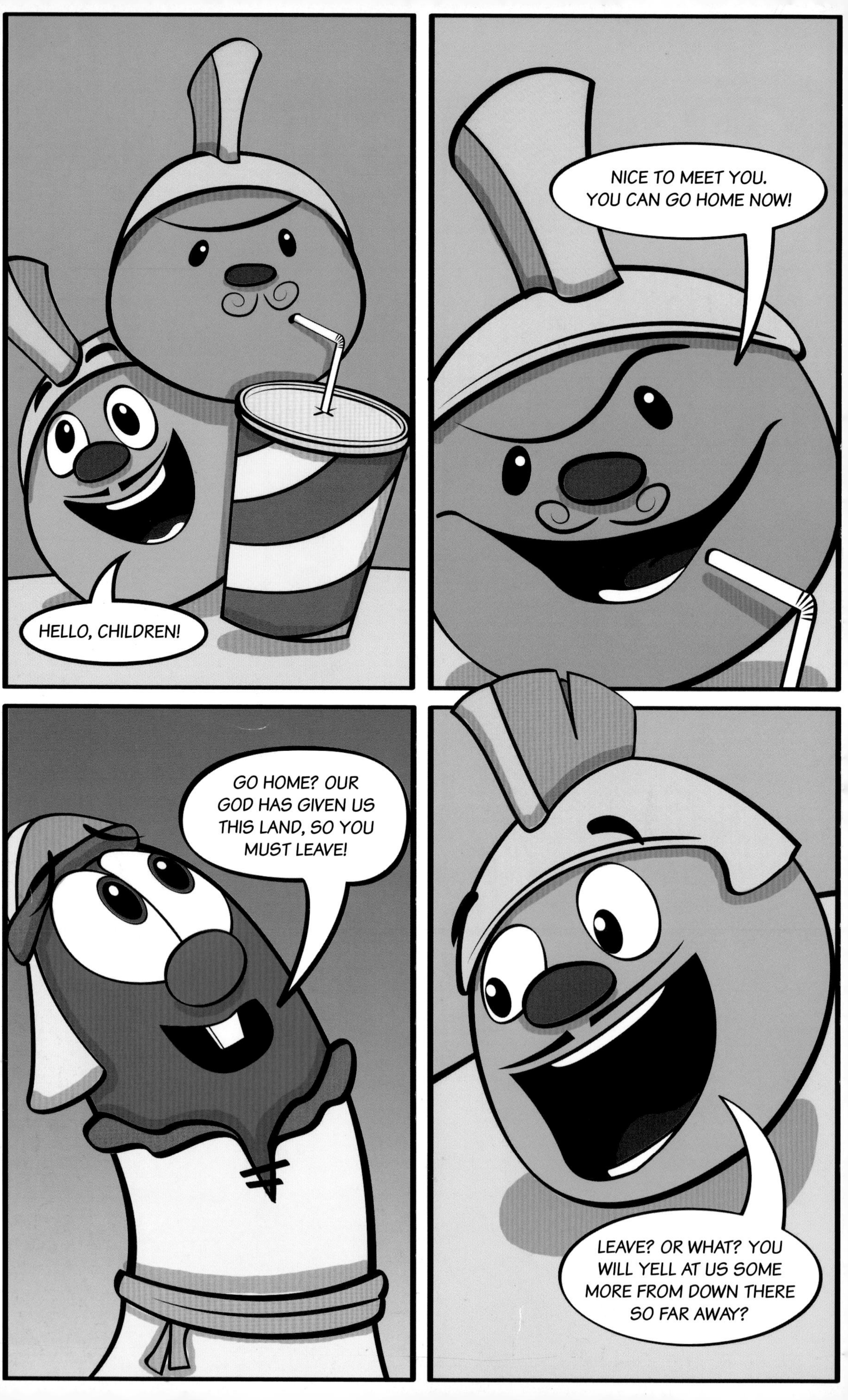
HELLO, CHILDREN!
NICE TO MEET YOU. YOU CAN GO HOME NOW!
GO HOME? OUR GOD HAS GIVEN US THIS LAND, SO YOU MUST LEAVE!
LEAVE? OR WHAT? YOU WILL YELL AT US SOME MORE FROM DOWN THERE SO FAR AWAY?

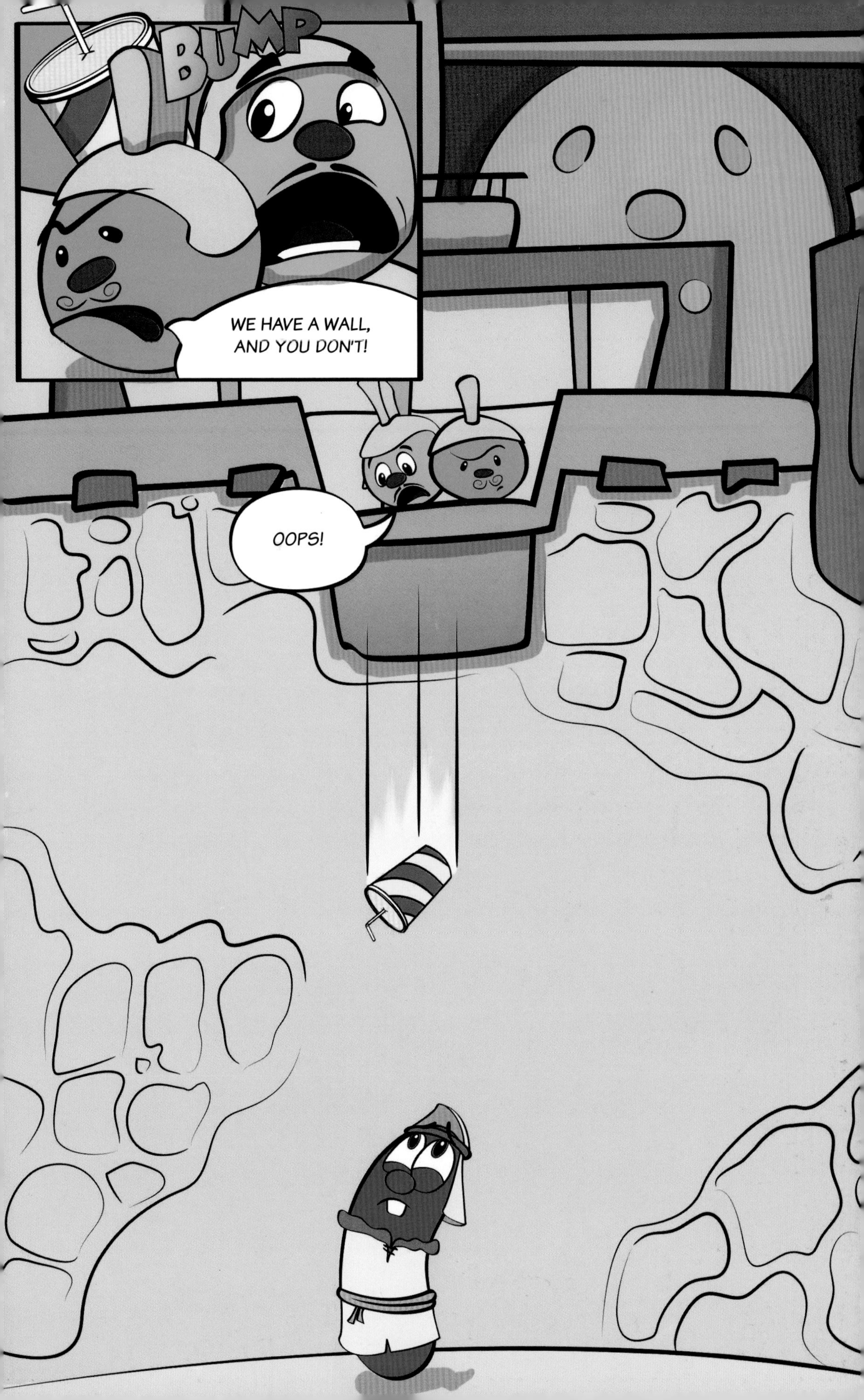
BUMP
WE HAVE A WALL, AND YOU DON'T!
OOPS!

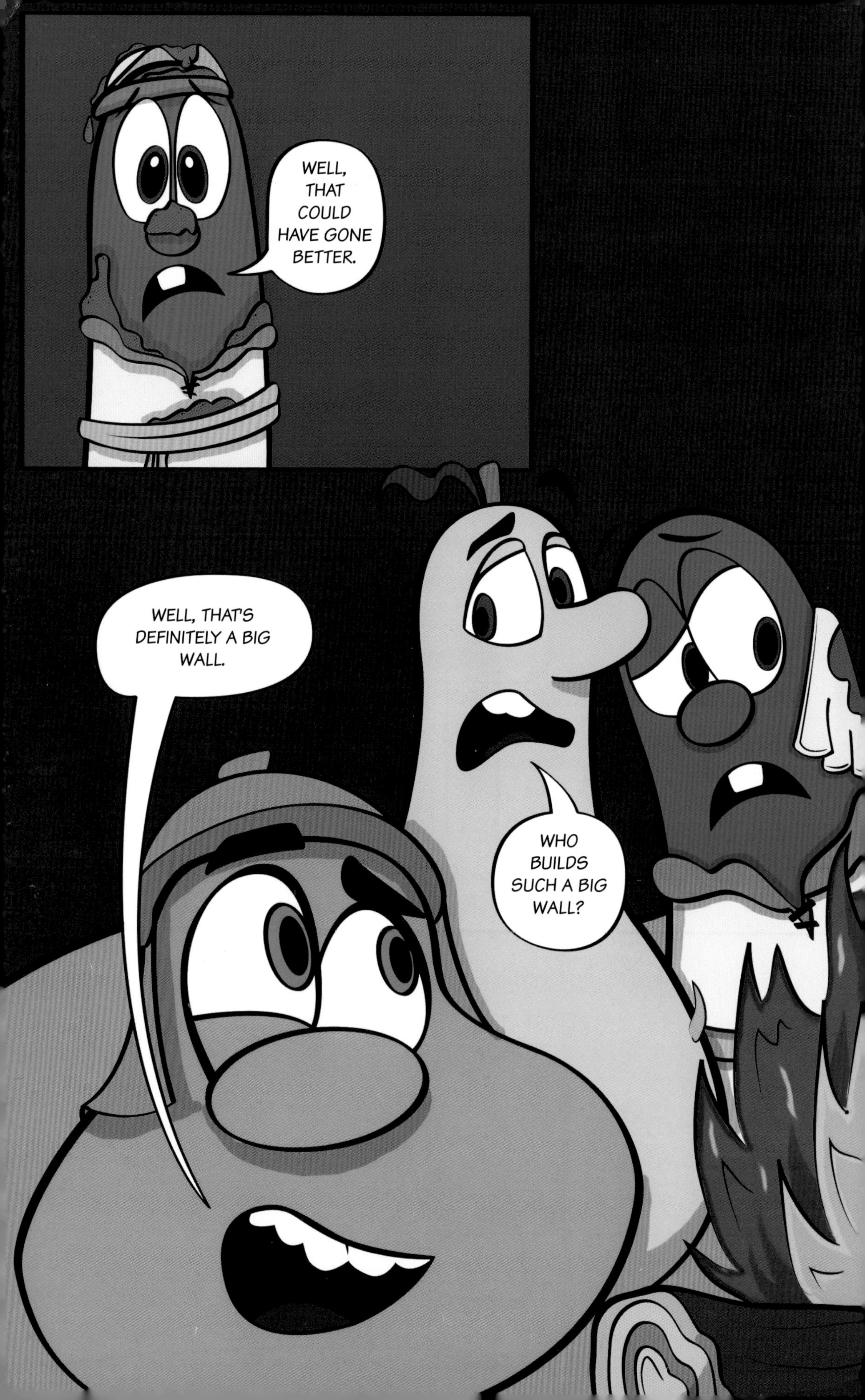
WELL, THAT COULD HAVE GONE BETTER.
WELL, THAT'S DEFINITELY A BIG WALL.
WHO BUILDS SUCH A BIG WALL?

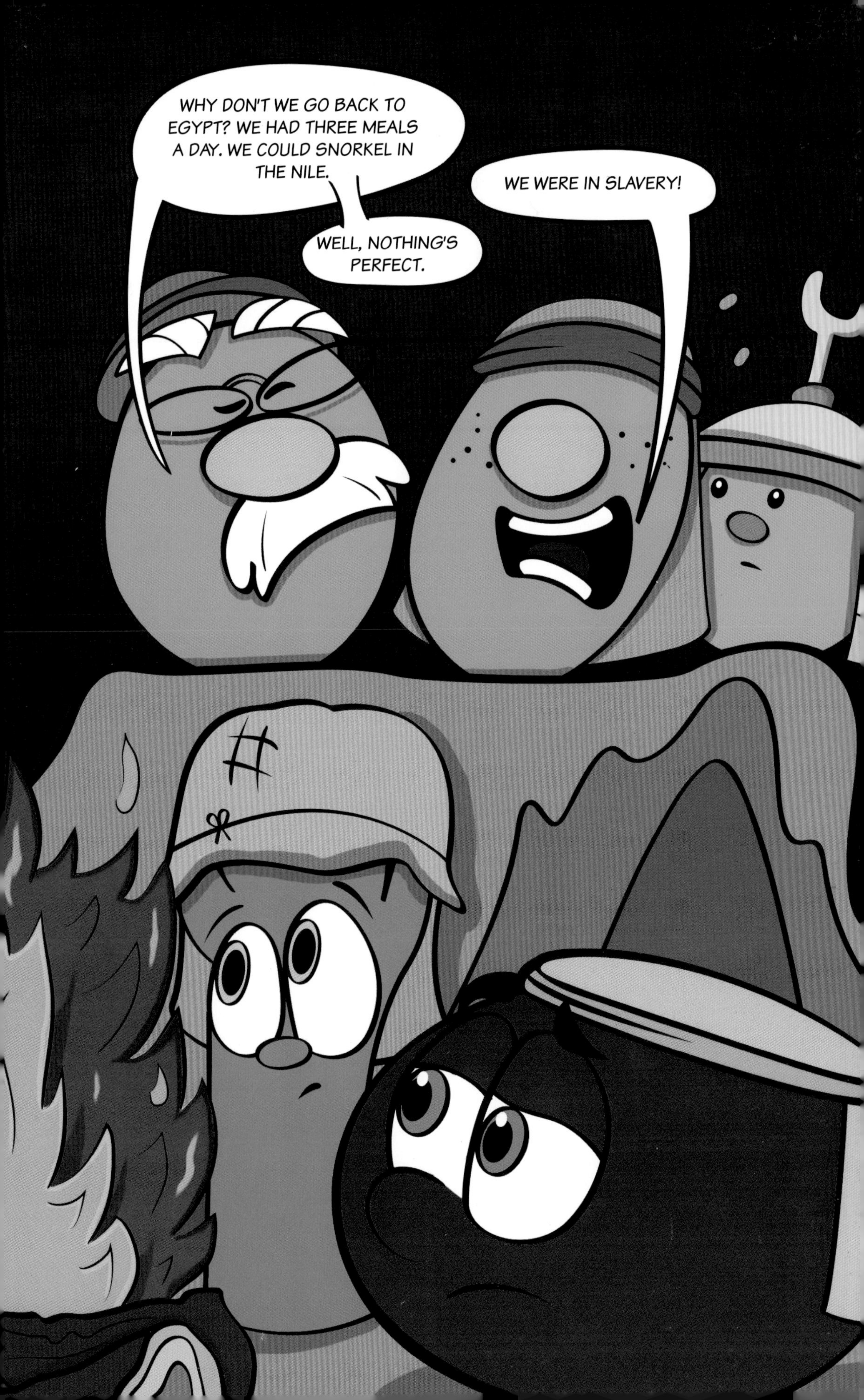
WHY DON'T WE GO BACK TO EGYPT? WE HAD THREE MEALS A DAY. WE COULD SNORKEL IN THE NILE.
WELL, NOTHING'S PERFECT.
WE WERE IN SLAVERY!

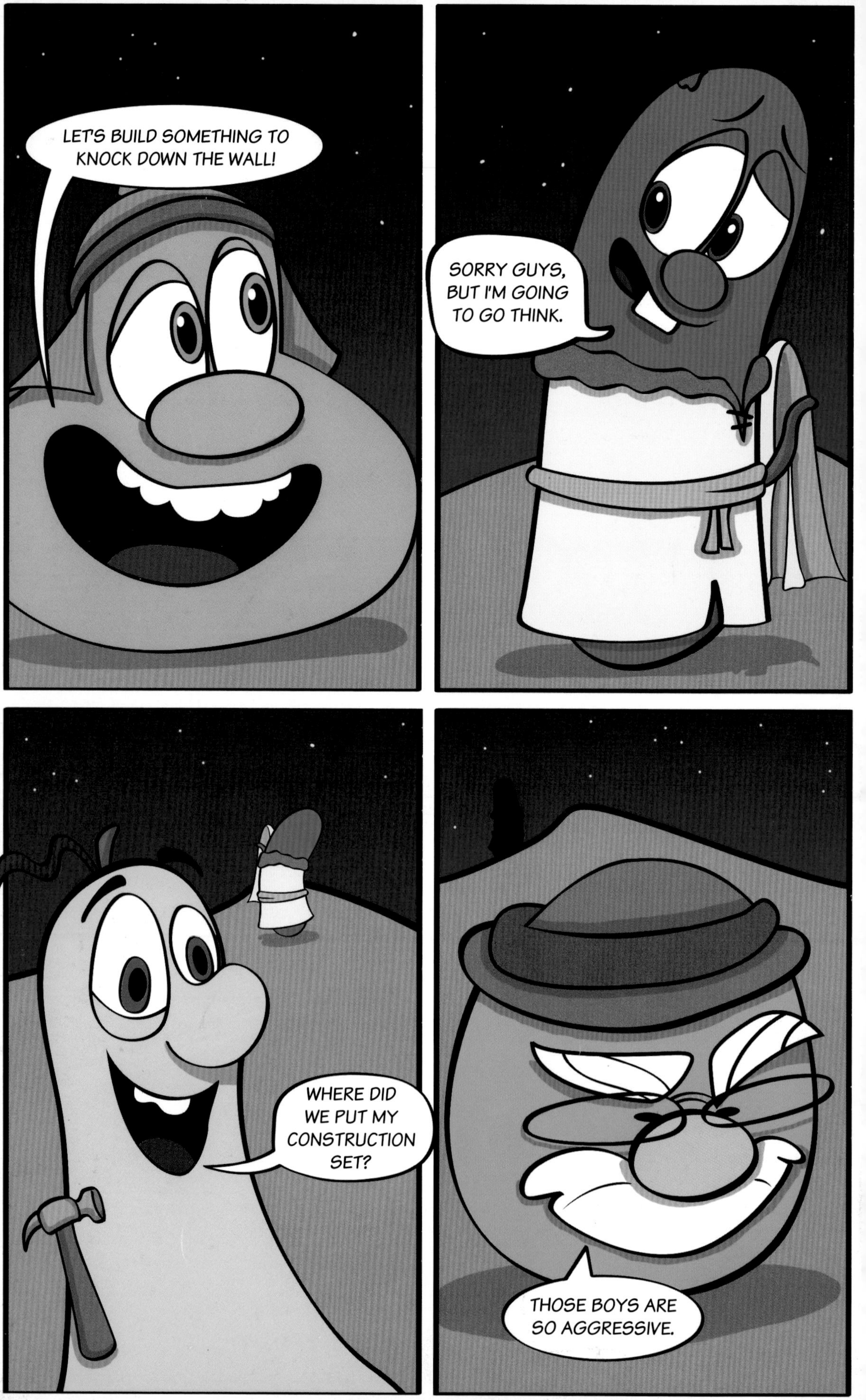
LET'S BUILD SOMETHING TO KNOCK DOWN THE WALL!
SORRY GUYS, BUT I'M GOING TO GO THINK.
WHERE DID WE PUT MY CONSTRUCTION SET?
THOSE BOYS ARE SO AGGRESSIVE.

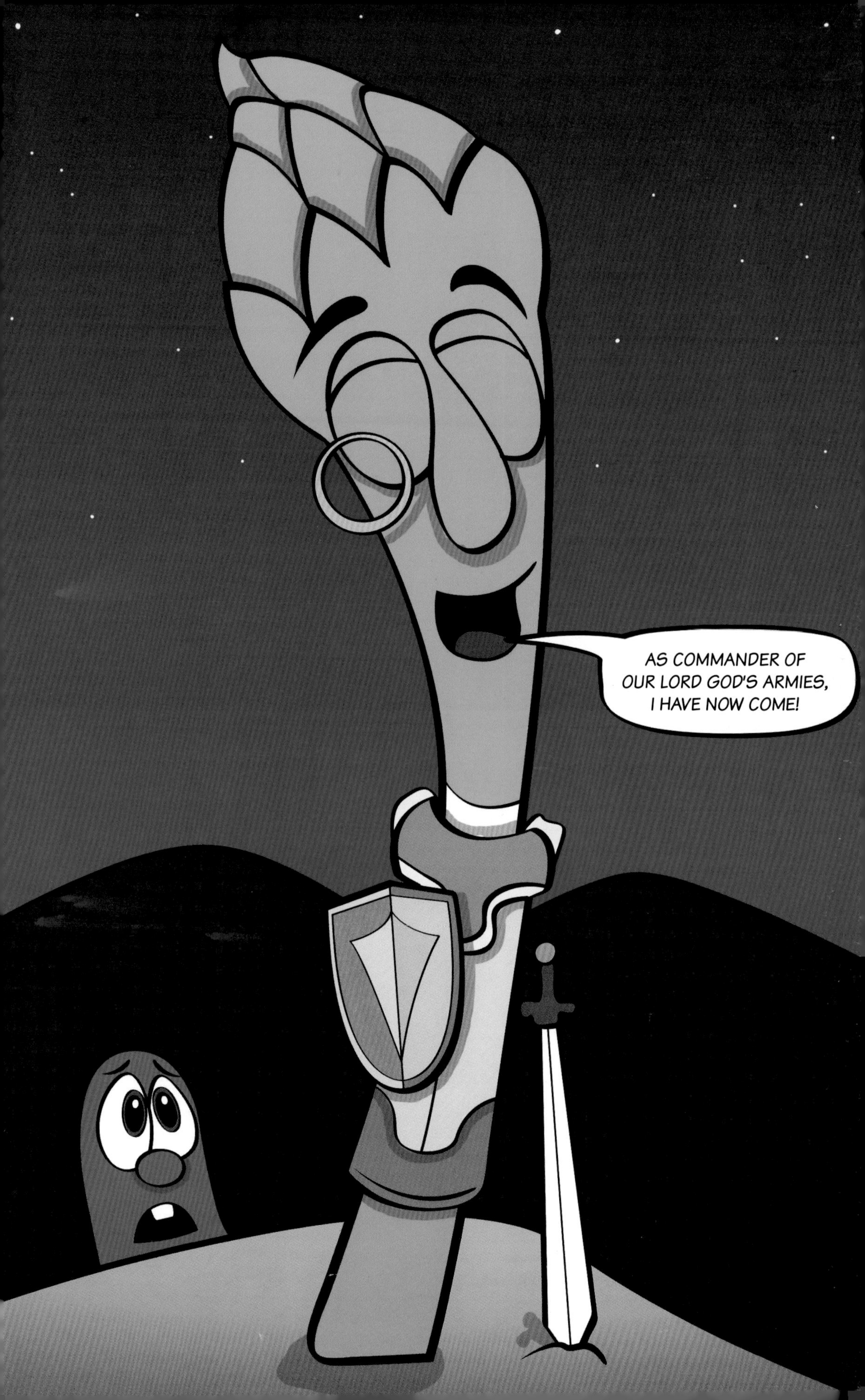
AS COMMANDER OF OUR LORD GOD'S ARMIES, I HAVE NOW COME!

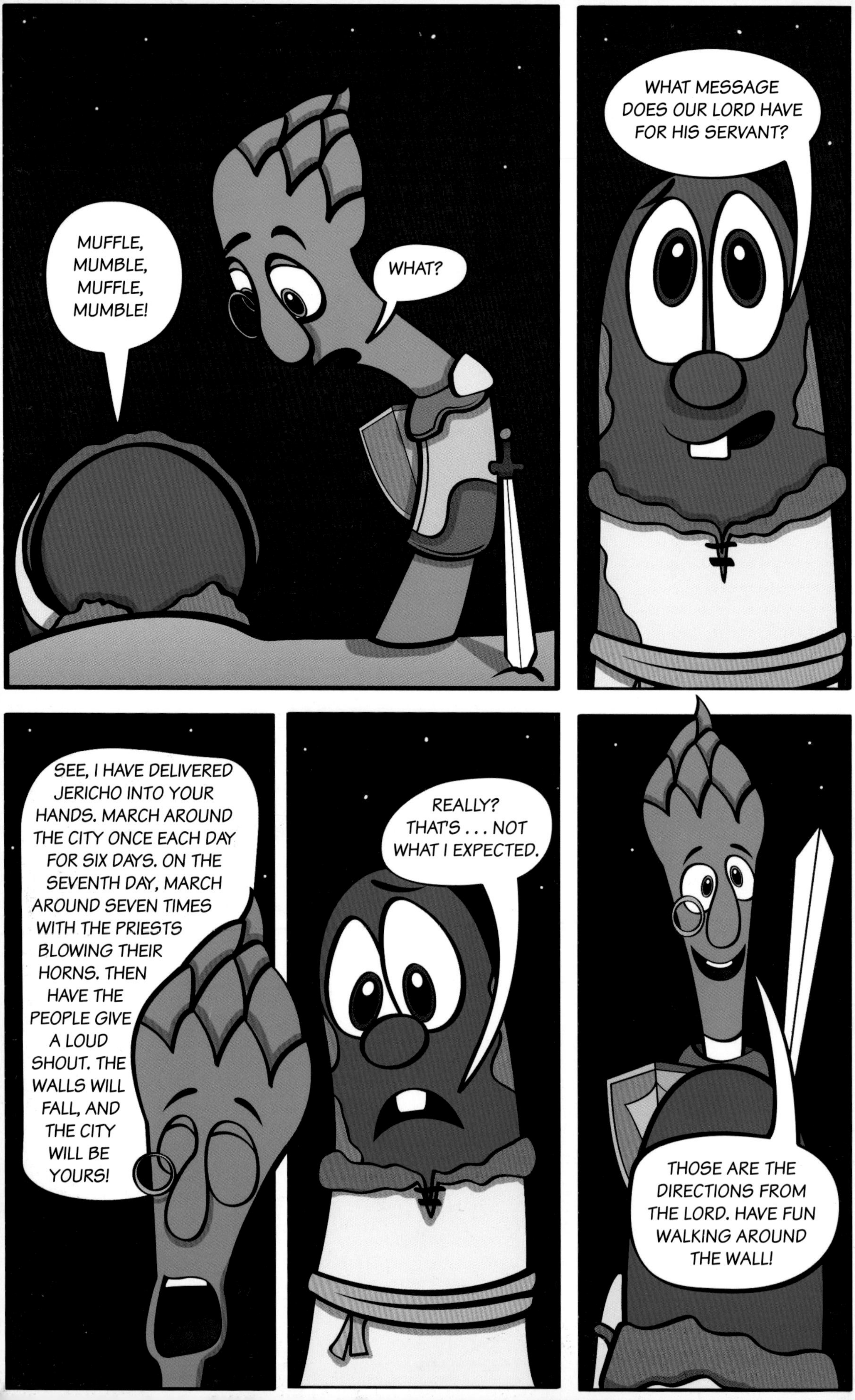
MUFFLE, MUMBLE, MUFFLE, MUMBLE!
WHAT?
WHAT MESSAGE DOES OUR LORD HAVE FOR HIS SERVANT?
SEE, I HAVE DELIVERED JERICHO INTO YOUR HANDS. MARCH AROUND THE CITY ONCE EACH DAY FOR SIX DAYS. ON THE SEVENTH DAY, MARCH AROUND SEVEN TIMES WITH THE PRIESTS BLOWING THEIR HORNS. THEN HAVE THE PEOPLE GIVE A LOUD SHOUT. THE WALLS WILL FALL, AND THE CITY WILL BE YOURS!
REALLY? THAT'S . . . NOT WHAT I EXPECTED.
THOSE ARE THE DIRECTIONS FROM THE LORD. HAVE FUN WALKING AROUND THE WALL!

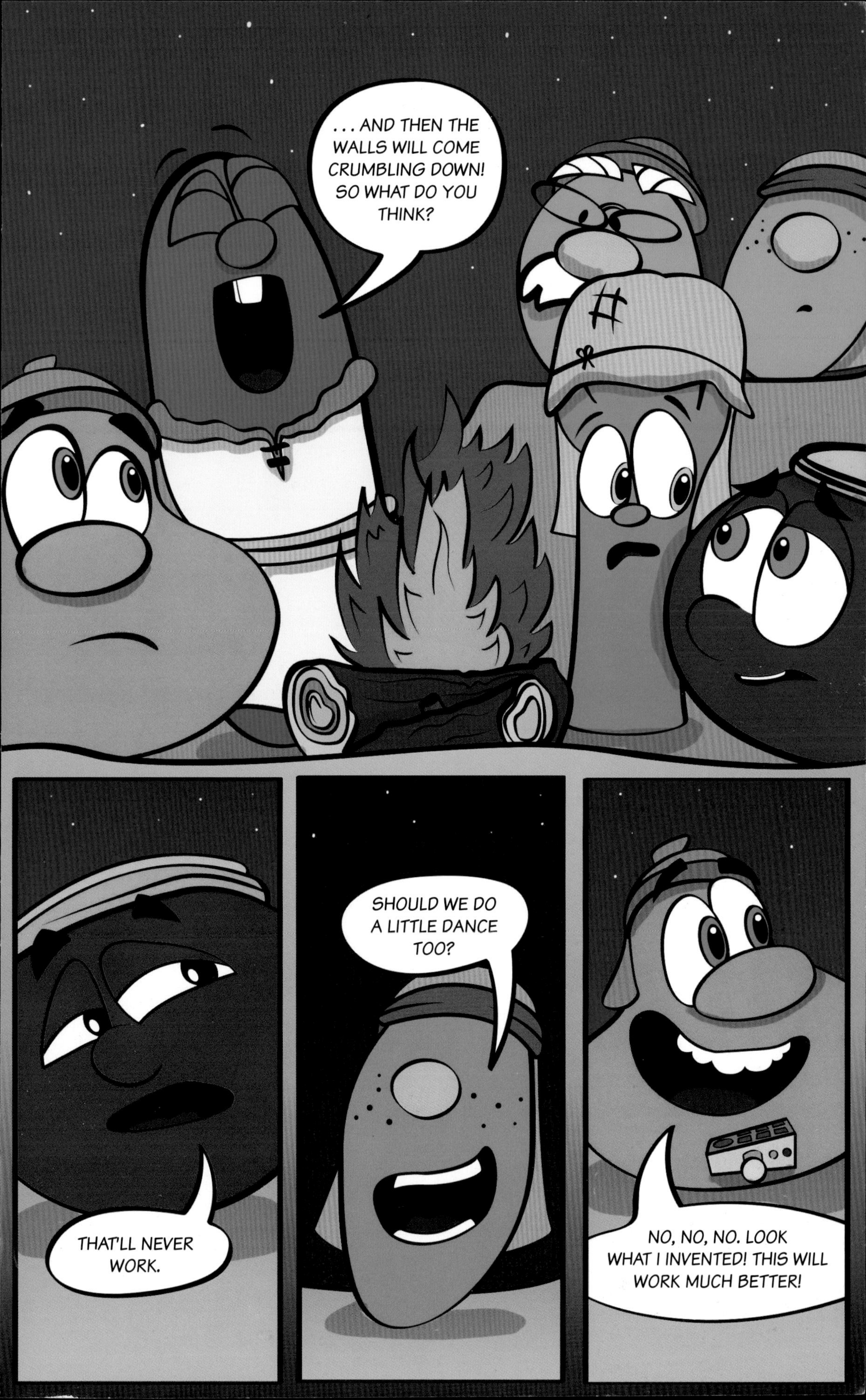
. . . AND THEN THE WALLS WILL COME CRUMBLING DOWN! SO WHAT DO YOU THINK?
THAT'LL NEVER WORK.
SHOULD WE DO A LITTLE DANCE TOO?
NO, NO, NO. LOOK WHAT I INVENTED! THIS WILL WORK MUCH BETTER!

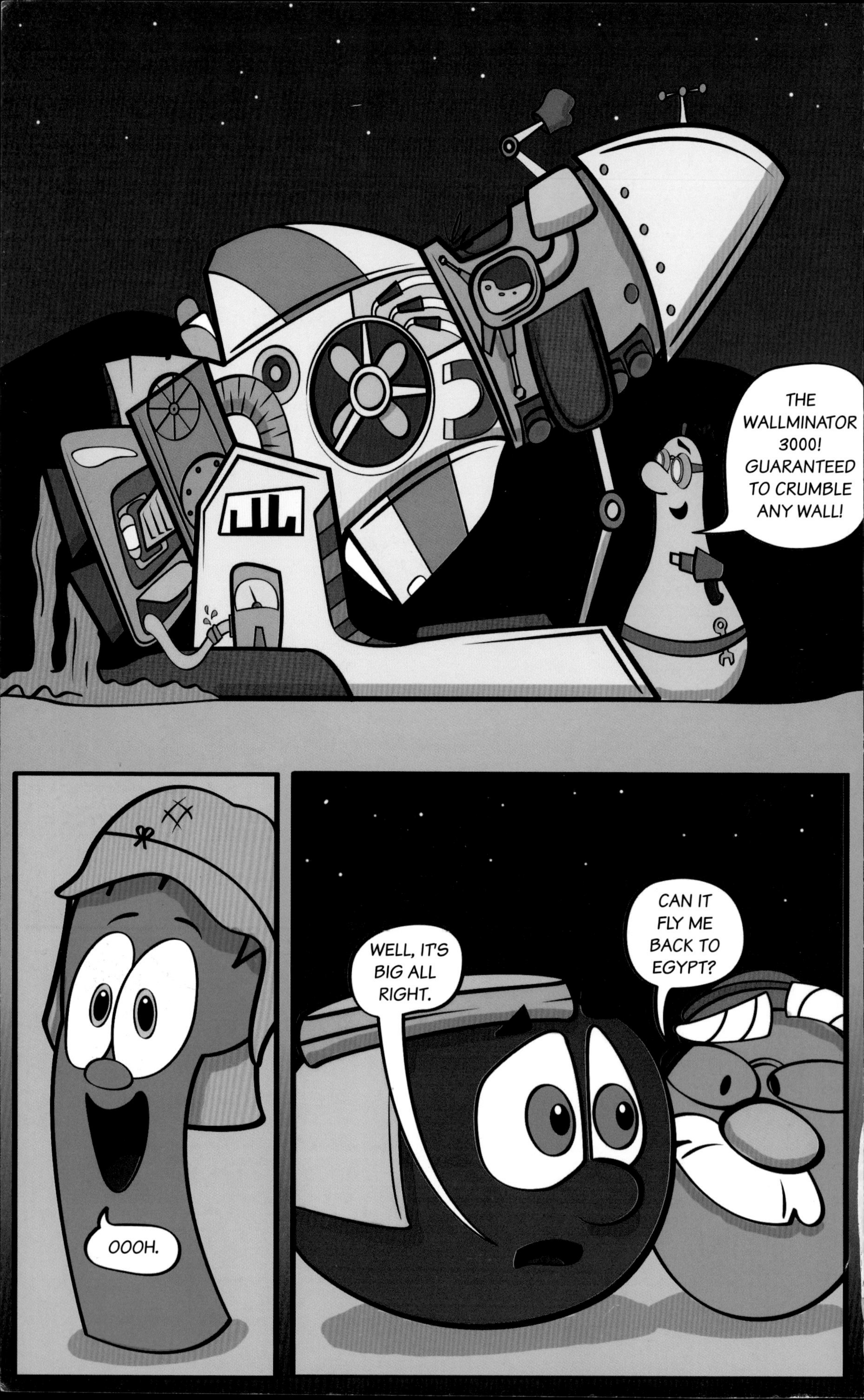
THE WALLMINATOR 3000! GUARANTEED TO CRUMBLE ANY WALL!
OOOH.
WELL, IT'S BIG ALL RIGHT.
CAN IT FLY ME BACK TO EGYPT?

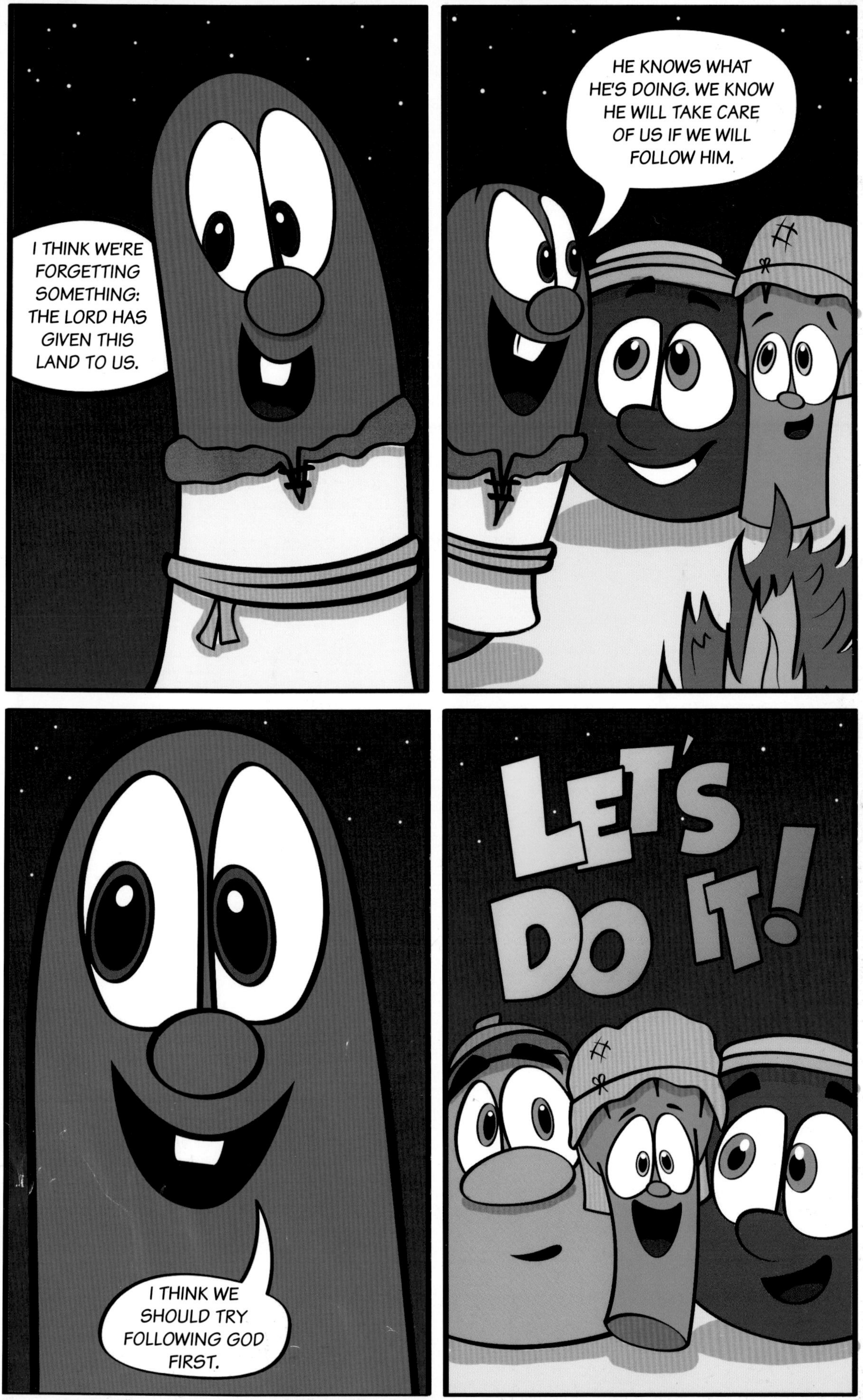
I THINK WE'RE FORGETTING SOMETHING: THE LORD HAS GIVEN THIS LAND TO US.
HE KNOWS WHAT HE'S DOING. WE KNOW HE WILL TAKE CARE OF US IF WE WILL FOLLOW HIM.
I THINK WE SHOULD TRY FOLLOWING GOD FIRST.
LET'S DO IT!

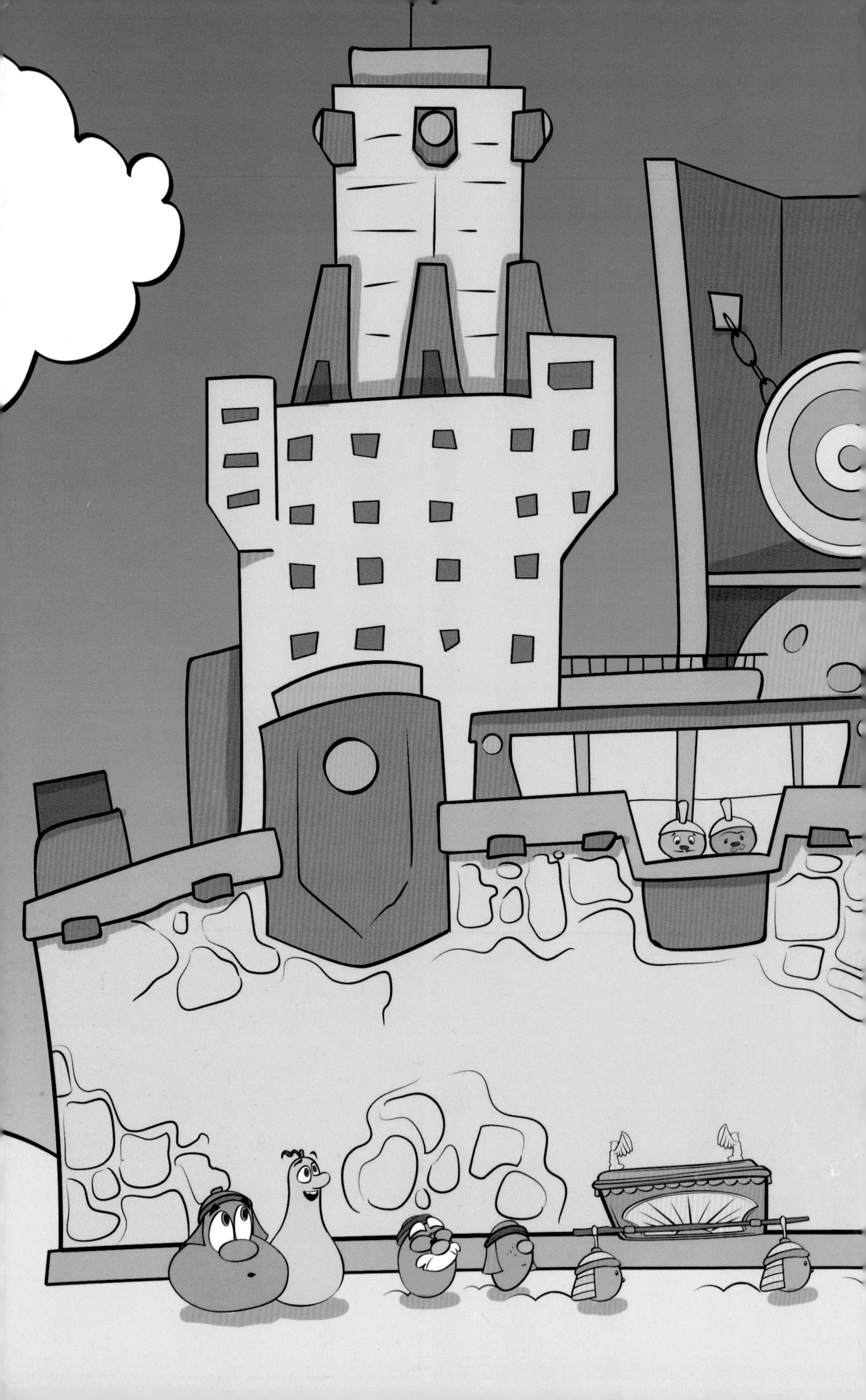

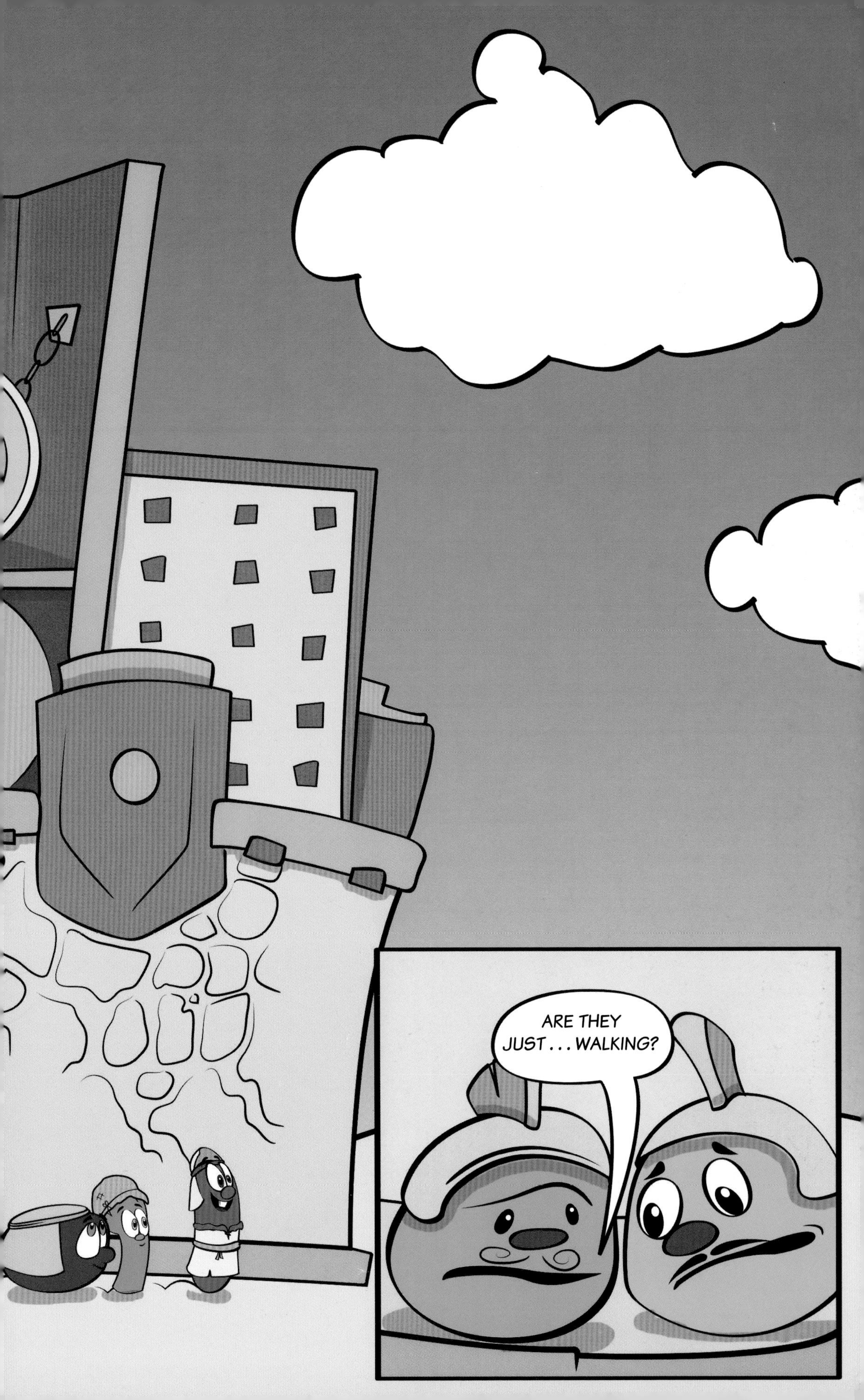
ARE THEY JUST . . . WALKING?

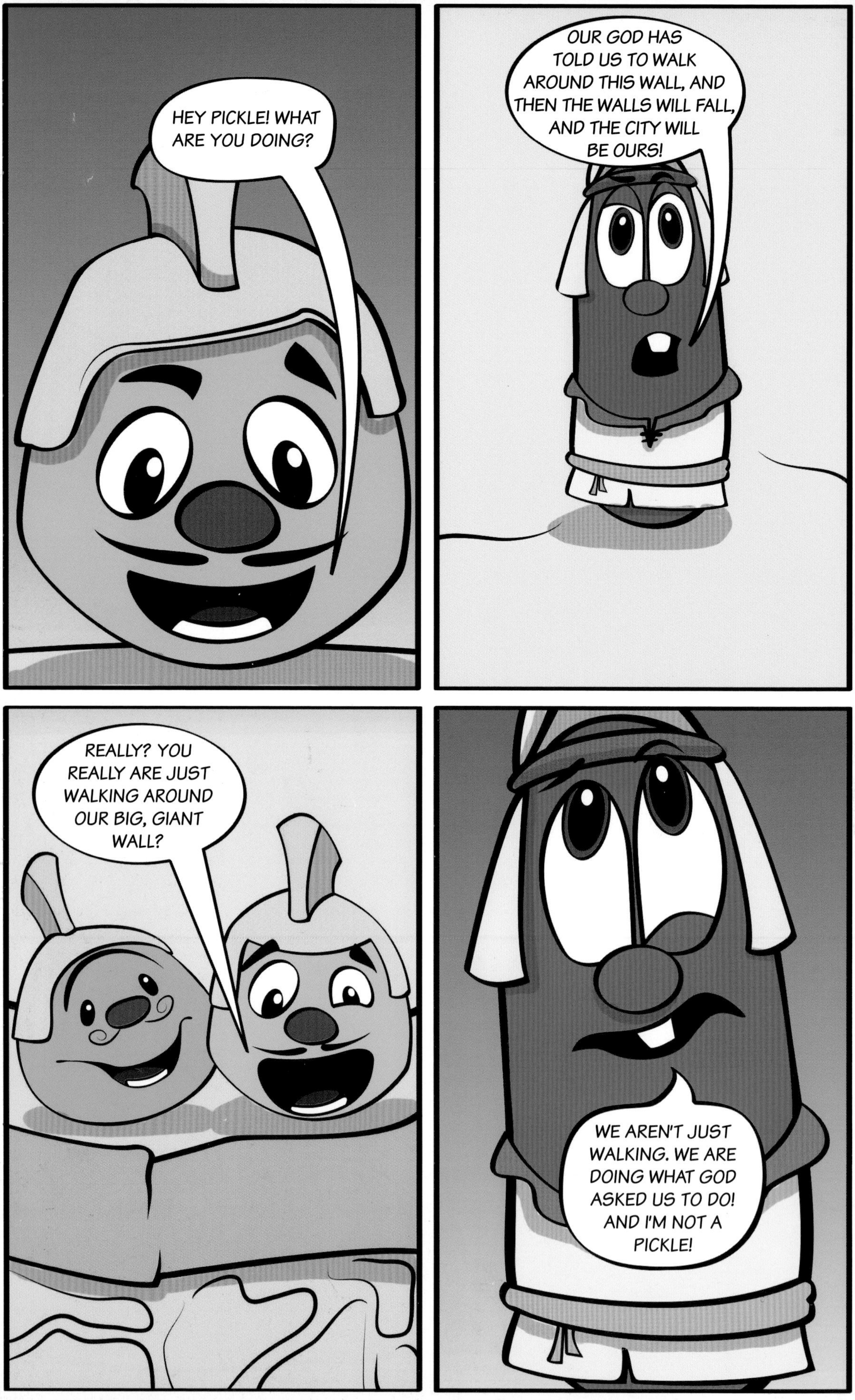
HEY PICKLE! WHAT ARE YOU DOING?
OUR GOD HAS TOLD US TO WALK AROUND THIS WALL, AND THEN THE WALLS WILL FALL, AND THE CITY WILL BE OURS!
REALLY? YOU REALLY ARE JUST WALKING AROUND OUR BIG, GIANT WALL?
WE AREN'T JUST WALKING. WE ARE DOING WHAT GOD ASKED US TO DO! AND I'M NOT A PICKLE!

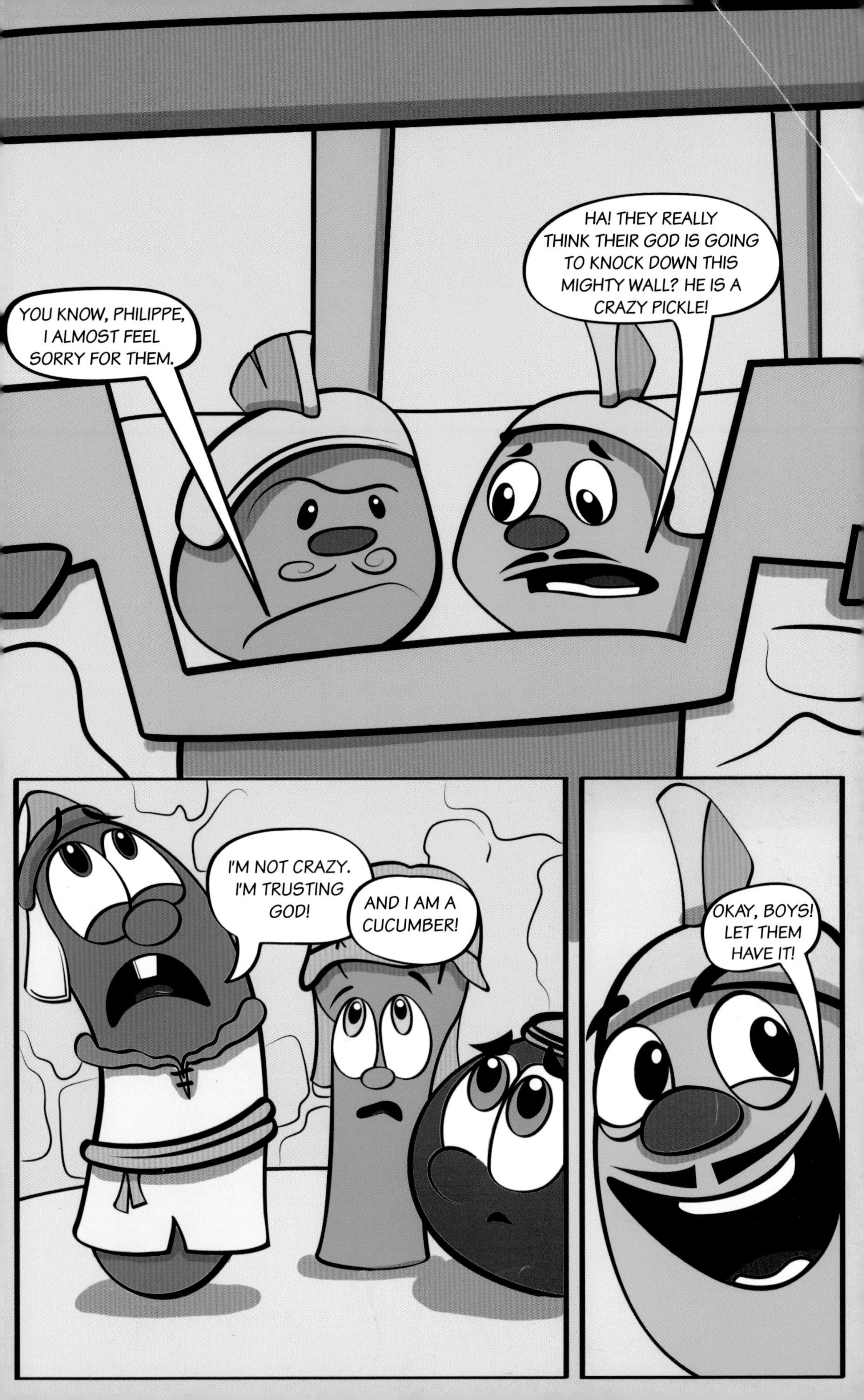
YOU KNOW, PHILIPPE, I ALMOST FEEL SORRY FOR THEM.
HA! THEY REALLY THINK THEIR GOD IS GOING TO KNOCK DOWN THIS MIGHTY WALL? HE IS A CRAZY PICKLE!
I'M NOT CRAZY. I'M TRUSTING GOD!
AND I AM A CUCUMBER!
OKAY, BOYS! LET THEM HAVE IT!

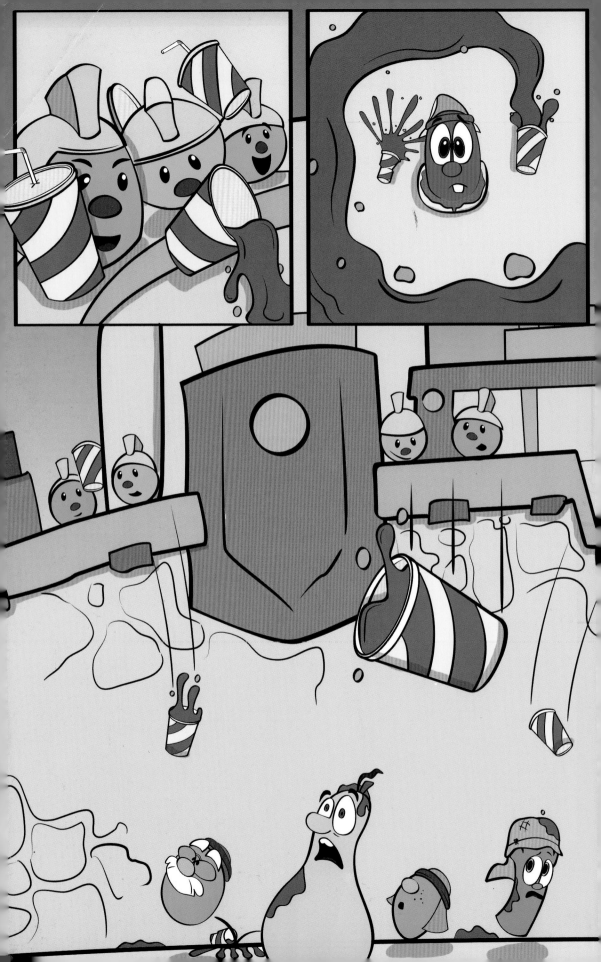

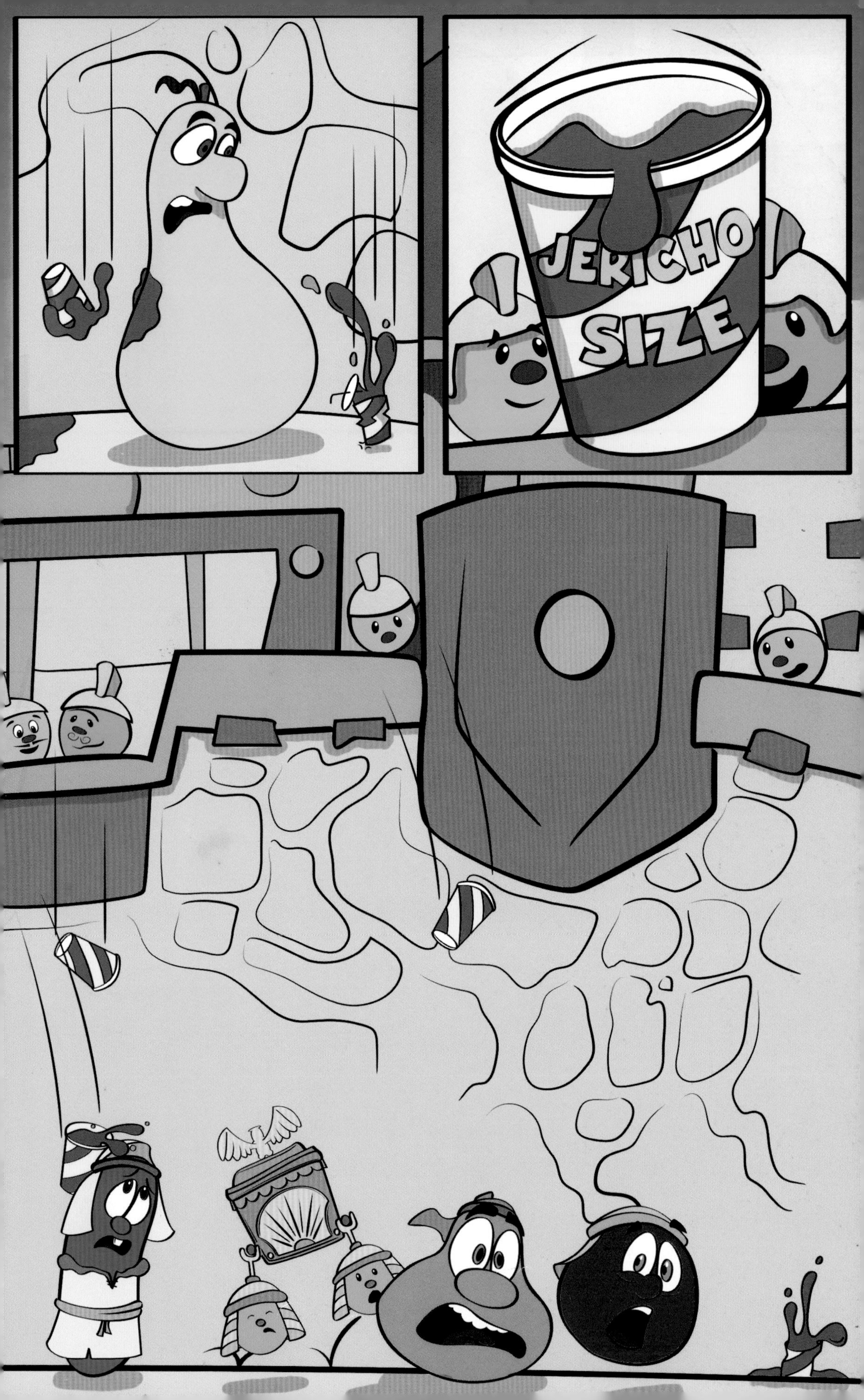
JERICHO
SIZE

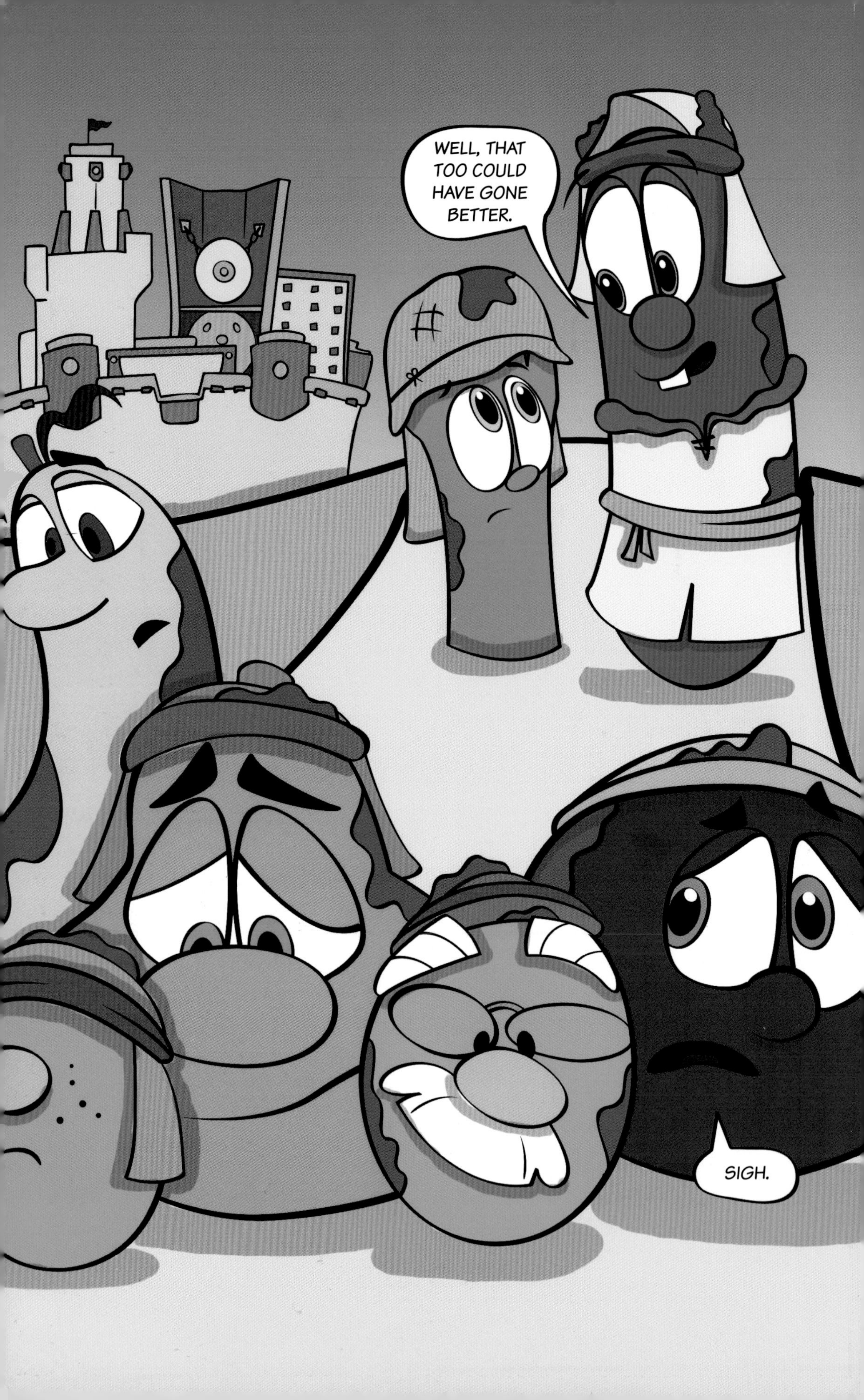
WELL, THAT TOO COULD HAVE GONE BETTER.
SIGH.

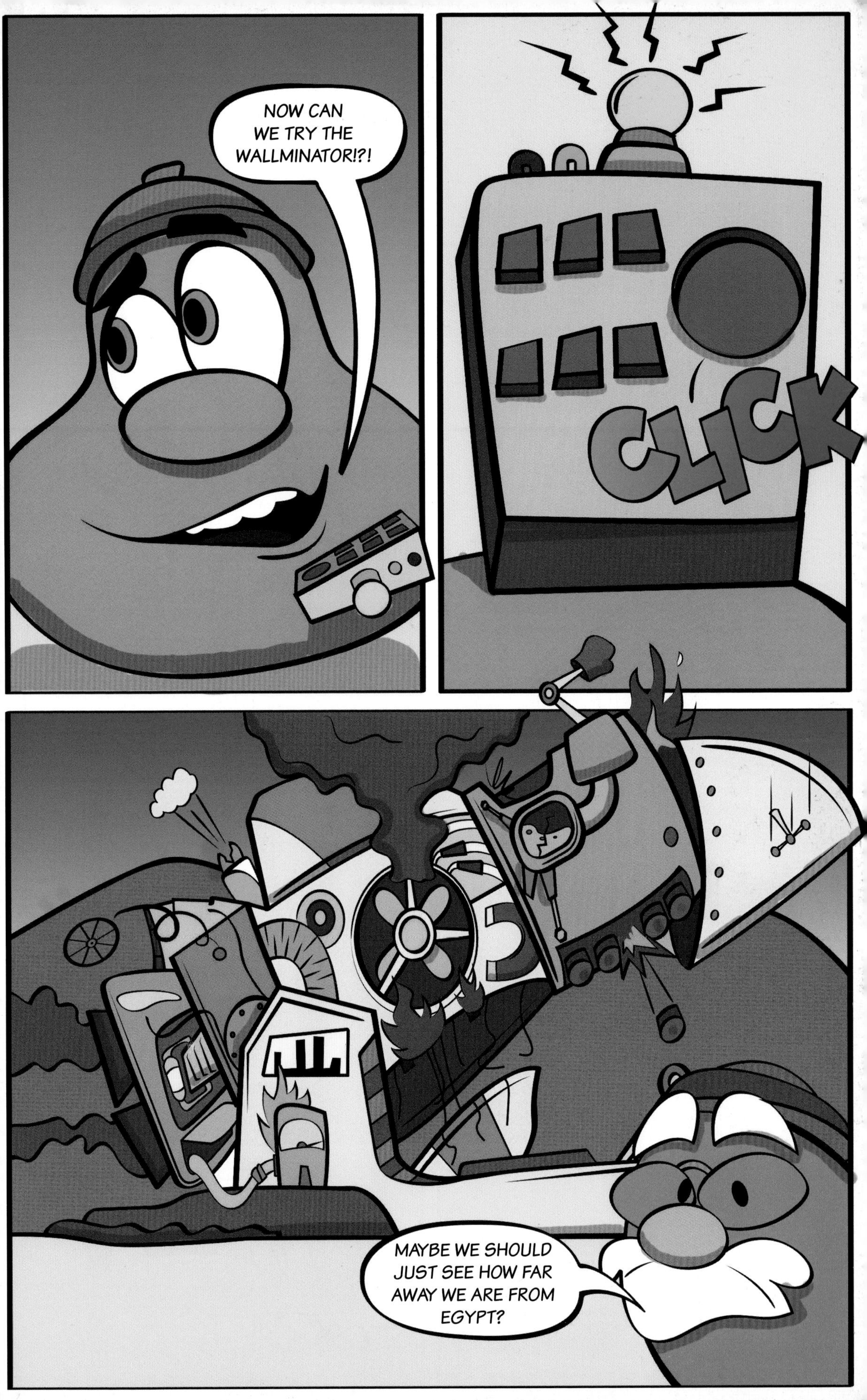
NOW CAN WE TRY THE WALLMINATOR!?!
CLICK
MAYBE WE SHOULD JUST SEE HOW FAR AWAY WE ARE FROM EGYPT?

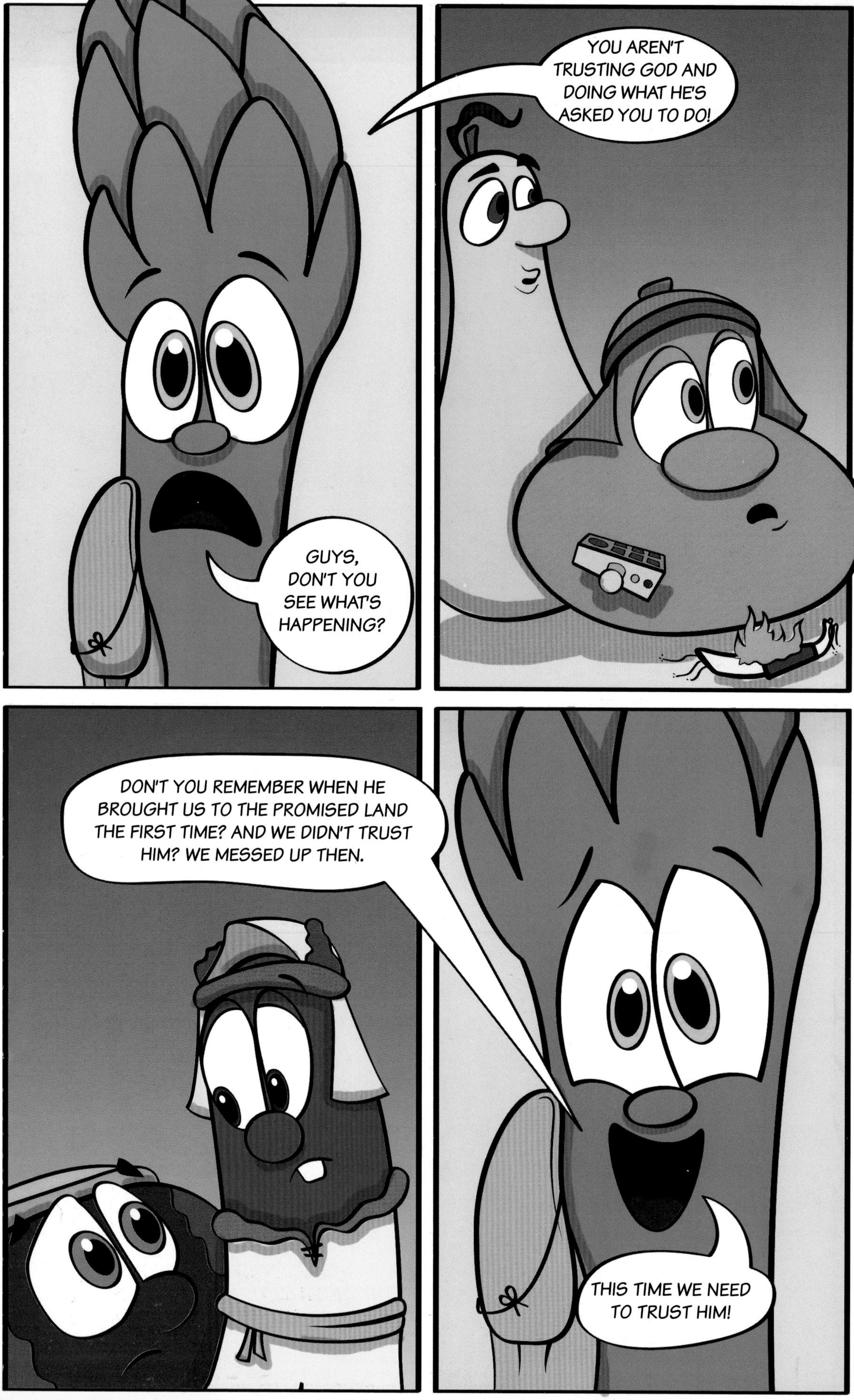
GUYS, DON'T YOU SEE WHAT'S HAPPENING?
YOU AREN'T TRUSTING GOD AND DOING WHAT HE'S ASKED YOU TO DO!
DON'T YOU REMEMBER WHEN HE BROUGHT US TO THE PROMISED LAND THE FIRST TIME? AND WE DIDN'T TRUST HIM? WE MESSED UP THEN.
THIS TIME WE NEED TO TRUST HIM!

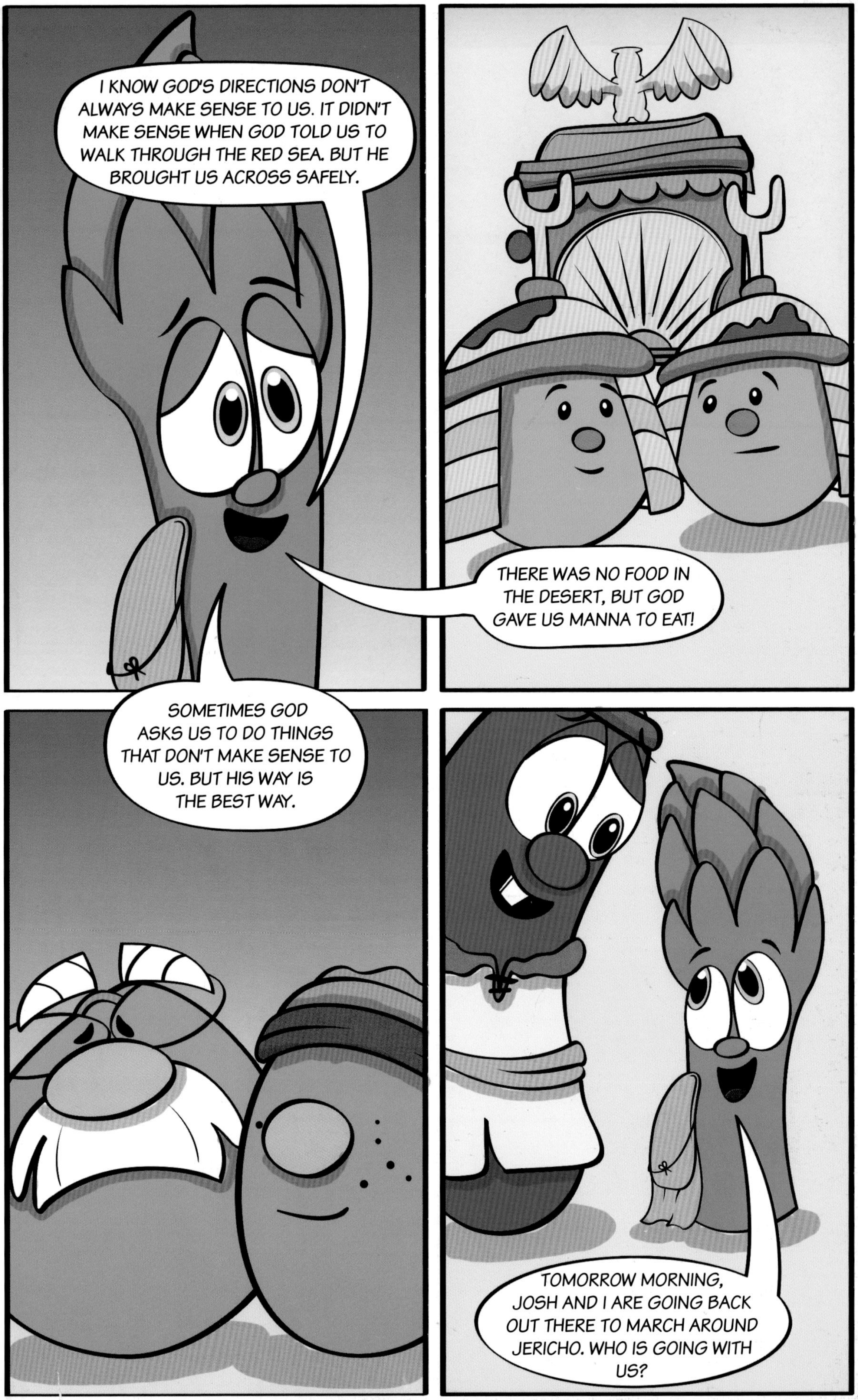
I KNOW GOD'S DIRECTIONS DON'T ALWAYS MAKE SENSE TO US. IT DIDN'T MAKE SENSE WHEN GOD TOLD US TO WALK THROUGH THE RED SEA. BUT HE BROUGHT US ACROSS SAFELY.
THERE WAS NO FOOD IN THE DESERT, BUT GOD GAVE US MANNA TO EAT!
SOMETIMES GOD ASKS US TO DO THINGS THAT DON'T MAKE SENSE TO US. BUT HIS WAY IS THE BEST WAY.
TOMORROW MORNING, JOSH AND I ARE GOING BACK OUT THERE TO MARCH AROUND JERICHO. WHO IS GOING WITH US?

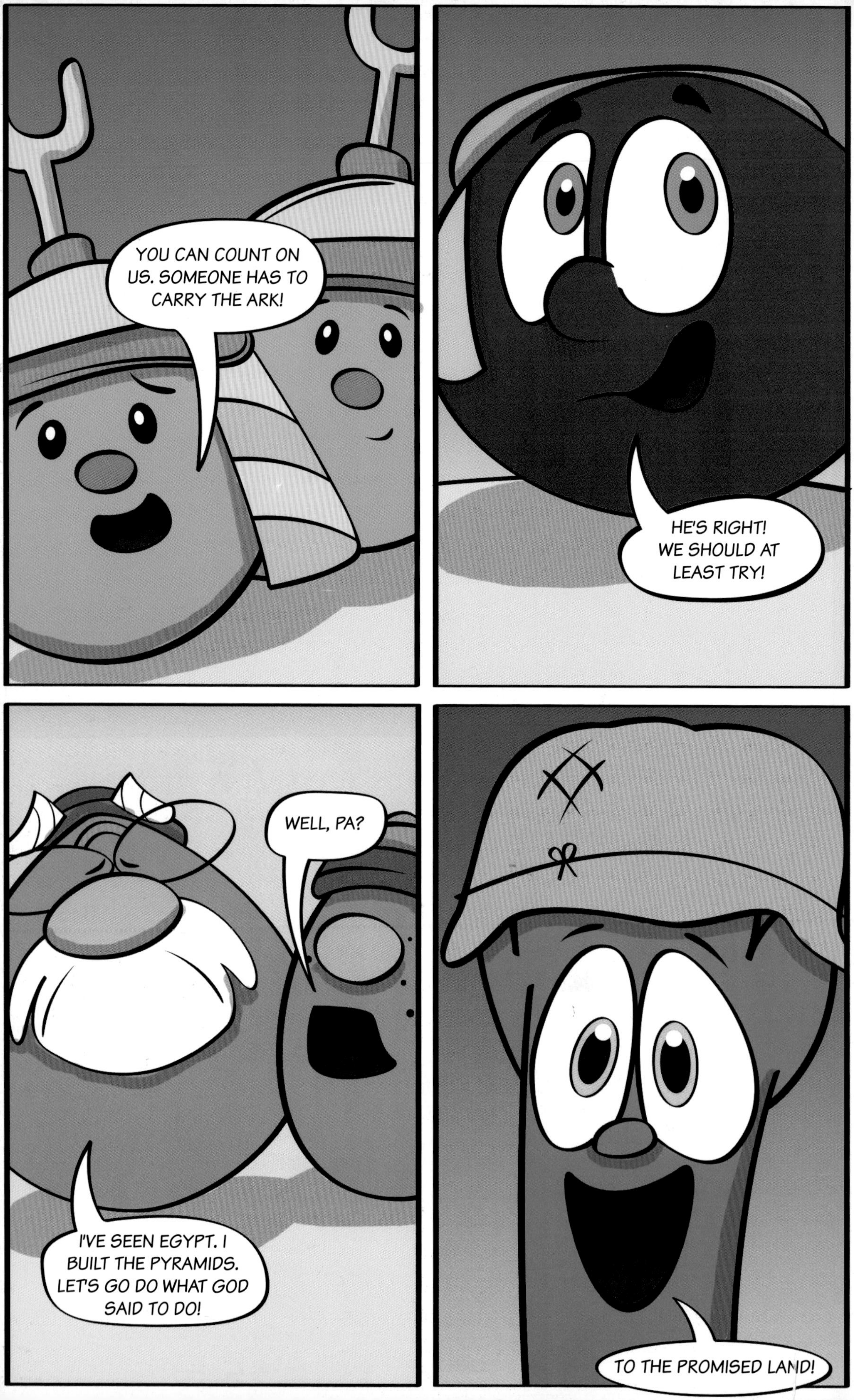
YOU CAN COUNT ON US. SOMEONE HAS TO CARRY THE ARK!
HE'S RIGHT! WE SHOULD AT LEAST TRY!
WELL, PA?
I'VE SEEN EGYPT. I BUILT THE PYRAMIDS. LET'S GO DO WHAT GOD SAID TO DO!
TO THE PROMISED LAND!

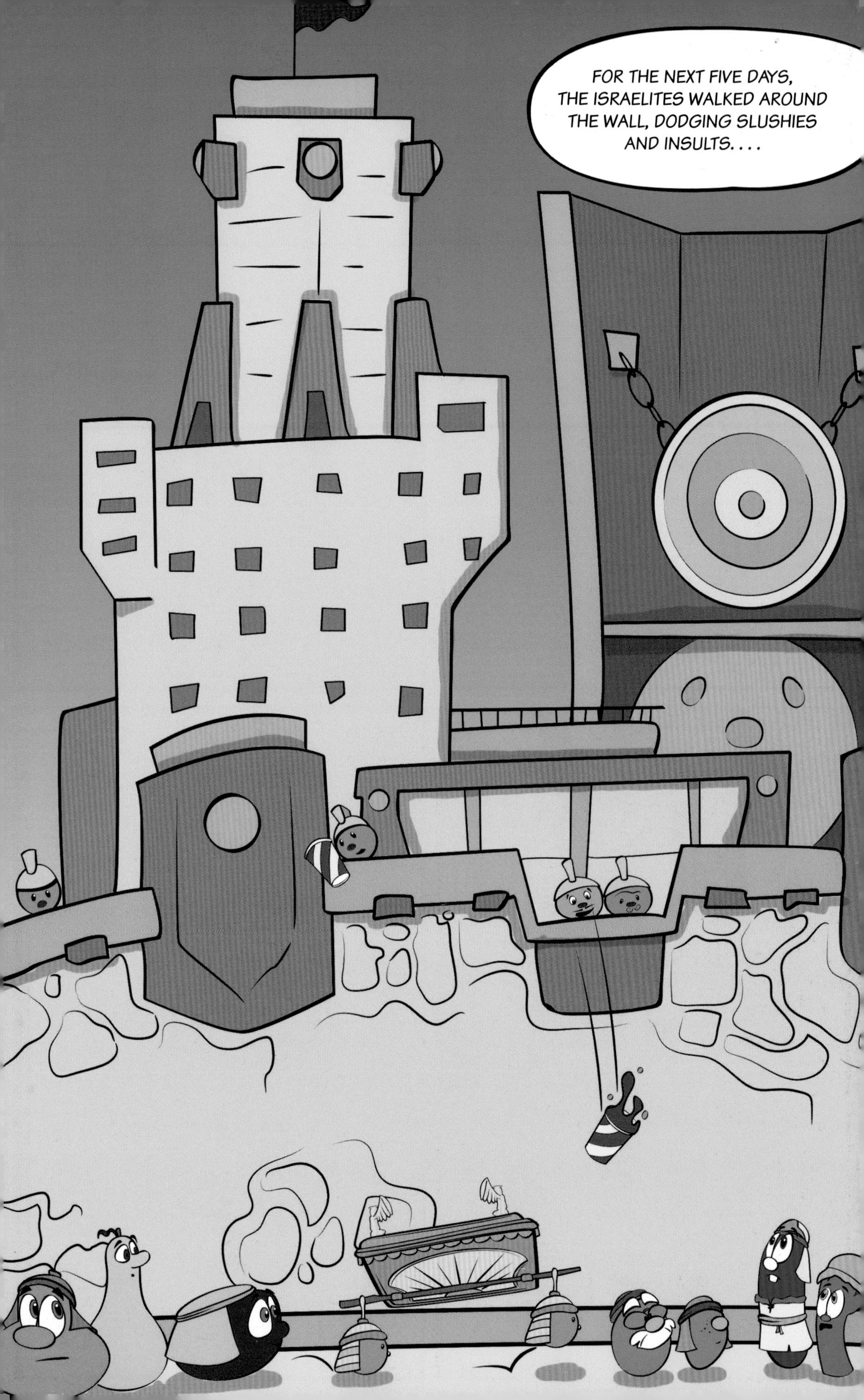
FOR THE NEXT FIVE DAYS,
THE ISRAELITES WALKED AROUND
THE WALL, DODGING SLUSHIES
AND INSULTS. . . .

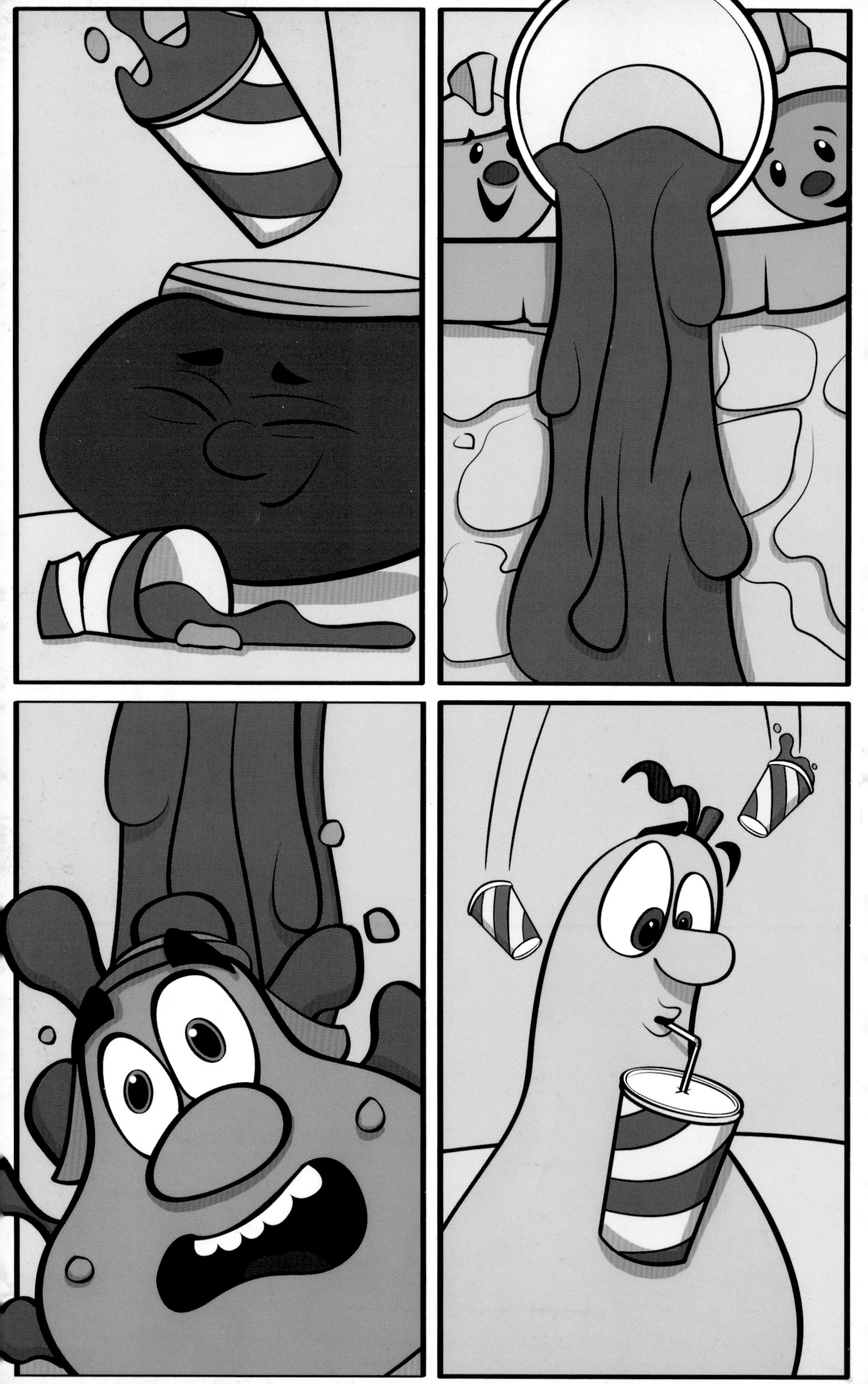

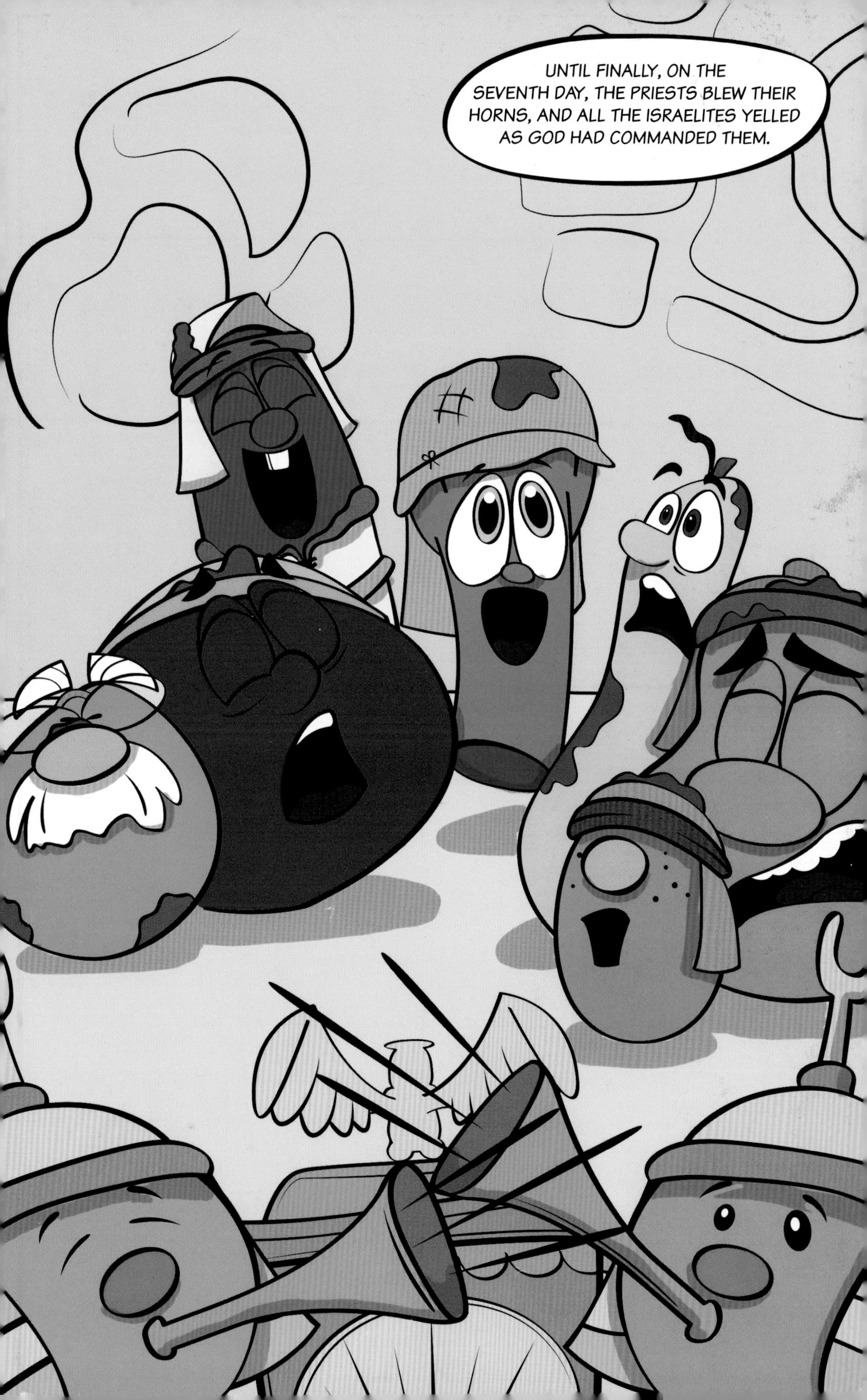
UNTIL FINALLY, ON THE SEVENTH DAY, THE PRIESTS BLEW THEIR HORNS, AND ALL THE ISRAELITES YELLED AS GOD HAD COMMANDED THEM.

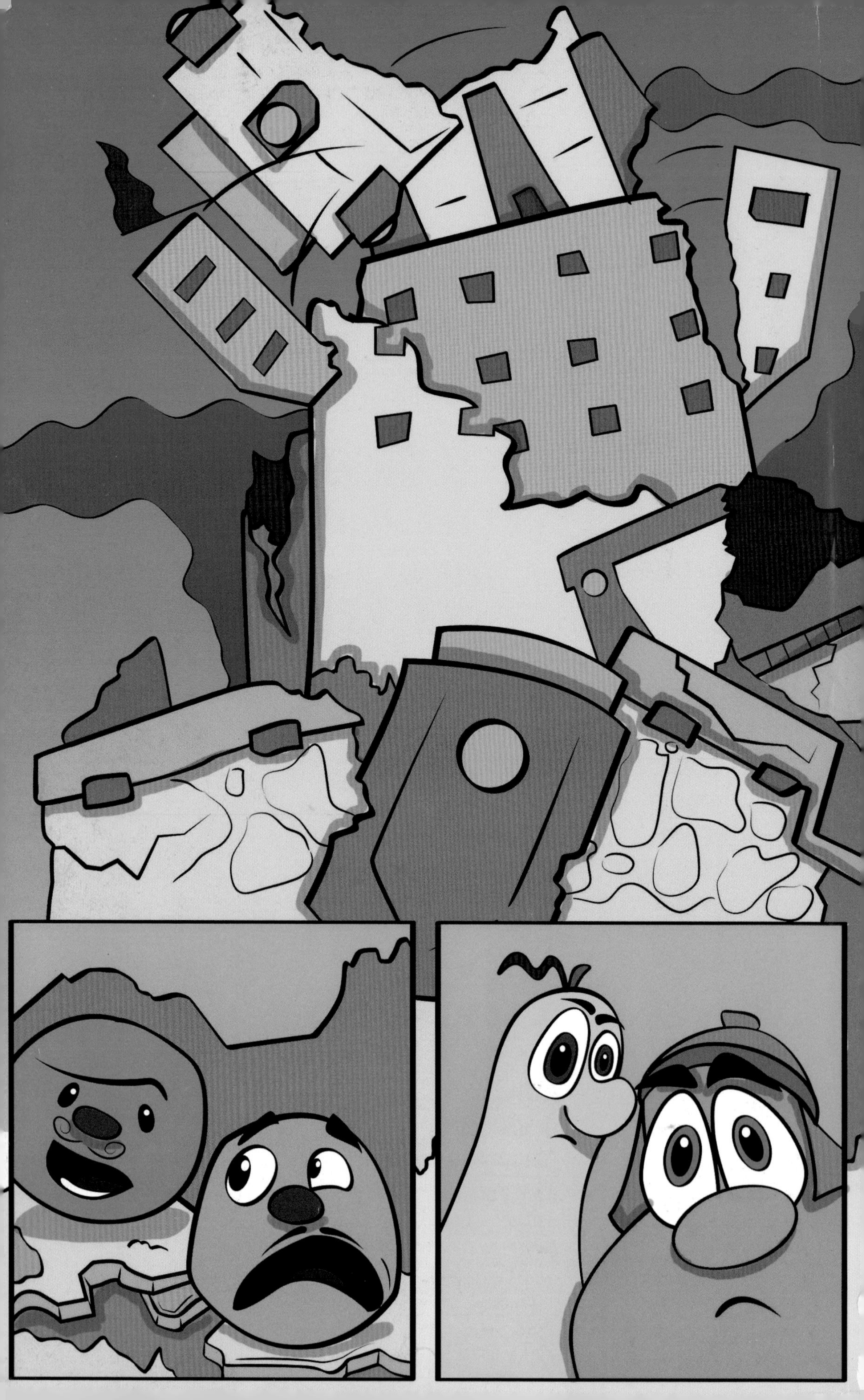

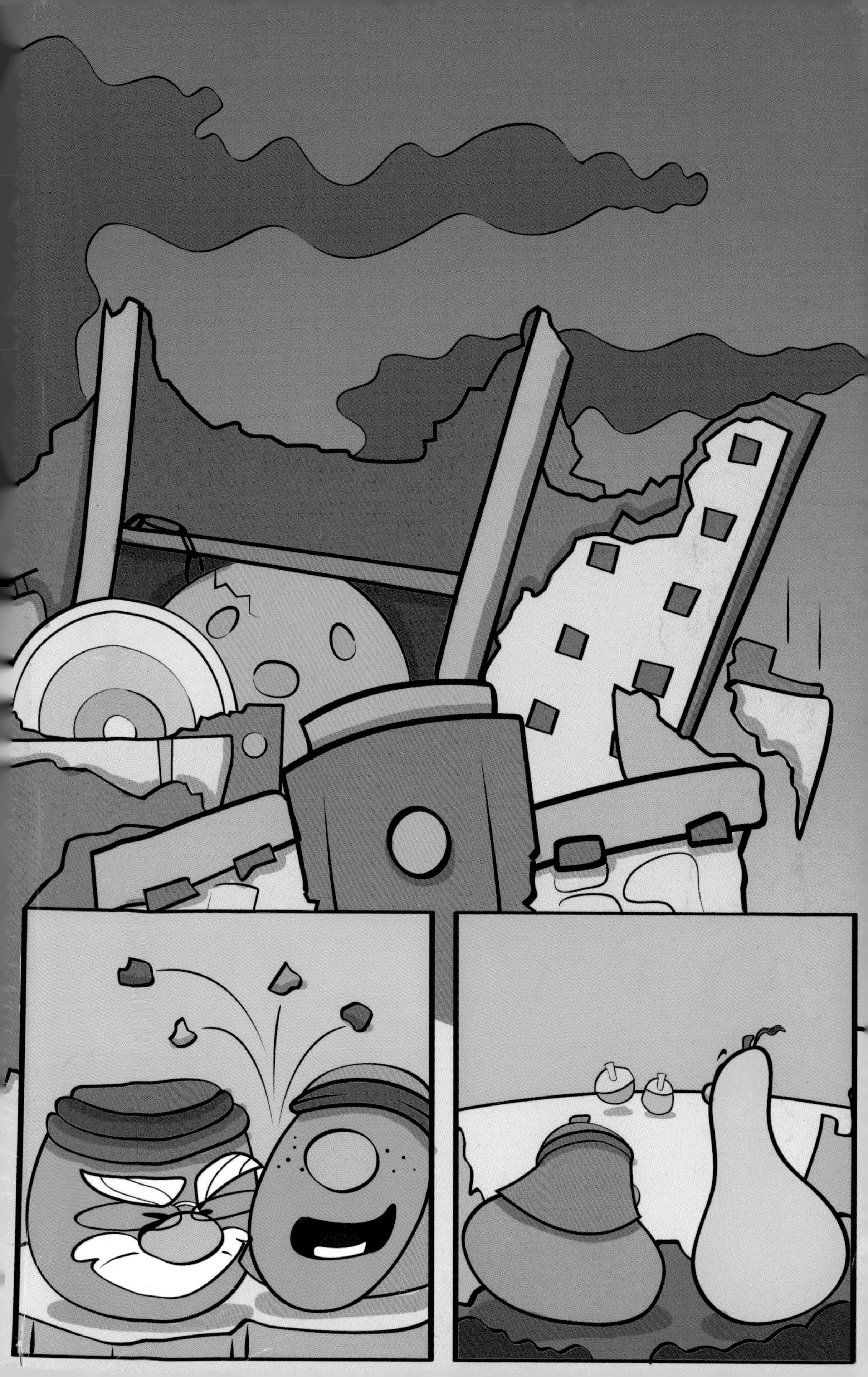

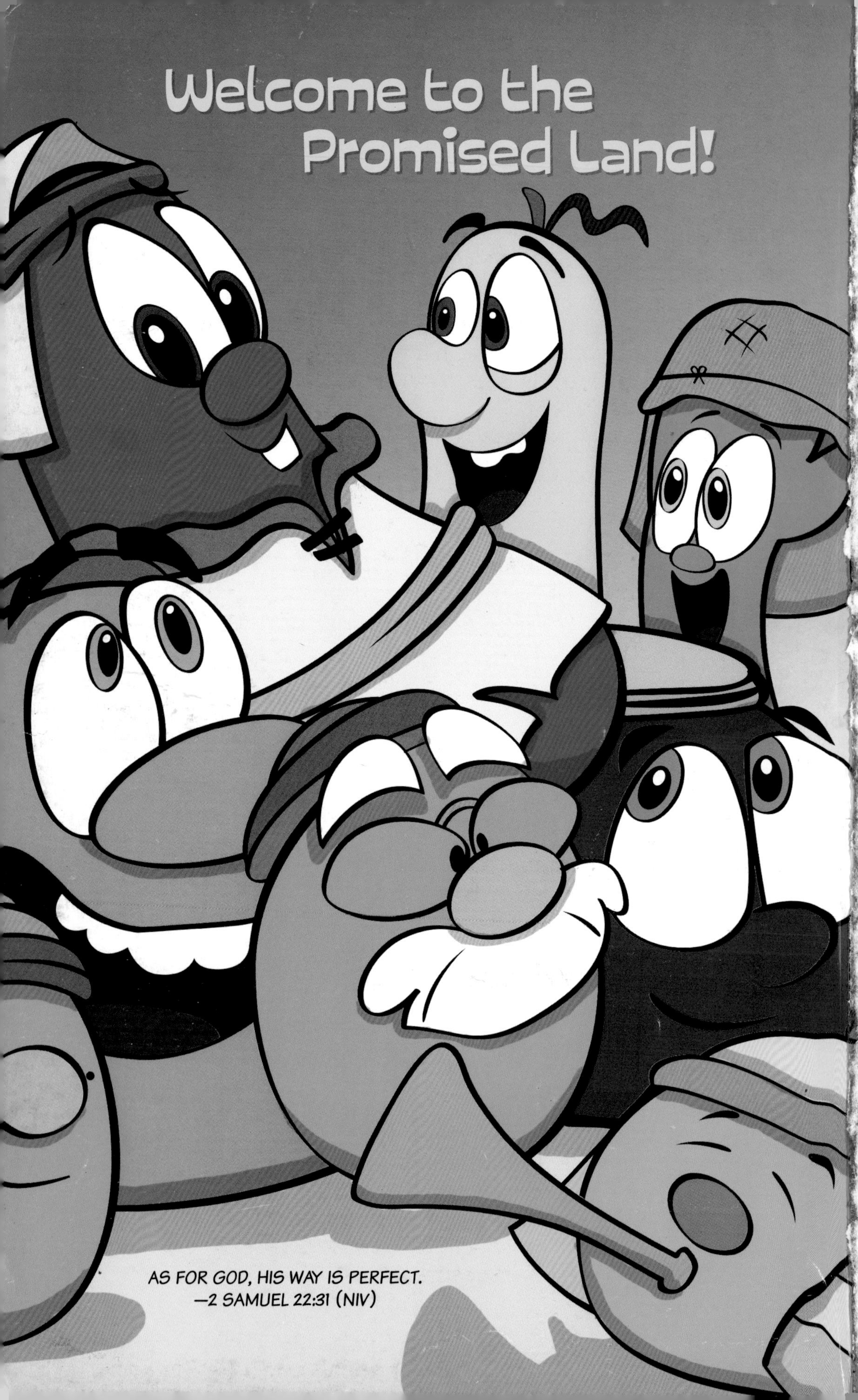
Welcome to the Promised Land!
AS FOR GOD, HIS WAY IS PERFECT.
—2 SAMUEL 22:31 (NIV)